HOTHOUSE

HOTHOUSE

Brian W. Aldiss

Introduction by
DAVID WINGROVE

JOHN GOODCHILD PUBLISHERS
WENDOVER

John Goodchild Publishers,
70 Carrington Crescent,
Wendover,
Buckinghamshire,
HP22 6AN

First published 1962
First published in the SF Alternatives series 1984

© Copyright Brian W. Aldiss 1962, 1984
Introduction © John Goodchild Publishers 1984

Cover design by David Harrop

Printed by Nene Litho, Wellingborough, Northants.
Bound by Woolnough Bookbinding, Wellingborough, Northants.

British Library Cataloguing in Publication Data
    Aldiss, Brian W.
        Hothouse.—(SF alternatives)
        I. Title   II. Series
        813'.914[F]   PR6051.L3

    ISBN 0-86391-023-8

Introduction

THE SECOND PART OF GROWTH

"My vegetable love should grow
Vaster than empires and more slow."

With these two lines from Andrew Marvell's *To His Coy Mistress*, Brian Aldiss introduced the opulent far-future world of 'Hothouse' to the readers of *The Magazine Of Fantasy And Science Fiction*. It was February 1961 and the science fiction field was bursting with creative energy and rich inventiveness. 1960 had seen Philip Jose Farmer publishing FLESH, which challenged the sexual taboos of the field. In the same year Walter M. Miller had produced A CANTICLE FOR LEIBOWITZ, one of the classic studies of religious conservativism in a post-Apocalypse world. 1961 saw the publication of further classic works: Galouye's haunting DARK UNIVERSE, Lem's innovative SOLARIS, and Heinlein's STRANGER IN A STRANGE LAND, which won that year's Hugo Award for best science fiction novel, introduced the word 'grok' into the vocabulary of America's youth and – years later – was to become an inspirational handbook for the Sharon Tate murderer, Charles Manson.

Aldiss's 'Hothouse' series ran in five issues of *Fantasy And Science Fiction* that year, overlapping with Anne McCaffrey's THE SHIP WHO SANG, also serialised in its pages. The novellas appeared throughout the year, 'Nomansland' in April, 'Undergrowth' in July, 'Timberland' in September and, finally, 'Evergreen' in December. It was immensely popular, and at the World Science Fiction Convention, Chicon III, held in Chicago the next year, the fans voted for the series as the best short fiction of 1961, favouring it over works by popular American authors like James H. Schmitz, Lloyd Biggle Jr., Fritz Leiber and Mack Reynolds. But it was a controversial decision and forced a change of rules which has meant that no other series has won the coveted Hugo. What is not in dispute is the quality of HOTHOUSE, the finest offering from a rich year and certainly a better written and more entertaining work than Heinlein's cultish power fantasy. But then, Heinlein had been in vogue since the early 40s and Aldiss was simply a new young English writer who had had his first science fiction story, 'Criminal Record', published only seven years previously in 1954.

Aldiss's first science fiction novel, NON-STOP (STARSHIP in the States – a title which ruined the novel's concealed environment mystery!) appeared in 1958, followed by two minor works, EQUATOR and THE INTERPRETER in the next three years. HOTHOUSE, in its polished form, was only his sixth full-length work and remains, more than twenty novels later, his most popular with science fiction fans. In his previous work Aldiss had shown himself capable of writing fast-moving and yet thoughtful adventure stories which worked on more than one level. The exuberant love of pure story-telling evident in HOTHOUSE can be seen in other works of this period, the fantastical novella, 'Legends Of Smith's Burst' amongst them. It was a time when Aldiss's imagination seemed as fecund as the teeming world depicted in HOTHOUSE, with its fabulous creations, half nonsense, half assonance – wiltmilts and leatherfeathers, colderpolders and pluggyrugs, trappersnappers and fuzzypuzzles, leapy-creepers and burnurns, dripperlips and speedseeds, not to mention the magnificent Sodal Ye of the catch-carry-kind – and its vivid and memorable imagery of an Earth at the far end of Time. But memorable and fascinating as these are, the novel's true strengths are not so readily apparent.

HOTHOUSE is perceptibly a fantasy, written in a fantastic rather than a realistic mode. It is a work which has its origins in the poetic imagination rather than in scientific speculation – owing more to Marvell, Pope and Wordsworth than to Newton, Einstein and Lovell. There is no mistaking its delightfully exaggerated tone, akin to Lewis Carroll. And yet HOTHOUSE has been consistently criticised – by James Blish at the time of its publication and most recently by David Langford – for its scientific inaccuracies. The Earth and Moon trapped and held immobile, face to face, circling the sun? Impossible! Creatures as vast and heavy as the space-travelling traversers? Preposterous! The existence of an intelligent morel fungus? Ridiculous! And so they are if viewed unimaginatively. Yet all three are potent symbols – symbols of Time-frozen, of vast, alien perspectives, and of the constant battle within the human mind. The landscapes through which we travel in HOTHOUSE are landscapes of the mind, landscapes of dream. The riotous growth, hideous and fascinating by turns, is something we recognise instinctively, for beyond our conscious lives lies another, less ordered, more chaotic existence, timeless and sprawling, illogical and plastic in its ever-melting, ever-shifting forms. In effect, HOTHOUSE is the world of our unconscious, its two hemispheres – one perpetually dark, the other forever brightly lit – analogous to our known and unknown selves. In this sense it is a work which owes much to the influence of Carl Jung; something tangentially acknowledged when the morel searches deep in Gren's mind and discovers Jung's collective unconscious, that vast store of racial instincts and memories. To criticise the novel for failing to measure up to scientific standards is, in this light, not merely an irrelevancy but a mis-reading of the novel.

In HOTHOUSE Aldiss engages us immediately and dramatically with some of the greatest problems and mysteries facing Man. Where does 'Mind' come from? Is 'Mind' a healthy or unhealthy phenomenon? And what is the relationship of innocence to intelligence? Does the acquisition of knowledge necessitate a kind of 'Fall'? These are questions which have fascinated Aldiss throughout his career and can be found in works as diverse as NON-STOP, 'Man On Bridge', MOREAU'S OTHER ISLAND, 'Brothers Of The Head' and the emergent HELLICONIA trilogy. Sometimes, as in ENEMIES OF THE SYSTEM, there has been too great an emphasis on the question and too little on the quest (a criticism that could also be levelled at THE EIGHTY MINUTE HOUR), but in HOTHOUSE Aldiss turned the question into a full-blooded, can't-put-it-down adventure, as perhaps it ought always to be. The result was not a reduction but an enrichment. The tale of Gren and the morel is also the story of Everyman and his mental inheritance: it is an adventure both felt and thought.

Aldiss made few changes in HOTHOUSE between magazine and novel publication, unlike the massive changes in his later serialised and novelised work, BAREFOOT IN THE HEAD. What few alterations there are consist of pargraphs added to link material and odd words and sentences deleted to assist the story's flow. The story itself is unchanged in any significant detail. Changed, however, was the novel's epigraph, Marvell's words superceded by Pope's – words that have their echo in one important passage towards the end of the book.

"Growing is symmetry, up and down, and what was called decay is not decay but the second part of growth."

The speaker is the Sodal Ye, that fantastical dolphin-like creature, part mystic, part scientist, part burden on the back of Mankind. His words permeate all we see and experience in HOTHOUSE – all the vast tapestry of death and life, light and dark, huge and small: all is suffused in greenness. From all decay ultimately comes growth – "Annihilating all that's made to a green thought in a green shade", to quote Marvell again. HOTHOUSE is about greenness just as GREYBEARD, Aldiss's more contemporary post-Civilization novel depicts a "world turned green", a world which Man exists within and yet, somehow, because of 'Mind', the morel, is kept apart from. This exile from Nature, from greenness itself, is captured in that moment when Gren experiences the 'Mirage' in the cave:

Time stopped. The world turned green. The tummy-belly man by the cave mouth, perched on one leg in a flying attitude, turned green, petrified in his absurd position. The rain behind him turned green. Everything: green and immobile.

And shrinking. To dwindle. To shrivel and contract. To become a drop of rain falling forever down the lungs of the heavens. Or to be a grain of sand marking an eternal tumble through hourglasses of endless time. To be a proton speeding inexhaustibly through its own pocket-sized version of limitless space. Finally to reach the infinite immensity of being nothing . . . the infinite richness of non-existence . . . and thus of becoming God . . . and thus of being the top and tail of one's own creation.

. . . of summoning up a billion worlds to rattle along the green links of every second . . . of flying through uncreated stacks of green matter that waited in a vast antechamber of being for its hour or eon of use . . .

And when the eyes in the cave close, releasing Gren, he realises that he is outside. Man, made conscious and self-aware by 'Mind', is an outsider, excluded from the state of blissful unawareness, from greenness itself. It is a pattern familiar to anyone who has undergone the pains and pangs of adolescence and suggests perhaps yet another explanation for HOT-HOUSE's great popularity.

Most science fiction fans (so the booksellers, publishers and pundits tell us) are adolescents who are bitten hard by the sf bug in their early teens and then shake off the habit within a handful of years. That specific period of their lives, with its strong sense of lost innocence and alienation, is reflected in Gren's story. They, like he, are exiled from their selves, unbalanced by the sudden onset of awareness. If they are fortunate they pass through this rite of passage unscathed and, like Gren, find a balance. 'Evergreen', the final five chapters of the book, is more than the obligatory up-beat ending; it is the final part of this process – depicting Gren's reintegration following his freedom from enslavement to 'Mind'. From the decay of his character (charted by Yattmur's reactions to him) comes growth, the second part of growth. Even as the Earth winds down and the Sun prepares to go nova there is life spiralling out across the vacuum of space to other planets, preserving and promising new worlds of greenness – and all to some vast, inscrutable purpose. It is all very reminiscent of Thomas Hardy's vast natural perspectives and is, like Hardy's, a magnificently affirmative vision for all its small tragedies.

> The long afternoon of eternity wore on, that long golden road of an afternoon that would somewhen lead to an everlasting night. Motion there was, but motion without event – except for those negligible events that seemed so large to the creatures participating in them.

Aldiss's seemingly impersonal aside contains a delightful irony, of course – one Hardy would have appreciated – for the fact is that Gren's story is far from negligible to us. His decision to return to the richly green middle branches of the great banyan tree, taking his wife Yattmur and his child Laren with him, provides the essential human perspective to set beside the Cosmic view. Like Hardy, Aldiss appreciated the need for contrast. So did Aldiss's American publishers, who called the novel THE LONG AFTERNOON OF EARTH.

Aldiss has progressed as a writer since the early days of HOTHOUSE, as works like the excellent and equally opulent THE MALACIA TAPESTRY clearly illustrate, yet his most recent writing has shown a return to the fast-paced yet intelligent adventure of his early years – a revitalization of his work which recently won him the John W. Campbell Memorial Award for his 1982 novel, HELLICONIA SPRING. Those years of experimentation in the mid and late 60s which produced REPORT ON PROBABILITY A and BAREFOOT IN THE HEAD – two of the most extreme stylistic exercises in the sf field – and the works of reassessment and 'homage' of the 70s such as FRANKENSTEIN UNBOUND and ENEMIES OF THE SYSTEM seem now, in retrospect, to have been not so much a period of decay after the energetic creativity of his early career, but a second kind of growth. Like his creation, Gren, Brian Aldiss seems to have returned to the sprawling middle branches of the sf banyan, having explored the darkness and ice of self-awareness at its fringes – and has returned with the confidence and maturity to produce his finest work yet in the emergent HELLICONIA trilogy.

For those who like to see patterns in things, it was all there in the plot of HOTHOUSE, exposed on the pages of *Fantasy and Science Fiction* back in 1961. Or, again, we might see Aldiss as another Scart, hero of PILE, Aldiss's 1979 poem, a synthesist of Science and Art, who undergoes a symbolic rebirth into the "bright world" following a descent into darkness, remembering that work's final lines:

> For every one of us it is the same,
> Worlds end or open as we go.

Those words, like the utterance of the Sodal Ye, reverberate throughout the work of Brian Aldiss. In HOTHOUSE those opening worlds – rich, teeming worlds of bright creation – remain in our minds long after the story of Gren and the morel has ended, creating new growth in us.

DAVID WINGROVE

SELECTED BIBLIOGRAPHY

Space, Time and Nathaniel (1957; Collection)
Non-Stop (1958)
Galaxies Like Grains Of Sand (1960; Collection – US)
Hothouse (1962)
The Dark-Light Years (1964)
Greybeard (1964)
The Saliva Tree and other Strange Growths (1964; Collection)
An Age (1967)
Report On Probability A (1968)
Barefoot In The Head (1969)
The Moment Of Eclipse (1970)
Billion Year Spree: The History Of Science Fiction (1973)
Frankenstein Unbound (1973)
The Malacia Tapestry (1976)
Brothers Of The Head (1977)
Last Orders (1977; Collection)
Enemies Of The System (1978)
New Arrivals, Old Encounters (1979; Collection)
Helliconia Spring (1982)
Helliconia Summer (1983)

PART I

I

Obeying an inalienable law, things grew, growing riotous and strange in their impulse for growth.

The heat, the light, the humidity—these were constant and had remained constant for . . . but nobody knew how long. Nobody cared any more for the big question that begin "How long . . .?" or "Why . . .?" It was no longer a place for mind. It was a place for growth, for vegetables. It was like a hothouse.

In the green light, some of the children came out to play. Alert for enemies, they ran along a branch, calling to each other in soft voices. A fast-growing berrywhisk moved upwards to one side, its sticky crimson mass of berries gleaming. Clearly it was intent on seeding and would offer the children no harm. They scuttled past. Beyond the margin of the group strip, some nettle-moss had sprung up during their period of sleep. It stirred as the children approached.

"Kill it," Toy said simply. She was the head child of the group. She was ten, had lived through ten fruitings of the fig tree. The others obeyed her, even Gren. Unsheathing the sticks every child carried in imitation of every adult, they scraped at the nettlemoss. They scraped at it and hit it. Excitement grew in them as they beat down the plant, squashing its poisoned tips.

Clat fell forward in her excitement. She was only five, the youngest of the group's children. Her hands fell among the poisonous stuff. She cried aloud and rolled aside. The other children also cried, but did not venture into the nettlemoss to save her.

9

Struggling out of the way, little Clat cried again. Her fingers clutched at the rough bark—then she was tumbling from the branch.

The children saw her fall on to a great spreading leaf several lengths below, clutch it, and lie there quivering on the quivering green. She looked pitifully up at them, afraid to call.

"Fetch Lily-yo," Toy told Gren. Gren sped back along the branch to get Lily-yo. A tigerfly swooped out of the air at him, humming its anger deeply. He struck it aside with a hand, not pausing. He was nine, a rare man child, very brave already, and fleet and proud. Swiftly he ran to the Headwoman's hut.

Under the branch, attached to its underside, hung eighteen great homemaker nuts. Hollowed out they were, and cemented into place with the cement distilled from the acetoyle plant. Here lived the eighteen members of the group, one to each homemaker's nut, the Headwoman, her five women, their man, and the eleven surviving children.

Hearing Gren's cry, out came Lily-yo from her nuthut, climbing up a line to stand on the branch beside him.

"Clat has fallen!" cried Gren.

With her stick, Lily-yo rapped sharply on the bough before running on ahead of the child.

Her signal called out the other six adults, the women Flor, Daphe, Hy, Ivin, and Jury, and the man Haris. They hastened from their nuthuts, weapons ready, ready for attack or flight.

As Lily-yo ran, she whistled on a sharp split note.

Instantly to her from the thick foliage nearby came a dumbler, flying to her shoulder. The dumbler rotated, a fleecy umbrella whose separate spokes controlled its direction. It matched its flight to her movement.

Both children and adults gathered round Lily-yo when she looked down at Clat, still sprawled some way below on her leaf.

"Lie still, Clat! Do not move!" called Lily-yo. "I will come to you." Clat obeyed that voice, though she was in pain and fear, staring up hopefully towards the source of hope.

Lily-yo climbed astride the hooked base of the dumbler, whistling softly to it. Only she of the group had fully mastered the art of commanding dumblers. These dumblers were the half-sentient fruits of the whistlethistle. The tips of their feathered spokes carried seeds; the seeds were strangely shaped, so that a light breeze whispering in them made them into ears that listened to every advantage of the wind that would spread their propagation. Humans, after long years of practice, could use these crude ears for their own purposes and instructions, as Lily-yo did now.

The dumbler bore her down to the rescue of the helpless child. Clat lay on her back, watching them come, hoping to herself. She was still looking up when green teeth sprouted through the leaf all about her.

"Jump, Clat!" Lily-yo cried.

The child had time to scramble to her knees. Vegetable predators are not as fast as humans. Then the green teeth snapped shut about her waist.

Under the leaf, a trappersnapper had moved into position, sensing the presence of prey through the single layer of foliage. The trappersnapper was a horny, caselike affair, just a pair of square jaws, hinged and with many long teeth. From one corner of it grew a stalk, very muscular and thicker than a human, and resembling a neck. Now it bent, carrying Clat away down to its true mouth, which lived with the rest of the plant far below on the unseen forest Ground, in darkness and decay.

Whistling, Lily-yo directed her dumbler back up to the home bough. Nothing now could be done for Clat. It was the way.

Already the rest of the group was dispersing. To stand in a bunch was to invite trouble, trouble from the unnumbered enemies of the forest. Besides, Clat's was not the first death they had witnessed.

Lily-yo's group had once consisted of seven underwomen and two men. Two women and one man had fallen to the green. Between them, the eight women had borne twenty-two children to the group, five of them being man children. Deaths of children were many, always. Now that Clat was gone, over half the children had fallen to the green. Lily-yo knew that this was a shockingly high fatality rate, and as leader she blamed herself for it. The dangers in the branches might be many, but they were familiar, and could be guarded against. She rebuked herself all the more because of the surviving offspring, only three man children were left, Gren, Poas, and Veggy. Of them, she felt obscurely that Gren was born for trouble.

Lily-yo walked back along the branch in the green light. The dumbler drifted from her unheeded, obeying the silent instructions of the forest air, listening for word of a seeding place. Never had there been such an overcrowding of the world. No bare places existed. Sometimes the dumblers floated through the jungles for centuries, waiting to alight, epitomizing a vegetable loneliness.

Coming to a point above one of the nuthuts, Lily-yo lowered herself down by the creeper into it. This had been Clat's nuthut. The headwoman could hardly enter it, so small was the door. Humans kept their doors as narrow as possible, enlarging them only as they grew. It helped to keep out unwanted visitors.

All was tidy in Clat's nuthut. From the soft fibre of the inside a bed had been cut; there the five-year-old had slept, when a feeling for sleep came among the unchanging forest green. On the cot lay Clat's soul. Lily-yo took it and thrust it into her belt.

She climbed out on to the creeper, took her knife, and began to slash at the place where the bark of the tree had been cut away and the nuthut was attached to the living wood. After several slashes, the cement gave. Clat's nuthut hinged down, hung for a moment, then fell.

As it disappeared among huge coarse leaves, there was a flurry of foliage. Something was fighting for the privilege of devouring the huge morsel.

Lily-yo climbed back on to the branch. For a moment she

paused to breathe deeply. Breathing was more trouble than it had been. She had gone on too many hunts, borne too many children, fought too many fights. With a rare and fleeting knowledge of herself, she glanced down at her bare green breasts. They were less plump than they had been when she first took the man Haris to her; they hung lower. Their shape was less beautiful.

By instinct she knew her youth was over. By instinct she knew it was time to Go Up.

The group stood near the Hollow, awaiting her. She ran to them, outwardly as active as ever, though her heart felt dead. The Hollow was like an upturned armpit, formed where the branch joined the trunk. In the Hollow a water supply had collected.

The group was watching a line of termights climb the trunk. One of the termights now and again signalled greetings to the humans. The humans waved back. As far as they had allies at all, the termights were their allies. Only five great families survived among the rampant green life; the tigerflies, the treebees, the plantants and the termights were social insects mighty and invincible. And the fifth family was man, lowly and easily killed, not organized as the insects were, but not extinct, the last animal species remaining in all the all-conquering vegetable world.

Lily-yo came up to the group. She too raised her eyes to follow the moving line of termights until it disappeared into the layers of green. The termights could live on any level of the great forest, in the Tips or down on the Ground. They were the first and last of insects; as long as anything lived, the termights and tigerflies would.

Lowering her eyes, Lily-yo called to the group.

When they looked, she brought out Clat's soul, lifting it above her head to show to them.

"Clat has fallen to the green," she said. "Her soul must go to the Tips, according to the custom. Flor and I will take it at once, so that we can go with the termights. Daphe, Hy, Ivin, Jury, you guard well the man Haris and the children till we return."

The women nodded solemnly. Then they came one by one to touch Clat's soul.

The soul was roughly carved of wood into the shape of a woman. As a child was born, so with rites its male parent carved it a soul, a doll, a totem soul—for in the forest when one fell to the green there was scarcely ever a bone surviving to be buried. The soul survived for burial in the Tips.

As they touched the soul, Gren adventurously slipped from the group. He was nearly as old as Toy, as active and as strong. Not only had he power to run. He could climb. He could swim. Further, he had a will of his own. Ignoring the cry of his friend Veggy, he scampered into the Hollow and dived into the pool.

Below the surface, opening his eyes, he saw a world of bleak clarity. A few green things like clover leaves grew at his approach, eager to wrap round his legs. Gren avoided them with a flick of his hands as he shot deeper. Then he saw the crocksock—before it saw him.

The crocksock was an aquatic plant semi-parasitic by nature. Living in hollows, it sent down its saw-toothed suckers into the trees' sap. But the upper section of it, rough and tongue-shaped like a sock, could feed also. It unfolded, wrapping round Gren's left arm, its fibres instantly locking to increase the grip.

Gren was ready for it. With one slash of his knife, he clove the crocksock in two, leaving the lower half to thrash uselessly at him as he swam away.

Before he could rise to the surface, Daphe the skilled huntress was beside him, her face angered, bubbles flashing out silver like fish from between her teeth. Her knife was ready to protect him.

He grinned at her as he broke surface and climbed out on to the dry bank. Nonchalantly he shook himself as she climbed beside him.

"Nobody runs or swims or climbs alone," Daphe called to

him, quoting one of the laws. "Gren, have you no fear? Your head is an empty burr!"

The other women too showed anger. Yet none of them touched Gren. He was a man child. He was tabu. He had the magic powers of carving souls and bringing babies—or would have when fully grown, which would be soon now.

"I am Gren, the man child!" he boasted to them, thumping his chest. His eyes sought Haris's for approval. Haris merely looked away. Now that Gren was so big, Haris did not cheer him on as once he had, though the boy's deeds were braver than before.

Slightly deflated, Gren jumped about, waving the strip of crocksock still wrapped round his left arm. He called and boasted at the woman to show how little he cared for them.

"You are a baby yet," hissed Toy. She was ten, his senior by one year. Gren fell quiet. The time would come to show them all that he was someone special.

Scowling, Lily-yo said, "The children grow too old to manage. When Flor and I have been to the Tips to bury Clat's soul, we shall return and break up the group. Time has come for us to part. Guard yourselves!"

She saluted them and turned about with Flor beside her.

It was a subdued group that watched their leader go. All knew that the group had to split; none cared to think about it. Their time of happiness and safety—so it seemed to all of them— would be finished, perhaps for ever. The children would enter a period of lonely hardship, fending for themselves before joining other groups. The adults embarked on old age, trial, and death when they Went Up into the unknown.

2

Lily-yo and Flor climbed the rough bark easily. For them it was like going up a series of more or less symmetrically placed rocks. Now and again they met some kind of vegetable enemy, a thinpin or a pluggyrug, but these were small fry, easily despatched into the green gloom below. Their enemies were the termights' enemies, and the moving column had already dealt with the foes in its path. Lily-yo and Flor climbed close to the termights, glad of their company.

They climbed for a long while. Once they rested on an empty branch, capturing two wandering burrs, splitting them, and eating their oily white flesh. On the way up, they had glimpsed one or two groups of humans on different branches; sometimes these groups waved shyly, sometimes not. Eventually they climbed too high for humans.

Nearer the Tips, new dangers threatened. In the safer middle layers of the forest the humans lived, avoided the perils of the Tips or the Ground.

"Now we move on," Lily-yo told Flor, getting to her feet when they had rested. "Soon we will be at the Tips."

A commotion silenced the two women. They looked up, crouching against the trunk for protection. Above their heads, leaves rustled as death struck.

A leapycreeper flailed the rough bark in a frenzy of greed, attacking the termight column. The leapycreeper's roots and stems were also tongues and lashes. Whipping round the trunk, it thrust its sticky tongues into the termights.

Against this particular plant, flexible and hideous, the insects had little defence. They scattered but kept doggedly climbing up, each perhaps trusting in the blind law of averages to survive.

For the humans, the plant was less of a threat—at least when met on a branch. Encountered on a trunk, it could easily dislodge them and send them helplessly falling to the green.

"We will climb on another trunk," Lily-yo said.

She and Flor ran deftly along the branch, once jumping a bright parasitic bloom round which treebees buzzed, a forerunner of the world of colour above them.

A far worse obstacle lay waiting in an innocent-looking hole in the branch. As Flor and Lily-yo approached, a tigerfly zoomed

16

up at them. It was all but as big as they were, a terrible thing that possessed both weapons and intelligence—and malevolence. Now it attacked only through viciousness, its eyes large, its mandibles working, its transparent wings beating. Its head was a mixture of shaggy hair and armour-plating, while behind its slender waist lay the great swivel-plated body, yellow and black, sheathing a lethal sting in its tail.

It dived between the women, aiming to hit them with its wings. They fell flat as it sped past. Angrily, it tumbled against the branch as it turned on them again; its golden-brown sting flicked in and out.

"I'll get it!" Flor said. A tigerfly had killed one of her babes.

Now the creature came in fast and low. Ducking, Flor reached up and seized its shaggy hair, swinging the tigerfly off balance. Quickly she raised her sword. Bringing it down in a mighty sweep, she severed that chitinous and narrow waist.

The tigerfly fell away in two parts. The two women ran on.

The branch, a main one, did not grow thinner. Instead, it ran on and grew into another trunk. The tree, vastly old, the longest lived organism ever to flourish on this little world, had a myriad trunks. Very long ago—two thousand million years past—trees had grown in many kinds, depending on soil, climate, and other conditions. As temperatures climbed, the trees proliferated and came into competition with each other. On this continent, the banyan, thriving in the heat and using its complex system of self-rooting branches, gradually established ascendancy over the other species. Under pressure, it evolved and adapted. Each banyan spread out farther and farther, sometimes doubling back on itself for safety. Always it grew higher and crept wider, protecting its parent stem as its rivals multiplied, dropping down trunk after trunk, throwing out branch after branch, until at last it learnt the trick of growing into its neighbour banyan, forming a thicket against which no other tree could strive. Their complexity became unrivalled, their immortality established.

On the continent where the humans lived, only one banyan tree grew now. It had become first King of the forest, then the forest itself. It had conquered the deserts and the mountains and the swamps. It filled the continent with its interlaced scaffolding. Only before the wider rivers or at the margins of the sea, where the deadly seaweeds could assail it, did the tree not go.

And at the terminator, where all things stopped and night began, there too the tree did not go.

The women climbed slowly now, alert as the odd tigerfly zoomed in their direction. Splashes of colour grew everywhere, attached to the tree, hanging from lines, or drifting free. Lianas and fungi blossomed. Dumblers moved mournfully through the tangle. As they gained height, the air grew fresher and colour rioted, azures and crimsons, yellows and mauves, all the beautifully tinted snares of nature.

A dripperlip sent its scarlet dribbles of gum down the trunk. Several thinpins, with vegetable skill, stalked the drops, pounced, and died. Lily-yo and Flor went by on the other side.

Slashweed met them. They slashed back and climbed on.

Many fantastic plant forms there were, some like birds, some like butterflies. Ever and again, whips and hands shot out, taking them in mid-flight.

"Look!" Flor whispered. She pointed above their heads.

The tree's bark was cracked almost invisibly. Almost invisibly, a part of it moved. Thrusting her stick out at arm's length, Flor eased herself up until stick and crack were touching. Then she prodded.

A section of the bark gaped wide, revealing a pale deadly mouth. An oystermaw, superbly camouflaged, had dug itself into the tree. Jabbing swiftly, Flor thrust her stick into the trap. As the jaws closed, she pulled with all her might, Lily-yo steadying her. The oystermaw, taken by surprise, was wrenched from its socket.

Opening its maw in shock, it sailed outward through the air. A rayplane took it without trying.

18

Lily-yo and Flor climbed on.

The Tips was a strange world of its own, the vegetable kingdom at its most imperial and most exotic.

If the banyan ruled the forest, *was* the forest, then the traversers ruled the Tips. The traversers had formed the typical landscape of the Tips. Theirs were the great webs trailing everywhere, theirs the nests built on the tips of the tree.

When the traversers deserted their nests, other creatures built there, other plants grew, spreading their bright colours to the sky. Debris and droppings knitted these nests into solid platforms. Here grew the burnurn plant, which Lily-yo sought for the soul of Clat.

Pushing and climbing, the two women finally emerged on to one of these platforms. They took shelter from the perils of the sky under a great leaf and rested from their exertions. Even in the shade, even for them, the heat of the Tips was formidable. Above them, paralysing half the heaven, burned a great sun. It burnt without cease, always fixed and still at one point in the sky, and so would burn until that day—now no longer impossibly distant—when it burnt itself out.

Here in the Tips, relying on that sun for its strange method of defence, the burnurn ruled among stationary plants. Already its sensitive roots told it that intruders were near. On the leaf above them, Lily-yo and Flor saw a circle of light move; it wandered over the surface, paused, contracted. The leaf smouldered and burst into flames. By focusing one of its urns on them, the plant was fighting them with its terrible weapon—fire.

"Run!" Lily-yo commanded, and they dashed behind the top of a whistlethistle, hiding beneath its thorns, peering out at the burnurn plant.

It was a splendid sight.

High reared the plant, displaying perhaps half a dozen cerise flowers, each flower larger than a human. Other flowers, fertilized, had closed together, forming many-sided urns. Later stages still could be seen, where the colour drained from the urns as seed swelled at the base of them. Finally, when the seed was ripe, the urn—now hollow and immensely strong—turned transparent as glass and became a heat weapon the plant could use even after its seeds were scattered.

Every vegetable and creature shrank from fire—except the humans. They alone could deal with the burnurn plant and use it to advantage.

Moving cautiously, Lily-yo stole forth and cut off a big leaf which grew through the platform on which they stood. It was taller than she was. Clutching it to her, she ran straight for the burnurn, hurling herself among its foliage and shinning to the top of it without pause, before it could turn its urn-shaped lenses up to focus on her.

"Now!" she cried to Flor.

Flor was already on the move, sprinting towards her.

Lily-yo raised the leaf above the burnurn, holding it between the plant and the sun, so that the menacing urns were in shadow. As if realizing that this ruined its method of defence, the plant drooped in the shade, a picture of vegetable dejection with its flowers and its urns hanging limply.

With a grunt of approval, Flor darted forward and cut off one of the great transparent urns. They carried it between them as they ran back for the cover of the whistlethistle. As the shadowing leaf fell away from over it, the burnurn came back to furious life, flailing its urns as they sucked in the sun again.

The two women reached cover just in time. A vegbird swooped out of the sky at them—and impaled itself on a thorn.

In no time, a dozen scavengers were fighting for its body. Under cover of the confusion, Lily-yo and Flor attacked the urn they had won. Using both their knives and all their strength, they prised up one side enough to put Clat's soul inside the urn. The side instantly snapped back into place again, an airtight join. The soul stared woodenly out at them through the transparent facets.

"May you Go Up and reach heaven," Lily-yo said.

It was her business to see the soul stood at least a sporting chance of doing so. With Flor, she carried the urn across to one of the cables spun by a traverser. The top end of the urn, where the seed had been, exuded gum and was enormously sticky. The urn adhered easily to the cable and hung there glittering in the sun.

Next time a traverser climbed up the cable, the urn stood an excellent chance of sticking like a burr to one of its legs. Thus it would be carried away to heaven.

As they finished the work, a shadow fell over them. A mile long body drifted down towards them. A traverser, that gross vegetable equivalent of a spider, was descending to the Tips.

Hurriedly, the women burrowed their way through the platform of leaves. The last rites for Clat had been carried out: it was time to return to the group.

Before they climbed down again to the green world of middle layers, Lily-yo looked back over her shoulder.

The traverser was descending slowly, a great bladder with legs and jaws, fibery hair covering most of its bulk. To her it was like a god, with the powers of a god. It came down a cable. It floated nimbly down a cable which trailed up into the sky.

Other cables could be seen, stretching up from the jungle close by or distantly. All slanted up, pointing like slender drooping fingers into heaven. Where the sun caught them, they shone. It could be seen that they trailed up in a certain direction. In that direction, a silver half globe floated, remote and cool, but visible even in the sunshine.

Unmoving, steady, the half moon remained always in that sector of the sky.

Throughout the eons, the pull of this moon had gradually slowed the axial revolution of its parent planet to a standstill, until day and night slowed, becoming fixed forever: one on one side of the planet, one on the other. At the same time, a reciprocal braking effect had checked the moon's apparent flight. Drifting farther from Earth, it had shed its role as satellite and rode along in a Trojan position, an independent planet in its own right hugging one angle of a vast equilateral triangle which held the Earth and the sun at its other angles. Now Earth and Moon, for what was left of the afternoon of eternity, faced each other in the same relative position. They were locked face to face, and so would be, until the sands of time ceased to run, or the sun ceased to shine.

And the multitudinous strands of cable floated across the gap between them, uniting the worlds. Back and forth the traversers could shuttle at will, vegetable astronauts huge and insensible, with Earth and Luna both enmeshed in their indifferent net.

With surprising suitability, the old age of the Earth was snared about with cobwebs.

3

The journey back to the group was fairly uneventful. Lily-yo and Flor travelled at an easy pace, sliding down again into the middle layers of the tree. Lily-yo did not press forward as hard as usual, for she was reluctant to face the break-up of the group that had to come.

She could not express her thoughts. In this green millenary, there were few thoughts and fewer words.

"Soon we must Go Up like Clat's soul," she said to Flor, as they climbed down.

"It is the way," Flor answered, and Lily-yo knew she would get no deeper a word on the matter than that. Nor could she frame deeper words herself; human understandings trickled shallow these days. It was the way.

The group greeted them soberly when they returned. Being weary, Lily-yo offered them a brief salutation and retired to her nuthut. Jury and Ivin soon brought her food, setting not so much as a finger inside her home, that being tabu. When she had eaten and slept, she climbed again on to the home strip of branch and summoned the others.

22

"Hurry!" she called, staring fixedly at Haris, who was not hurrying. How he could vex her, when he knew she favoured him most! Why should a difficult thing be so precious—or a precious thing so difficult?

At that moment, while her attention was diverted, a long green tongue licked out from behind the tree trunk. Uncurling, it hovered daintily for a second. It took Lily-yo round the waist, pinning her arms to her side, lifting her off the branch, while she kicked and cried in a fury at having been less than alert.

Haris pulled a knife from his belt, leapt forward with eyes slitted, and hurled the blade. Singing, it pierced the tongue and pinned it to the rough trunk of the tree.

Haris did not pause after throwing. As he ran towards the pinioned tongue, Daphe and Jury ran behind him, while Flor scuttled the children to safety. In its agony, the tongue eased its grip on Lily-yo.

Now a terrific thrashing had set in on the other side of the tree trunk: the forest seemed full of its vibrations. Lily-yo whistled up two dumblers, fought her way out of the green coils round her, and got safely back on the branch. The tongue, writhing in pain, flicked about meaninglessly. Weapons out, the four humans moved forward to deal with it.

The tree itself shook with the wrath of the creature trapped by its tongue. Edging cautiously round the trunk, they saw it. Its great vegetable mouth distorted, a wiltmilt stared back at them with the hideous palmate pupil of its single eye. Furiously it hammered itself against the tree, foaming and mouthing. Though they had faced wiltmilts before, yet the humans trembled at the sight.

The wiltmilt was many times the girth of the tree trunk at its present extension. If necessary, it could have extended itself up almost to the Tips, stretching and becoming thinner as it did so. Like an obscene jack-in-the-box, it sprang up from the Ground in search of food, armless, brainless, gouging its slow way over the forest floor on wide and rooty legs.

"Pin it!" Lily-yo cried. "Don't let the monster break away!"

Concealed all along the branch were sharp stakes that the group kept for emergencies. With these they stabbed the tongue still cracking like a whip about their heads. At last they had a good length of it secured, staked down to the tree. However much the wiltmilt writhed, it could never get free now.

"Now we must leave and Go Up," Lily-yo said.

No human could ever kill a wiltmilt, for its vital parts were inaccessible. But already its struggles were attracting predators, the thinpins—those mindless sharks of the middle layers—ray-planes, trappersnappers, gargoyles, and smaller vegetable vermin. They would tear the wiltmilt to living pieces until nothing of it remained—and if they happened on a human at the same time . . . well, it was the way. So the group melted quickly away into the curtains of green.

Lily-yo was angry. She had brought on this trouble. She had been caught off guard. Alert, she would never have been trapped by a slow-moving wiltmilt. Her mind had been tied with thought of her own bad leadership. For she had caused two dangerous trips to be made to the Tips where one would have done. If she had taken all the group with her when Clat's soul was disposed of, she would have saved the second ascent that now lay before them. What ailed her brain that she did not see this beforehand?

She clapped her hands. Standing for shelter under a giant leaf, she made the group come about her. Sixteen pairs of eyes stared trustingly at her, awaiting her words. She was angry to see how they trusted her.

"We adults grow old," she told them. "We grow stupid. I grow stupid—I let a slow wiltmilt catch me. I am not fit to lead you any more. The time is come for the adults to Go Up and return to the gods who made us. Then the children will be on their own. They will be the new group. Toy will lead the group. By the time you are sure of your group, Gren and soon Veggy will be old enough to give you children. Take care of the man

24

children. Let them not fall to the green, or the group dies. Better to die yourself than let the group die."

Lily-yo had never made, the others had never heard, so long a speech. Some of them did not understand it all. What of this talk about falling to the green? One did or one did not: it needed no talk. Whatever happened was the way, and talk could not touch it.

May, a girl child, said cheekily, "On our own we can enjoy many things."

Reaching out, Flor clapped her on an ear.

"First you make the hard climb to the Tips," she said.

"Yes, move," Lily-yo said. She gave the order for climbing, who should lead, who follow. There was no further discussion between them, no curiosity; only Gren said wonderingly, "Lily-yo would punish us all for her mistake."

About them the forest throbbed, green creatures sped and snapped through the greenery, as the wiltmilt was devoured.

"The climb is hard. Begin quickly," Lily-yo said, looking restlessly about her, and laying a particularly severe look on Gren.

"Why climb?" Gren asked rebelliously. "With dumblers we can fly easily to the Tips and suffer no pain."

It was too complicated to explain to him that a human drifting in the air was far more vulnerable than a human shielded by a trunk, with the good rough bark nodules to squeeze between in case of attack.

"While I lead, you climb," Lily-yo said. "You talk so much you must have a toad in your head." She could not hit Gren; he was a tabu man child.

They collected their souls from their nuthuts. There was no pomp about saying good-bye to their old home. Their souls went in their belts, their swords—the sharpest, hardest, thorns available—went in their hands. They ran along the branch after Lily-yo, away from the disintegrating wiltmilt, away from their past.

Slowed by the younger children, the journey up to the Tips

25

was long. Although the humans fought off the usual hazards, the tiredness growing in small limbs could not be fought. Half way to the Tips, they found a side branch to rest on, for there grew a fuzzypuzzle, and they sheltered in it.

The fuzzypuzzle was a beautiful, disorganized fungus. Although it looked like nettlemoss on a larger scale, it did not harm humans, drawing in its poisoned pistils as if with disgust when they came to it. Ambling in the eternal branches of the tree, fuzzypuzzles desired only vegetable food. So the group climbed into the middle of it and slept. Guarded among the waving viridian and yellow stalks, they were safe from nearly all forms of attack.

Flor and Lily-yo slept most deeply of the adults. They were tired by their previous journey. Haris the man was the first to awake knowing something was wrong. As he roused, he woke up Jury by poking her with his stick. He was lazy; besides, it was his duty to keep out of danger. Jury sat up. She gave a shrill cry of alarm and jumped at once to defend the children.

Four winged things had invaded the fuzzypuzzle. They had seized Veggy, the man child, and Bain, one of the younger girl children, gagging and tying them before the pair could wake properly.

At Jury's cry, the winged ones looked round.

They were flymen!

In some respects they resembled humans. That is to say, they had one head, two long and powerful arms, stubby legs, and strong fingers on hands and feet. But instead of smooth green skin, they were covered in a glittering horny substance, here black, here pink. And large scaly wings resembling those of a vegbird grew from their wrists to their ankles. Their faces were sharp and clever. Their eyes glittered.

When they saw the humans waking, the flymen grabbed up the two captive children. Bursting through the fuzzypuzzle, which did not harm them, they ran towards the edge of the branch to jump off.

Flymen were crafty enemies, seldom seen but much dreaded by the group. They worked by stealth. Though they did not kill unless forced to, they stole children, which was reckoned almost a graver crime. Catching them was hard. Flymen did not fly properly, but the crash glides they fell into carried them swiftly away through the forest, safe from human reprisal.

Jury flung herself forward with all her might, Ivin behind her. She caught one of the flymen's ankles before he could launch himself, seizing part of the leathery tendon of wing where it joined the foot, and clung on. The flyman staggered with her weight and turned to free himself, releasing his hold on Veggy. His companion, taking the full weight of the boy child, paused, dragging out a knife to defend himself.

Ivin flung herself at him with savagery. She had mothered Veggy: he should not be taken away. The flyman's blade came to meet her. She threw herself on it. It ripped her stomach till the brown entrails showed, and she toppled from the branch with no cry. There was a commotion in the foliage below as trapper-snappers fought for her as she fell.

Knocked backwards by Ivin's charge, the flyman dropped the bound Veggy and left his friend still struggling with Jury. He spread his wings, taking off heavily after the two who had borne Bain away between them into the green thicket.

All the group were awake now. Lily-yo silently untied Veggy, who did not cry, for he was a man child. Meanwhile, Haris knelt by Jury and her winged opponent, who fought without words to get away. Haris raised his knife to settle the struggle.

"Don't kill me. I will go!" cried the flyman. His voice was harsh, his words hardly understandable. The mere strangeness of him filled Haris with savagery, so that his lips curled back and his tongue came thickly between his teeth.

He thrust his knife deep between the flyman's ribs, four times over, till the blood poured across his clenched fist.

Jury stood up gasping and leant against Flor. "I grow old," she said. "Once it was no trouble to kill a flyman."

27

She looked at the man Haris with gratitude. He had more than one use.

With one foot she pushed the limp body over the edge of the branch. It rolled messily, then dropped. With its old wizened wings tucked uselessly about its head, the flyman fell to the green.

4

They lay among the sharp leaves of two whistlethistle plants, dazed by the bright sun but still alert for danger. Their climb had been completed. Now the nine children saw the Tips for the first time—and were struck mute by it.

Once more Lily-yo and Flor lay siege to a burnurn, with Daphe helping them to shade it with upheld leaves. As the plant slumped defencelessly, Daphe severed six of the great transparent pods that were to be their coffins. Hy helped her carry them to safety, after which Lily-yo and Flor dropped their leaves and ran for the shelter of the whistlethistles.

A cloud of paperwings drifted by, their colours startling to eyes generally submerged in green: sky blues and yellows and bronzes and a viridian that flashed like water.

One of the paperwings alighted fluttering on a tuft of emerald foliage near the watchers. The foliage was a dripperlip. Almost at once the paperwing turned grey as its small nourishment content was sucked out. It disintegrated like ash.

Rising cautiously, Lily-yo led the group over to the nearest cable of traverser web. Each adult carried her own urn.

The traversers, largest of all creatures, vegetable or otherwise, could never go into the forest. They spurted out their line among the upper branches, securing it with side strands.

Finding a suitable cable with no traverser in sight, Lily-yo turned, signalling for the urns to be put down. She spoke to Toy, Gren, and the seven other children.

"Now help us climb with our souls into our burnurns. See us tight in. Then carry us to the cable and stick us to it. And then good-bye. We Go Up, and leave the group in your hands. You are the living now!"

Toy momentarily hesitated. She was a slender girl, her breasts like pearfruit.

"Do not go, Lily-yo," she said. "We still need you, and you know we need you."

"It is the way," Lily-yo said firmly.

Prising open one of the facets of her urn, she slid into her coffin. Helped by the children, the other adults did the same. From habit, Lily-yo glanced to see that Haris the man was safe.

They were all in their transparent prisons at last. A surprising coolness and peace stole over them.

The children carried the coffins between them, glancing nervously up at the sky meanwhile. They were afraid. They felt helpless. Only the bold man child Gren looked as if he was enjoying their new sense of independence. He more than Toy directed the others in the placing of the urns upon the traverser's cable.

Lily-yo smelt a curious smell in the urn. As it soaked through her lungs, her senses became detached. Outside, the scene that had been clear clouded and shrank. She saw she hung suspended on a traverser cable above the tree tops, with Flor, Haris, Daphe, Hy and Jury in other urns nearby, hanging helplessly. She saw the children, the new group, run to shelter. Without looking back, they dived into the muddle of foliage on the platform and disappeared.

The traverser drifted very high above the Tips, safe from its enemies. All about it, space was indigo, and the invisible rays of space bathed it and nourished it. Yet the traverser was still dependent on the earth for nourishment. After many hours of vegetative dreaming, it swung itself over and climbed down a cable.

Other traversers hung motionless nearby. Occasionally one would blow a globe of oxygen or hitch a leg to try and dislodge a troublesome parasite. Their was a leisureliness never attained before. Time was not for them; the sun was theirs, and would ever be until it became unstable, turned nova, and burnt both them and itself out.

The traverser fell, its feet twinkling, hardly touching its cable. It fell straight to the forest, it plunged towards the leafy cathedrals of the forest. Here in the air lived its enemies, enemies many times smaller, many times more vicious, many times more clever. Traversers were prey to one of the last families of insect, the tigerflies.

Only tigerflies could kill traversers—in their own insidious, invincible way.

Over the long slow eons as the sun's radiation increased, vegetation had evolved to undisputed supremacy. The wasps had developed too, keeping pace with the new developments. They grew in number and size as the animal kingdom fell into eclipse and dwindled into the rising tide of green. In time they became the chief enemies of the spider-like traversers. Attacking in packs, they could paralyse the primitive nerve centres, leaving the traversers to stagger to their own destruction. The tigerflies also laid their eggs in tunnels bored into the stuff of their enemies' bodies; when the eggs hatched, the larvae fed happily on living flesh.

This threat it was, more than anything, that had driven the traversers farther and farther into space many millennia past. In this seemingly inhospitable region, they reached their full and monstrous flowering.

Hard radiation became a necessity for them. Nature's first astronauts, they changed the face of the firmament. Long after man had rolled up his affairs and retired to the trees from whence he came, the traversers reconquered that vacant pathway he had lost. Long after intelligence had died from its peak of dominance, the traversers linked the green globe and the white indissolubly —with that antique symbol of neglect, a spider's web.

The traverser scrambled down among foliage of the Tips,

erecting the hairs on its back, where patchy green and black afforded it natural camouflage. On its way down it had collected several creatures caught fluttering in its cables. It sucked them peacefully. When the soupy noises stopped, it vegetated.

Buzzing roused it from its doze. Yellow and black stripes zoomed before its crude eyes. A pair of tigerflies had found it.

With great alacrity, the traverser moved. Its massive bulk, contracted in the atmosphere, had an overall length of over a mile, yet it moved lightly as pollen, scuttling up a cable back to the safety of vacuum.

As it retreated, its legs brushing the web, it picked up various spores, burrs, and tiny creatures that adhered there. It also picked up six burnurns, each containing an insensible human, which swung unregarded from its shin.

Several miles up, the traverser paused. Recovering from its fright, it ejected a globe of oxygen, attaching it gently to a cable. It paused. Its palps trembled. Then it headed out towards deep space, expanding all the time as pressure dropped.

Its speed increased. Folding its legs, the traverser began to eject fresh web from the spinnerets under its abdomen. So it propelled itself, a vast vegetable almost without feeling, rotating slowly to stabilize its temperature.

Hard radiations bathed it. The traverser basked in them. It was in its element.

Daphe roused. She opened her eyes, gazing without intelligence. What she saw had no meaning. She only knew she had Gone Up. This was a new existence and she did not expect it to have meaning.

Part of the view from her urn was eclipsed by stiff yellowy wisps that might have been hair or straw. Everything else was uncertain, being washed either in blinding light or deep shadow. Light and shadow revolved.

Gradually Daphe identified other objects. Most notable was a splendid green half-ball mottled with white and blue. Was it a fruit? To it trailed cables, glinting here and there, many cables, silver or gold in the crazy light. Two traversers she recognized at some distance, travelling fast, looking mummified. Bright points of lights sparkled painfully. All was confusion.

This was the region of the gods.

Daphe had no feeling. A curious numbness kept her without motion or the wish to move. The smell in the urn was strange. Also the air seemed thick. Everything was like an evil dream. Daphe opened her mouth, her jaw sticky and slow to respond. She screamed. No sound came. Pain filled her. Her sides in particular ached.

Even when her eyes closed again, her mouth still hung open.

Like a great shaggy balloon, the traverser floated down to the moon.

It could hardly be said to think, being a mechanism or little more. Yet somewhere in it the notion stirred that its pleasant journey was too brief, that there might be other directions in which to sail. After all, the hated tigerflies were almost as many now, and as troublesome, on the moon as on the earth. Perhaps somewhere there might be a peaceful place, another of these half-round places with green stuff, in the middle of warm delicious rays. . . .

Perhaps some time it might be worth sailing off on a full belly and a new course. . . .

Many traversers hung above the moon. Their nets straggled untidily everywhere. This was their happy base, better liked than the earth, where the air was thick and their limbs were clumsy. This was the place they had discovered first—except for some puny creatures who had been long gone before they arrived. They were the last lords of creation. Largest and lordliest, they enjoyed their long lazy afternoon's supremacy.

The traverser slowed, spinning out no more cable. In leisurely fashion, it picked its way through a web and drifted down to the pallid vegetation of the moon. . . .

Here were conditions very unlike those on the heavy planet. The many-trunked banyans had never gained supremacy here; in the thin air and low gravity they outgrew their strength and collapsed. In their place, monstrous celeries and parsleys grew, and it was into a bed of these that the traverser settled. Hissing from its exertions, it blew off a cloud of oxygen and relaxed.

As it settled down into the foliage, its great sack of body rubbed against the stems. Its legs too scraped into the mass of leaves. From the legs and body a shower of light debris was dislodged—burrs, seeds, grit, nuts, and leaves caught up in its sticky fibres back on distant earth. Among this detritus were six seed casings from a burnurn plant. They rolled over the ground and came to a standstill.

Haris the man was the first to awaken. Groaning with an unexpected pain in his sides, he tried to sit up. Pressure on his forehead reminded him of where he was. Doubling up knees and arms, he pushed against the lid of his coffin.

Momentarily, it resisted him. Then the whole urn crumbled into pieces, sending Haris sprawling. The rigours of vacuum had destroyed its cohesive powers.

Unable to pick himself up, Haris lay where he was. His head throbbed, his lungs were full of an unpleasant odour. Eagerly he gasped in fresh air. At first it seemed thin and chill, yet he sucked it in with gratitude.

After a while, he was well enough to look about him.

Long yellow tendrils were stretching out of a nearby thicket, working their way gingerly towards him. Alarmed, he looked about for a woman to protect him. None was there. Stiffly, his arms so stiff, he pulled his knife from his belt, rolled over on one side, and lopped the tendrils off as they reached him. This was an easy enemy!

Haris cried as he saw his own flesh. He jumped unsteadily to his feet, yelling in disgust at himself. He was covered in scabs.

33

Worse, as his clothes fell in shreds from him, he saw that a mass of leathery flesh grew from his arms, his ribs, his legs. When he lifted his arms, the mass stretched out almost like wings. He was spoilt, his handsome body ruined.

A sound made him turn, and for the first time he remembered his fellows. Lily-yo was struggling from the remains of her burn-urn. She raised a hand in greeting.

To his horror, Haris saw that she bore disfigurements like his own. In truth, he scarcely recognized her at first. She resembled nothing so much as one of the hated flymen. He flung himself to the ground and wept as his heart expanded in fear and loathing.

Lily-yo was not born to weep. Disregarding her own painful deformities, breathing laboriously, she cast about round the indifferent legs of the traverser, seeking out the other four coffins.

Flor's was the first she found, half buried though it was. A blow with a stone shattered it. Lily-yo lifted up her friend, as hideously transformed as she, and in a short while Flor roused. Inhaling the strange air raucously, she too sat up. Lily-yo left her to seek the others. Even in her dazed state, she thanked her aching limbs for feeling so light of body.

Daphe was dead. She lay stiff and purple in her urn. Though Lily-yo shattered it and called aloud, Daphe did not stir. Her swollen tongue stayed dreadfully protruding from her mouth. Daphe was dead, Daphe who had lived, Daphe who had been the sweet singer.

Hy was also dead, a poor shrivelled thing lying in a coffin that had cracked on its arduous journey between the two worlds. When that coffin shattered under Lily-yo's blow, Hy too fell away to powder. Hy was dead, Hy who had born a man child, Hy always so fleet of foot.

Jury's urn was the last. She stirred as the headwoman reached her and brushed the burrs from her transparent box. A minute later, she was sitting up, eyeing her deformities with a stoical distaste, breathing the sharp air. Jury lived.

34

Haris staggered over to the women. In his hand he carried his soul.

"Four of us!" he exclaimed. "Have we been received by the gods or no?"

"We feel pain—so we live," Lily-yo said. "Daphe and Hy have fallen to the green."

Bitterly, Haris flung down his soul and trampled it underfoot. "Look at us! Better be dead!" he said.

"Before we decide that, we will eat," said Lily-yo.

Painfully, they retreated into the thicket, alerting themselves once more to the idea of danger. Flor, Lily-yo, Jury, Haris, each supported the other. The idea of tabu had somehow been forgotten.

5

"No proper trees grow here," Flor protested, as they pushed among giant celeries whose crests waved high above their heads.

"Take care!" Lily-yo said. She pulled Flor back. Something rattled and snapped, like a chained dog, missing Flor's leg by inches.

A trappersnapper, having missed its prey, was slowly reopening its jaws, baring its green teeth. This one was only a shadow of the terrible trappersnappers spawned on the jungle floors of earth. Its jaws were weaker, its movements far more circumscribed. Without the shelter of the giant banyans, the trappersnappers were disinherited.

Something of the same feeling overcame the humans. They and their ancestors for countless generations had lived in the high trees. Safety was arboreal. Trees there were here, but only celery and parsley trees offering neither the rock-steadiness nor the unlimited boughs of the giant trees.

So they journeyed, nervous, lost, in pain, knowing neither where they were nor why they were.

They were attacked by leapycreepers and sawthorns, and beat

35

them down. They skirted a thicket of nettlemoss taller and wider than any to be met with on earth. Conditions that worked against one group of vegetation favoured others. They climbed a slope and came on a pool fed by a stream. Over the pool hung berries and fruits, sweet to taste, good to eat.

"This is not so bad," Haris said. "Perhaps we can still live."

Lily-yo smiled at him. He was the most trouble, the most lazy; yet she was glad he was still here. When they bathed in the pool, she looked at him again. For all the strange scales that covered him, and the two broad sweeps of flesh that hung by his side, he was still good to look on just because he was Haris. She hoped she was also comely. With a burr she raked her hair back; only a little of it fell out.

When they had bathed, they ate. Haris worked then, collecting fresh knives from the bramble bushes. They were not so tough as the ones on earth, but they would have to do. Then they rested in the sun.

The pattern of their lives was completely broken. More by instinct than intelligence they had lived. Without the group, without the tree, without the earth, no pattern guided them. What was the way or what was not became unclear. So they lay where they were and rested.

As she lay, Lily-yo looked about her. All was strange, so that her heart beat faintly.

Though the sun shone bright as ever, the sky was as deep blue as a vandalberry. And the half-globe shining in the sky was streaked with green and blue and white, so that Lily-yo could not know it for somewhere she had lived. Phantom silver lines pointed to it, while nearer at hand the tracery of traverser webs glittered, veining the whole sky. Traversers moved over it like clouds, their great bodies slack.

All this was their empire, their creation. On their first journeys here, many millennia ago, the traversers had literally laid the seeds of this world. To begin with, they withered and died by the thousand on the inhospitable ash. But even the dead had brought their little levy of oxygen and other gases, soil, spores, and seed, some of which latter sprouted on the fruitful corpses. Under the weight of dozy centuries, these plants gained a sort of foothold.

They grew. Stunted and ailing in the beginning, they grew. With vegetal tenacity, they grew. They exhaled. They spread. They thrived. Slowly the broken wastes of the moon's lit face turned green. In the craters creepers began to flower. Up the ravaged slopes the parsleys crawled. As the atmosphere deepened, so the magic of life intensified, its rhythm strengthened, its tempo increased. More thoroughly than another dominant species had once managed to do, the traversers colonized the moon.

Little Lily-yo knew or cared about any of this. She turned her face from the sky.

Flor had crawled over to Haris the man. She lay against him in the circle of his arms, half under the shelter of his new skin, and she stroked his hair.

Furious, up jumped Lily-yo. She kicked Flor on the shin, then flung herself upon her, using teeth and nails to pull her away. Jury ran to join in.

"This is not time for mating!" Lily-yo cried. "How dare you touch Haris?"

"Let me go! Let me go!" cried Flor. "Haris touched me first."

Haris in his startlement jumped up. He stretched his arms, waved them, and rose effortlessly into the air.

"Look!" he shouted in alarmed delight. "Look what I can do!"

Over their heads he circled once, perilously. Then he lost his balance and came sprawling head first, mouth open in fright. Head first he pitched into the pool.

Three anxious, awe-struck, and love-struck female humans dived in in unison to save him.

37

While they were drying themselves they heard the noises in the forest. At once they became alert, their old selves. They drew their swords and looked to the thicket.

The wiltmilt when it appeared was not like its earthly brothers. No longer upright like a jack-in-the-box, it groped its way along like a caterpillar.

The humans saw its distorted eye break from the celeries. Then they turned and fled.

Even when the danger was left behind, they still moved rapidly, not knowing what they sought. Once they slept, ate, and then again pressed on through the unending growth, the undying daylight, until they came to where the jungle gaped.

Ahead of them, everything seemed to cease and then go on again.

Cautiously they went to see what they had arrived at. The ground underfoot had been uneven. Now it broke altogether into a wide crevasse. Beyond the crevasse the vegetation grew again—but how did humans span that gulf? The four of them stood anxiously where the ferns ended, looking across at the far side.

Haris the man screwed his face in pain to show he had a troublesome idea in his head.

"What I did before—going up in the air," he began awkwardly. "If we do it again now, all of us, we go in the air across to the other side."

"No!" Lily-yo said. "When you go up you come down hard. You will fall to the green!"

"I will do better than before. I think I have the art now."

"No!" repeated Lily-yo. "You are not to go. You are not safe."

"Let him go," Flor said. "He says he has the art."

The two women turned to glare at each other. Taking his chance, Haris raised his arms, waved them, rose slightly from the ground, and began to use his legs too. He moved forward over the crevasse before his nerve broke.

As he fluttered down, Flor and Lily-yo, moved by instinct, dived into the gulf after him. Spreading their arms, they glided about him, shouting. Jury remained behind, crying in baffled anger down to them.

Regaining a little control, Haris landed heavily on an outcropping ledge. The two women alighted chattering and scolding beside him. They looked up, pressing against the cliff for safety. Two lips fringed with fern sucked a narrow purple segment of sky above their heads. Jury could not be seen, though her cries still echoed down to them. They called back to her.

Behind the ledge on which they stood, a tunnel ran into the cliff. All the rock face was peppered with similar holes, so that it resembled a sponge. From the tunnel ran three flymen, two male and one female, ropes and spears in their hands.

Flor and Lily-yo were bending over Haris. Before they had time to recover, they were knocked sprawling and tied with ropes. Other flymen launched themselves from other holes and came gliding in to help secure them. Their flight seemed more sure, more graceful, than it had done on earth. Perhaps the fact that humans were lighter here had something to do with it.

"Bring them in!" the flymen cried to each other. Their sharp, clever faces jostled round eagerly as they hoisted up their captives and bore them into the gloom of tunnel.

In their alarm, Lily-yo, Flor and Haris forgot about Jury, still crouching on the lip of the crevasse. They never saw her again.

The tunnel sloped gently down. Finally it curved and led into another which ran level and true. This in its turn led into an immense cavern with regular sides and a regular roof. Grey daylight flooded in at one end, for the cavern stood at the bottom of the crevasse.

To the middle of this cavern the three captives were brought. Their knives were taken from them and they were released. As they huddled together uneasily, one of the flymen stood forward and spoke.

39

"We will not harm you unless we must," he said. "You come by traverser from the Heavy World. You are new here. When you learn our ways, you will join us."

"I am Lily-yo," Lily-yo proudly said. "You must let me go. We three are humans and you are flymen."

"Yes, you are humans, we are flymen. Also we are humans, you are flymen, for we are all the same. Just now you know nothing. Soon you will know more when you have seen the Captives. They will tell you many things."

"I am Lily-yo. I know many things."

"The Captives will tell you many more things," the flyman insisted.

"If there were many more things, then I should know them, for I am Lily-yo."

"I am Band Appa Bondi and I say come to see the Captives. Your talk is stupid Heavy World talk, Lily-yo."

Several flymen began to look aggressive, so that Haris nudged Lily-yo and muttered, "Let us do what he asks. Do not make more trouble."

Grumpily, Lily-yo let herself and her two companions be led to another chamber. This one was partially ruined, and stank. At the far end of it, a fall of cindery rock marked where the roof had collapsed, while a shaft of the unremitting sunlight burnt on the floor, sending up a curtain of golden light about itself. Near this light were the Captives.

"Do not fear to see them. They will not harm you," Band Appa Bondi said, going forward.

The encouragement was needed, for the Captives were not prepossessing.

Eight of them there were, eight Captives, kept in eight great burnurns big enough to serve them as narrow cells. The cells stood grouped in a semicircle. Band Appa Bondi led Lily-yo, Flor and Haris into the middle of this semicircle, where they could survey and be surveyed.

The Captives were painful to look on. All had some kind of

40

deformity. One had no legs. One had no flesh on his lower jaw. One had four gnarled dwarf arms. One had short wings of flesh connecting ear lobes and thumbs, so that he lived perpetually with hands half raised to his face. One had boneless arms dangling at his side and one boneless leg. One had monstrous wings which trailed about him like carpet. One was hiding his ill-shaped form away behind a screen of his own excrement, smearing it on to the transparent walls of his cell. And one had a second head, a small wizened thing growing from the first that fixed Lily-yo with a malevolent eye. This last captive, who seemed to lead the others, spoke now, using the mouth of his main head.

"I am the Chief Captive. I greet you, children, and invite you to know yourselves. You are of the Heavy World; we are of the True World. Now you join us because you are of us. Though your wings and your scars are new, you are welcome to join us."

"I am Lily-yo. We three are humans, while you are only fly-men. We will not join you."

The Captives grunted in boredom. The Chief Captive spoke again.

"Always this talk from you denizens of the Heavy World! Understand that you *have* joined us by becoming like us. You are flymen, we are human. You know little, we know much."

"But we——"

"Stop your stupid talk, woman!"

"We are——"

"Be silent, woman, and listen," Band Appa Bondi said.

"We know much," repeated the Chief Captive. "Some things we will tell you now to make you understand. All who make the journey from the Heavy World become changed. Some die. Most live and grow wings. Between the worlds are many strong rays, not seen or felt, which change our bodies. When you come here, when you come to the True World, you become a true human. The grub of the tigerfly is not a tigerfly until it changes. So humans change, becoming what you call flymen."

41

"I cannot know what he says," Haris said stubbornly, throwing himself down. But Lily-yo and Flor were listening.

"To this True World, as you call it, we came to die," Lily-yo said, doubtingly.

The Captive with the fleshless jaw said, "The grub of the tigerfly thinks it dies when it changes into a tigerfly."

"You are still young," said the Chief Captive. "You have entered a fresh life. Where are your souls?"

Lily-yo and Flor looked at each other. In their flight from the wiltmilt they had heedlessly thrown down their souls. Haris had trampled on his. It was unthinkable!

"You see. You needed your souls no more. You are still young, and may be able to have babies. Some of those babies may be born with wings."

The Captive with the boneless arms added, "Some may be born wrong, as we are. Some may be born right."

"You are too foul to live!" Haris growled. "Why are you not killed for your horrible shapes?"

"Because we know all things," the Chief Captive said. His second head roused itself and declared in a husky voice, "To be a standard shape is not all in life. To know is also important. Because we cannot move well, we can *think*. This tribe of the True World is good and understands the value of thought in any shape. So it lets us rule it."

Flor and Lily-yo muttered together.

"Do you say that you poor Captives *rule* the True World?" Lily-yo asked at last.

"We do."

"Then why are you captives?"

The flyman with ear lobes and thumbs connected, making his perpetual little gesture of protest, spoke for the first time in a rich and strangled voice.

"To rule is to serve, woman. Those who bear power are slaves to it. Only an outcast is free. Because we are Captives, we have the time to talk and think and plan and know. Those who know

42

command the knives of others. We are power, though we rule without power."

"No hurt will come to you, Lily-yo," Band Appa Bondi added. "You will live among us and enjoy your life free from harm."

"No!" the Chief Captive said with both mouths. "Before she can enjoy, Lily-yo and her companion Flor—this other man creature is plainly useless—must help our great plan."

"You mean we should tell them about the invasion?" Bondi asked.

"Why not? Flor and Lily-yo, you arrive here at a good time. Memories of the Heavy World and its savage life are still fresh in you. We need such memories. So we ask you to go back there on a great plan we have."

"Go back?" gasped Flor.

"Yes. We plan to attack the Heavy World. You must help to lead our force."

6

The long afternoon of eternity wore on, that long golden road of an afternoon that would somewhen lead to everlasting night. Motion there was, but motion without event—except for those negligible events that seemed so large to the creatures participating in them.

For Lily-yo, Flor and Haris there were many events. Chief of these was, that they learnt to fly properly.

The pains associated with their wings soon died away as the wonderful new flesh and tendon strengthened. To sail up in the light gravity became an increasing delight—the ugly flopping movements of flymen on the Heavy World had no place here.

They learnt to fly in packs, and then to hunt in packs. In time they were trained to carry out the Captives' plan.

The series of accidents that had first delivered humans to this world in burnurns had been a fortunate one, growing more fortunate as millennia rolled away. For gradually the humans adapted better to the True World. Their survival factor became greater, their power surer. All this: as on the Heavy World conditions grew more and more adverse to anything but vegetation.

Lily-yo at least was quick to see how much easier life was in these new conditions. She sat with Flor and a dozen others eating pulped pluggyrug, before they did the Captives' bidding and left for the Heavy World.

It was hard to express all she felt.

"Here we are safe," she said, indicating the whole green land that sweltered under the silver network of webs.

"Except from the tigerflies," Flor agreed.

They rested on a bare peak, where the air was thin and even the giant creepers had not climbed. The turbulent green stretched away below them, almost as if they were on Earth—although here it was continually checked by the circular formations of rock.

"This world is smaller," Lily-yo said, trying again to make Flor know what was in her head. "Here we are bigger. We do not need to fight so much."

"Soon we must fight."

"Then we can come back here again. This is a good place, with nothing so savage and without so many enemies. Here the groups could live without so much fear. Veggy and Toy and May and Gren and the other little ones would like it here."

"They would miss the trees."

"We shall soon miss the trees no longer. We have wings instead. Everything is a matter of custom."

This idle talk took place beneath the unmoving shadow of a rock. Overhead, silver blobs against a purple sky, the traversers drifted, walking their networks, descending only occasionally to celeries far below. As Lily-yo fell to watching these creatures, she thought in her mind of the grand plan the Captives had hatched, she flicked it over in a series of vivid pictures.

Yes, the Captives knew. They could see ahead as she could not.

44

She and those about her had lived like plants, doing what came to hand. The Captives were not plants. From their cells they saw more than those outside.

This, the Captives saw. That the few humans who reached the True World bore few children, because they were old, or because the rays that made their wings grow made their seed die. That it was good here, and would be better still with more humans. That one way to get more humans here was to bring babies and children from the Heavy World.

For countless time, this had been done. Brave flymen had travelled back to that other world and stolen children. The flymen who had once attacked Lily-yo's group on their climb to the Tips had been on that mission. They had taken Bain to bring her to the True World in burnurns—and had not been heard of since.

Many perils and mischances lay in that long double journey. Of those who set out, few returned.

Now the Captives had thought of a better and more daring scheme.

"Here comes a traverser," Band Appa Bondi said, rousing Lily-yo from her thoughts. "Let us be ready to move."

He walked before the pack of twelve flyers who had been chosen for this new attempt. He was the leader of them. Lily-yo, Flor, and Haris were in support of him, together with eight others, three male, five female. Only one of them, Band Appa Bondi himself, had been carried to the True World as a boy; the rest had arrived here in the same manner as Lily-yo.

Slowly the pack stood up, stretching their wings. The moment of their great adventure was here. Yet they felt little fear; they could not look ahead as the Captives did, except perhaps for Band Appa Bondi and Lily-yo. She strengthened her will by saying "It is the Way". Then they all spread their arms wide and soared off to meet the traverser.

The traverser had eaten.

45

It had caught one of its most tasty enemies, a tigerfly, in a web and sucked it till only the shell was left. Now it sank down into a bed of celeries, crushing them under its great bulk. Gently, it began to bud; then it could be heading out for the great black gulfs, where heat and radiance called it. It had been born on this world. Being young, it had never yet made that dreaded and desired journey to the other world.

Its buds burst up from its back, hung over, popped, fell to the ground, and scurried away to bury themselves in the pulp and dirt where they might begin their ten thousand years' growth in peace.

Young though it was, the traverser was sick. It did not know this. The enemy tigerfly had been at it, but it did not know this either. Its vast bulk held little sensation.

The twelve humans glided over and landed on its back, low down on the abdomen in a position hidden from the creature's cluster of eyes. They sank among the tough shoulder-high fibres that served the traverser as hair, and looked about them. A ray-plane swooped overhead and disappeared. A trio of tumble-weeds skittered into the fibres and were seen no more. All was as quiet as if they lay on a small deserted hill.

At length they spread out and moved along in line, heads down, eyes searching, Band Appa Bondi at one end, Lily-yo at the other. The great body was streaked and pitted and scarred, so that progress down the slope was not easy. The fibre grew in patterns of different shades, green, yellow, black, breaking up the traverser's bulk when seen from the air, serving it as natural camouflage. In many places, tough parasitic plants had rooted themselves, drawing their nourishment entirely from their host; most of them would die when the traverser launched itself out between worlds.

The humans worked hard. Once they were thrown flat when the traverser changed position. As the slope down which they moved grew steeper, so progress became more slow.

"Here!" cried Y Coyin, one of the women.

At last they had found what they sought, what the Captives sent them to seek.

Clustering round Y Coyin with their knives out, the pack looked down at a place where the fibres had been neatly champed away in swathes, leaving a bare patch as far across as a human was long. In this patch was a round scab. Lily-yo stooped and felt it. It was immensely hard.

Lo Jint put his ear to it. Silence.

They looked at each other.

No signal was needed, none given.

Together they knelt, prising with their knives round the scab. Once the traverser moved, and they threw themselves flat. A bud rose nearby, popped, rolled down the slope and fell to the distant ground. A thinpin devoured it as it ran. The humans continued prising.

The scab moved. They lifted it off. A dark and sticky tunnel was revealed to them.

"I go first," Band Appa Bondi said.

He lowered himself into the hole. The others followed. Dark sky showed roundly above them until the twelfth human was in the tunnel. Then the scab was drawn back into place. A soft slobber of sound came from it, as it began to heal back into position again.

They crouched where they were for a long time, in a cavity that pulsed slightly. They crouched, their knives ready, their wings folded round them, their human hearts beating strongly.

In more than one sense they were in enemy territory. At the best of times, traversers were only allies by accident; they ate humans as readily as they devoured anything else. But this burrow was the work of that yellow and black destroyer, the tigerfly. One of the last true insects to survive, the tough and resourceful tigerflies had instinctively made the most invincible of all living things its prey.

The female tigerfly alights and bores her tunnel into the traverser. Burrowing away, she stops at last and prepares a natal

47

chamber, hollowing it from the living traverser, paralysing its flesh with her needletail to prevent it healing again. There she lays her store of eggs before climbing back to daylight. When the eggs hatch, the larvae have fresh and living stuff to nourish them.

After a while, Band Appa Bondi gave a sign and the pack moved forward, climbing awkwardly down the tunnel. A faint luminescence guided their eyes. The air lay heavy and green in their chests. Very slowly, very quietly, they moved—for they heard movement ahead.

Suddenly the movement was on them.

"Look out!" Band Appa Bondi cried.

From the terrible dark, something launched itself at them.

Before they realized it, the tunnel had curved and widened into the natal chamber. The tigerfly's eggs had hatched. An uncountable number of larvae with jaws as wide as a man's reach turned on the intruders, snapping in fury and fear.

Even as Band Appa Bondi sliced his first attacker, another had his head off. He fell, and his companions launched themselves over him in the dark. Pressing forward, they dodged those clicking jaws.

Behind their hard heads, the larvae were soft and plump. One slash of a sword and they burst, their entrails flowing out. They fought, but knew not how to fight. Savagely the humans stabbed, ducked and stabbed. No other human died. With backs to the wall they cut and thrust, breaking jaws, ripping flimsy stomachs. They killed unceasingly with neither hate nor mercy until they stood knee deep in slush. The larvae snapped and writhed and died. Uttering a grunt of satisfaction, Haris slew the last of them.

Wearily then, eleven humans crawled back to the tunnel, there to wait until the mess drained away—and then to wait a longer while.

The traverser stirred in its bed of celeries. Vague impulses drifted through its being. Things it had done. Things it had to do. The things it had done had been done before, the things it had to do were still to do. Blowing off oxygen, it heaved itself up.

Slowly at first, it swung up a cable, climbing to the network where the air thinned. Always, always before in the eternal afternoon it had stopped here. This time there seemed no reason for stopping. Air was nothing, heat was all, the heat that blistered and prodded and chafed and coaxed increasingly with height. . . .

It blew a jet of cable from a spinneret. Gaining speed, gaining intention, it rocketed its mighty vegetable self out and away from the place where the tigerflies flew. Ahead of it at an unjudgable distance floated a semicircle of light, white and blue and green, that was a useful thing to head towards.

For this was a lonely place for a young traverser, a terrible-wonderful bright-dark place, so full of nothing. Turn as you speed and you fry well on all sides . . . nothing to trouble you . . .

. . . Except that deep in your core a little pack of humans use you as an ark for their own purposes. You carry them unknowingly back to a world that once—so staggeringly long ago—belonged to their kind.

7

Throughout most of the forest, silence ruled.

The silence seemed to carry as much weight as that deep mass of foliage which covered all the land on the day side of the planet. It was a silence built of millions upon millions of years, intensifying as the sun overhead poured forth more and more energy in the first stages of its decline. Not that the silence signified lack of life. Life was everywhere, life on a formidable scale. But the increased solar radiation that had brought the extinction of most of the animal kingdom had spelt the triumph of plant life. Everywhere, in a thousand forms and guises, the plants ruled. And vegetables have no voices.

The new group with Toy leading moved along the number-

49

less branches, disturbing that deep silence not at all. They travelled high in the Tips, patterns of light and shade falling across their green skins. Continually alert for danger, they sped along with all possible discretion. Fear drove them with apparent purpose, although in fact they had no destination. Travel gave them a needful illusion of safety, so they travelled.

A white tongue made them halt.

The tongue lowered itself gradually down to one side of them, keeping close to a sheltering trunk. Noiselessly it sank, pointing down from the Tips whence it had come towards the distant Ground, a fibrous cylindrical thing like a snake, tough and naked. The group watched it go, watched its tip sink out of sight through the foliage towards the dark floor of the forest, watched its visible length paying out.

"A suckerbird!" Toy said to the others. Although her leadership was still unsure, most of the other children—all of them but Gren—clustered round her and looked anxiously from her to the moving tongue.

"Will it harm us?" Fay asked. She was five, and the youngest by a year.

"We will kill it," Veggy said. He was a man child. He jumped up and down on the branch so that his soul rattled. "I know how to kill it, I will kill it!"

"*I* will kill it," Toy said, firmly asserting her leadership. She stepped forward, unwinding a fibre rope from her waist as she did so.

The others watched in alarm, not yet trusting to Toy's skill. Most of them were already young adults, with the broad shoulders, strong arms, and long fingers of their kind. Three of them—a generous proportion—were men children: the clever Gren, the self-assertive Veggy, the quiet Poas. Gren was the oldest of the three. He stepped forward now.

"I also know how to trap the suckerbird," he told Toy, eyeing the long white tube that still lowered itself into the depths. "I will hold you to keep you safe, Toy. You need help."

50

Toy turned to him. She smiled because he was beautiful and because one day he would mate with her. Then she frowned because she was leader.

"Gren, you are man now. It is tabu to touch you, except during the courtship seasons. I will trap the bird. Then we will all go up to the Tips to kill and eat it. It shall be a great feast for us, to celebrate that I now lead."

Gren's and Toy's gaze met challengingly. But just as she had not yet settled into her role as leader, so he had hardly assumed —and was indeed reluctant to assume—the role of rebel. He disagreed with her ideas, but tried as yet not to show it. He fell back, fingering the soul that dangled from his belt, the little wooden image of himself that gave him confidence.

"Do as you please," he said—but Toy had already turned away.

On the topmost branches of the forest perched the suckerbird. Being of vegetable origin, it had little intelligence and only a rudimentary nervous system. What it lacked in this respect, it made up for in bulk and longevity.

Shaped like a mighty two-winged seed, the suckerbird could never fold its wings. They were capable of little movement, although the sensitive flexible fibres with which they were covered, and their overall span of some two hundred metres, made them masters of the breezes that stirred their hothouse world.

So the suckerbird perched, paying out that incredible tongue from its pouch down to the nourishment it needed in the obscure depths of the forest. At last the tender buds on its tip hit Ground.

Cautiously, slowly, the sensitive feelers of the tongue explored, ready to shrink from any of the many dangers of that gloomy region. Deftly, it avoided giant mildews and funguses. It found a patch of naked earth, soggy and heavy and full of nourishment. It bored down. It began to suck.

"Right!" Toy said when she was ready. She felt the excitement of the others behind her. "Nobody make a sound."

Her rope was knotted to her knife. Now she leant forward and slipped the loose end about the white hose, knotting it in a slip knot. She sank her blade into the tree, thus securing the arrangement. After a moment, the tongue bulged and expanded up its length as soil was sucked up inside it to the suckerbird's "stomach". The noose tightened. Though the suckerbird did not realize it, it was now a prisoner, and could not fly from its perch.

"That's well done!" Poyly said admiringly. She was Toy's closest friend, emulating her in everything.

"Quick, to the Tips!" Toy called. "We can kill the bird now it cannot get away."

They all began climbing the nearest trunk, to get to the suckerbird—all except Gren. Though not disobedient by nature, he knew there were easier ways than climbing to get to the Tips. As he had learnt to do from some of his elders in the old group, from Lily-yo and Haris the man, he whistled from the corner of his lips.

"Come on, Gren!" Poas called back to him. When Gren shook his head, Poas shrugged and climbed on up the tree after the others.

A dumbler came floating to Gren's command, twirling laconically down through the foliage. Its vanes spun, and on the end of each spoke of its flight umbrella grew the curiously-shaped seeds.

Gren climbed on to his dumbler, clinging tightly to its shaft, and whistled his instructions. Obeying him sluggishly, it carried him upwards, so that he arrived in the Tips just after the rest of the group, unruffled when they were panting.

"You should not have done that," Toy told him angrily. "You were in danger."

"Nothing ate me," Gren replied. Yet suddenly he felt a chill, for he knew Toy was right. Climbing a tree was laborious but safe. Floating among the leaves, where hideous creatures might momentarily appear and drag one down into the green depths, was both easy and wildly dangerous. Still, he was safe now. They would see his cleverness soon enough.

The cylindrical white tongue of the suckerbird still pulsed nearby. The bird itself squatted just above them, keeping its immense crude eyes swivelled for enemies. It was headless. Slung between the stiffly extended wings was a heavy bag of body, peppered with the corneal protuberances of its eyes and its bud corms; among these latter hung the pouch from which the tongue now extended. By deploying her forces, Toy had her party attacking this monstrous creature from several sides at once.

"Kill it!" Toy cried. "Now, jump! Quick, my children!"

They leapt on it where it lay gracelessly among the upper branches, yelping in excitement in a way that would have earnt Lily-yo's fury.

The suckerbird's body heaved, its wings fluttered in a vegetal parody of fright. Eight humans—all but Gren—hurled themselves among the feathery leafage of its back, stabbing deep into the epicarp to wound its rudimentary nervous system. Among that leafage lay other dangers. Disturbed from its slumbers, a tigerfly crawled from under the low-lying growth and came almost face to face with Poas.

Confronted with a yellow and black enemy as big as himself, the man child fell back squealing. On this later-day Earth, drowsing through the late afternoon of its existence, only a few families of the old orders of hymenoptera and diptera survived in mutated form: most dreadful of these were the tigerflies.

Veggy dashed to his friend's aid. Too late! Poas sprawled over on his back: the tigerfly was on to him. As the circular plates of its body arched, a ginger-tipped sabre of sting flashed out, burying itself into Poas's defenceless stomach. Its legs and arms gripped the boy, and with a hurried whirr of wings the tigerfly was bearing its paralysed burden away. Veggy hurled his sword uselessly after it.

No time could be spared for bemoaning this accident. As the

equivalents of pain filtered through to it, the suckerbird strove to fly away. Only Toy's frail noose held it down, and that might soon pull free.

Still crouching under the creature's belly, Gren heard Poas's cry and knew something was amiss. He saw the shaggy body heave, heard the wings creak in their frames as they beat the air. Twigs showered down on him, small branches snapped, leaves flew. The limb to which he clung vibrated.

Panic filled Gren's mind. All he knew was that the suckerbird might escape, that it must die as soon as possible. Inexperienced, he stabbed out blindly at the sucker tongue that now threshed against the tree trunk in its efforts to break free.

He sliced with his knife again and again. A gash appeared in the living white hose. Earth and mud, sucked from the Ground and intended for the vegbird's nourishment, spurted out of it, plastering Gren with filth. The vegbird heaved convulsively and the wound widened.

For all his fear, Gren saw what was about to happen. He flung himself up, his long arms outstretched, grasped one of the bird's bud protuberances, and clung to it shaking. Anything was better than to be left alone in the mazes of the forest—where he might wander for half a lifetime without coming on another group of humans.

The suckerbird fought to release itself. In its struggles, it enlarged the gash Gren had made, tugging until it pulled its tongue off. Free at last, it sailed into the air.

In mortal terror, hugging fibres and leafage, Gren crawled on to its great back, where seven other frightened humans crouched. He joined them without a word.

The suckerbird swung upwards into the blinding sky. There blazed the sun, slowly building up towards the day when it would turn nova and burn itself and its planets out. And beneath the suckerbird, which was twirling like the sycamore seed it resembled, swung endless vegetation that rose, rose as remorselessly as boiling milk to greet its life-source.

Toy was shouting to the group.

"Slay the bird!" she called at them, rising on her knees, waving her sword. "Slay it fast! Chop it to bits. Kill it, or we shall never get back to the jungle."

With the sun bronze on her green skin, she looked wonderful. Gren slashed for her sake. Veggy and May worked together, carving a great hole through the tough rind of the bird, kicking away chunks of it. As the chunks fell they were snapped up by predators before hitting the forest.

For a long while the suckerbird flew on unperturbed. The humans tired before it did. Yet even semi-sentience has its limits of endurance; when the suckerbird was leaking sap from many gashes, its wings faltered in their broad sweeping movement. It began to sink down.

"Toy! Toy! Living shades, look what we are coming to!" Driff cried. She pointed ahead at the shining entanglements towards which they were falling.

None of the young humans had seen the sea; intuition, and a marrow-deep knowledge of the hazards of their planet, told them that they were being carried towards grave dangers.

A stretch of coast rose up to meet them—and here was waged the most savage of all battles for survival, where the things of the land met the things of the ocean.

Clinging to the suckerbird's leafage, Gren worked his way over to where Toy and Poyly lay. He realized that he was much ot blame for their present predicament, and longed to be helpful.

"We can call dumblers and fly to safety with them," he said. "They will carry us safely home."

"That's a good idea, Gren," Poyly said encouragingly, but Toy looked blankly at him.

"You try and call a dumbler, Gren," she said.

He did as he was bidden, distorting his face to whistle. The air rushing past them carried the sound away. They were in any case travelling too high for the whistlethistle seeds. Sulkily,

Gren lapsed into silence, turning away from the others to see where they were getting to.

"I'd have thought of that idea if it had been any good," Toy told Poyly. She was a fool, thought Gren, and he ignored her.

The suckerbird was now losing height more slowly; it had reached a warm updraught of air and drifted along in it. Its lame and late efforts to turn inland again only carried it parallel with the coast, so that the humans had the doubtful privilege of seeing what awaited them there.

Highly organized destruction was in progress, a battle without generals waged for uncounted thousands of years. Or perhaps one side had a general, for the land was covered with that one inexhaustible tree which had grown and spread and sprawled and swallowed everything from shore to shore. Its neighbours had been starved, its enemies overgrown. It had conquered the whole continent as far as the terminator that divided Earth's day from its night side; it had almost conquered time, for its numberless trunks afforded it a life-span the end of which could not be foreseen; but the sea it could not conquer. At the sea's edge, the mighty tree stopped and drew back.

At this point, away among the rocks, sands, and swamps of the coast, species of tree defeated by the banyan had made their last stand. The shore was their inhospitable home. Withered, deformed, defiant, they grew as they could. Where they grew was called Nomansland, for they were beseiged on both sides by enemies.

On their land side, the silent force of the tree opposed them. On their other side they had to face poisonous seaweeds and other antagonists that assailed them perpetually.

Over everything, indifferent begetter of all this carnage, shone the sun.

Now the wounded suckerbird dropped more rapidly, until the humans could hear the slap of the seaweeds below. They all gathered close, waiting helplessly to see what would happen.

More steeply fell the bird, slipping sideways. It veered over the sea, all the fringes of which were dappled by the vegetation growing in its tideless waters. Labouring, it swerved towards a narrow and stony peninsula that jutted into the sea.

"Look! There's a castle below!" cried Toy.

The castle stood out on the peninsula, tall, thin, and grey, seeming to tilt crazily as the suckerbird flapped towards it. They swerved down. They were going to hit it. Evidently the dying creature had sighted the clear space at the base of the castle, had marked it as the only nearby place of safety, and was heading there.

But now its creaking wings like old sails in a storm paid no heed to their controls. The great body lumbered earthwards, Nomansland and sea lurched up to meet it, castle and peninsula jarred towards it.

"Hold tightly, all!" Veggy yelled.

Next moment they crashed into the spire of the castle, the impact flinging them all forward. One wing split and tore as the suckerbird clung to a soaring buttress.

Toy saw what would happen next: the suckerbird must fall, taking the humans with it. Agile as a cat, she jumped down to one side, into a depression formed between the irregular tops of two buttresses and the main bulk of the castle. Then she called to the others to join her.

One by one they leapt across to her narrow platform, were caught and steadied. May was the last across. Clutching her wooden soul, she jumped to safety.

Helplessly, the suckerbird swivelled a striated eye at them. Toy had time to notice that the recent violent impact had split it clean across the great bulb of its body. Then it began to slip.

Its crippled wing slithered across the castle wall. Its grip relaxed. It fell.

They leant over the natural rampart and watched it go.

The suckerbird hit the clear ground by the base of the castle and rolled over. With the tenacity to life of its kind, it was far from dead; it pulled itself up and staggered away from the grey pile, moving in a drunken semicircle, trailing its wings as it went.

One wing brushed over the stony edge of the peninsula, reflecting its tip in the motionless sea.

The face of the water puckered and from it emerged great leathery strands of seaweed. These strands were punctuated along their length by bladder-like execrescences. Almost hesitantly, they began to lash at the wing of the suckerbird.

Although the lashing was at first lethargic, it quickly worked up to a faster tempo. More and more of the sea, up to a quarter of a mile out, became covered with the flailing seaweed that punished and struck at the water repeatedly in idiot hatred of all life but its own.

Directly it was struck, the suckerbird attempted to drag itself out of the way. But the reach of the seaweed once it became active was surprisingly long, and the suckerbird's attempts to lurch to safety were of no avail, struggle though it might under the battery of blows.

Some of the bladder-like protrusions that flogged the luckless being landed so hard that they burst. A dark iodine-like liquid sprayed up from them, foaming and gushing into the air.

Where the poison landed on the suckerbird, it gave off a rank brown steam.

The suckerbird could utter no cries to relieve its promptings of pain. At something between flight and a hobble, it set off along the peninsula, heading for the shore, bounding into the air when it could to escape the seaweed. Its wings smouldered.

More than one kind of seaweed fringed that macabre coast. The frenzied bludgeoning stopped and the bladder weeds sank below the waves, their autotrophic beings temporarily exhausted.

In their stead, a long-toothed weed leapt out of the waters, raking the peninsula with its thorny teeth. Several fragments of rind were torn from the fleeing bird by these flails, but it almost gained the shore before it was properly hooked.

The teeth had it. More and more seaweed put out wavering

58

arms and tugged at the suckerbird's wing. By now it could fight only feebly. It heeled over and hit the confused water. The whole sea developed mouths to meet it.

Eight frightened humans watched all this from the top of the castle.

"We can never get back to the safety of the trees," Fay whimpered. She was the youngest; she began to cry.

The seaweed had earned but not yet won its prey, for the plants of Nomansland had scented the prize. Squeezed as they were between jungle and sea, some of them, mangrove-like in form, had long ago waded out boldly into the water. Others, more parasitic by nature, grew on their neighbours and sent out great stiff brambles that hung down towards the water like fishing rods.

These two species, with others rapidly joining them, put forth claim to the victim, trying to snatch it from their marine enemies. From under the sea they threw up gnarled roots like the limbs of some antidiluvian squid. They seized the sucker-bird, and battle was joined.

At once the whole coastline came alive. A fearful array of flails and barbs burst into action. Everything writhed deliriously. The sea was whipped into a spray that added to the horror by partially concealing it. Flying creatures, leatherfeathers and ray-planes, soared overhead out of the forest to pick their own advantage from the fray.

In the mindless carnage, the suckerbird was pulverized and forgotten. Its flesh was tossed and lost in spume.

Toy stood up, full of decision.

"We must go now," she said. "This is the time for us to get to the shore."

Seven agonized faces regarded her as if she were mad.

"We shall die down there," Poyly said.

"No," Toy said fiercely. "*Now* we shall not die. Those things fight each other, so they will be too busy to hurt us. Later may be too late."

59

Toy's authority was not absolute. The group was unsure of itself. When she saw them beginning to argue, Toy fell into a rage and boxed Fay and Shree on the ears. But her chief opponents were Veggy and May.

"We shall be killed there at any time," Veggy said. "There is no way to safety. Haven't we just seen what happened to the suckerbird that was so strong?"

"We cannot stay here and die," Toy said angrily.

"We can stay and wait till something happens," May said. "Please let's stay!"

"Nothing will happen," Poyly said, taking her friend Toy's part. "Only bad things. It is the way. We must look after ourselves."

"We shall be killed," Veggy repeated stubbornly.

In despair, Toy turned to Gren, the senior man child.

"What do you say?" she asked.

Gren had watched all the destruction with a set face. It did not relax as he turned it towards Toy.

"You lead the group, Toy. Those who can obey you must do it. That is law."

Toy stood up.

"Poyly, Veggy, May, you others—follow me! We will go now while the things are too busy to see us. We must get back to the forest."

Without hesitation she swung a leg over the domed top of the buttress and began sliding down its steep side. Sudden panic filled the others in case they were left behind. They followed Toy. They swarmed over the top, slipping and scrambling down after her.

At the bottom, dwarfed by the grey height of the castle, they stood momentarily in a silent group. Awe held them there.

Their world held an aspect of flat unreality. Because the great sun burnt overhead, their shadows lay like disregarded dirt below their feet. Everywhere was this same lack of shadow, lending the landscape its flat look. It was as dead as a poor painting.

60

The coastal battle raged like a fever. There was in this era (as in a sense there had always been) only Nature. Nature was supreme mistress of everything; and in the end it was as if she had laid a curse on her handiwork.

Overcoming her fears, Toy moved forward.

As they ran after Toy and away from that mysterious castle, their feet tingled; the stones beneath their feet were stained with brown poison. In the heat it had dried to harmlessness.

Noise of battle filled their ears. Spume drenched them—but the combatants paid them no attention, so absorbed were they in their mindless antagonism. Frequent explosions now ploughed the sea's face. Some of the Nomansland trees, beleagured for century after century in their narrow strip of territory, had plunged their roots down into the meagre sands to find not only nourishment but a way of defence against their enemies. They had discovered charcoal, they had drawn up sulphur, they had mined potassium nitrate. In their knotty entrails they had refined and mixed them.

The gunpowder that resulted had been carried up through sappy veins to nut cases in the topmost branches. These branches now hurled their explosive weapons at the seaweeds. The torpid sea writhed under the bombardment.

Toy's plan was not a good one: it succeeded through luck rather than judgment. To one side of the land end of the peninsula, a great mass of seaweed had threshed itself far out of the water and covered a gunpowder tree. By sheer weight, it was pulling the tree down, and a fight to the death raged about it. The little humans burst past, and fled into the shelter of tall couch grass.

Only then did they realize Gren was not with them.

8

Gren still lay in the blinding sun, hunched behind the ramparts of the castle.

Fear had been the chief but not the only cause for his remaining behind. He had felt, as he had told Toy, that obedience was important. Yet he was by nature hard put to it to obey. Particularly so in this case, when the plan Toy offered seemed to hold such slight hope for survival. Also, he had an idea of his own, though he found it impossible to express verbally.

"Oh, how can anyone speak!" he said to himself. "There seem so few words. Once there must have been more words!"

His idea concerned the castle.

The rest of the group were less thoughtful than Gren. Directly they had landed on it, their attention had been directed elsewhere. Not so Gren's; he realized that the castle was not of rock. It had been built with intelligence. Only one species could have built it and that species would have a safe way from the castle to the coast.

So in a little while, after Gren had watched his companions run down the stony path, he rapped with his knife handle on the wall beside him.

At first the knock went unanswered.

Without warning, a section of the tower behind Gren swung open. He turned at the faint sound, to face eight termights emerging from darkness.

Once declared enemies, now termight and human faced each other almost in kinship, as though the teeming millennia of change had wrought a bond between them. Now that men were the outcasts rather than the inheritors of Earth, they met the insects on equal terms.

The termights surrounded Gren and inspected him, their mandibles working. He stood still, motionless as their white bodies brushed round him. They were nearly as big as he was. He could smell their smell, acrid but not unpleasant.

When they had satisfied themselves that Gren was harmless, the termights marched to the ramparts. From all appearances they were staring out at the battle. Whether they could see or not in glaring daylight Gren did not know, but at least they

62

could hear the sounds of the sea struggle clearly enough.

Tentatively, Gren moved over to the opening in the tower. A strange cool odour drifted from it.

Two of the termights came rapidly across and barred his way, their jaws level with his throat.

"I want to go down," he told them. "I will be no trouble. Let me come inside."

One of the creatures disappeared down the hole. In a minute it returned with another termight. Gren shrank back. The new termight had a gigantic growth on its head.

The growth was a leprous brown in colour, spongy in texture, and pitted like the honeycomb the treebees made. It proliferated over the termight's cranium, growing round its neck in a ruff. Despite this fearsome burden, the termight seemed active enough. It came forward and the others made way for it. It seemed to stare at Gren, then turned away.

Scratching in the grit underfoot, it began to draw. Crudely but clearly, it sketched a tower and a line, and connected the two by a narrow strip formed with two parallel lines. The single line was evidently intended to represent the coast, the strip the peninsula.

Gren was completely surprised by this. He had never heard of such artistic abilities in insects before. He walked round gazing at the lines.

The termight stepped back and seemed to regard Gren. Obviously something was expected of him. Pulling himself together, he stooped down and falteringly added to the sketch. He drew a line from the top of the tower down the middle of it, through the middle of the strip and to the coast. Then he pointed to himself.

Whether the creatures understood this or not was hard to say. They simply turned and hurried back into the tower. Deciding there was nothing else for it, Gren followed them. This time they did not stop him; evidently his request had been understood.

That strange sunless smell enveloped him.

It was nerve-wracking in the tower when the entrance closed above them. After the sun-flooded brilliance outside, everything here was pitch dark.

Descending the tower was easy for one as agile as Gren, since it was much like climbing down a natural chimney, with plenty of protrusions on all sides to cling on to. He swarmed down hand over fist with growing confidence.

As his eyes accustomed themselves to the dark, Gren saw that a faint luminescence clung to the bodies of the termights, giving them ghostly shape. Many of them were present in the tower, utterly silent. Like phantoms they seemed to move on every side, noiseless rows of them trundling up into the dark, noiseless rows of them trundling down. He could not guess what they were busy at.

Eventually he and his guides reached the bottom of the castle and stood on level ground. According to Gren's estimation, they must now be below the level of the sea. The atmosphere was moist and heavy.

Only the termight with the growth accompanied Gren now; the others moved off in military order without looking back. Gren noted a curious green light composed as much of shadow as of illumination; at first he could not detect its source. He was hard put to it to follow his guide. The corridor they traversed was uneven and full of traffic. Termights were everywhere, moving purposefully: there were also other small creatures about, herded along by the hosts, sometimes singly, sometimes in flocks.

"Not so fast," Gren cried, but his guide kept to its steady pace, paying him no attention.

The green light was stronger now. It lay mistily on either side of their route. Gren saw it filtered through irregular mica sheets evidently set there by the creative genius of the tunnelling insects. These mica sheets formed windows looking out into the sea, through which the activities of the menacing seaweed could be viewed.

The industry of this underground place amazed him. At least the denizens were so busy that they kept to themselves; not one paused to inspect him, until one of the creatures belonging to the termights approached. Four-legged and furry, it possessed a tail and luminous yellow eyes and stood almost as high as Gren. Eyeing him through its glowing pupils, the creature cried "Miaow!" and tried to rub against him. Its whiskers brushed his arm. Shuddering, he dodged it and pressed on.

The furry creature looked back at him almost with a quality of regret. Then it turned to follow some termights, the species that now tolerated and fed it. A moment later Gren saw several more of these mewing things; some of them were infected with and almost covered by the fungus growth.

Gren and his guide came at last to where the broad tunnel divided into several lesser ones. Unhesitatingly, the guide chose a fork that sloped upwards into darkness. The darkness was broken suddenly as the termight pushed up a flat stone that covered the tunnel mouth and crawled into daylight.

"You've been very kind," Gren said as he crawled out too. He kept as much distance as possible between himself and the brown growth.

The termight scurried back into the hole, pulling the stone into place with never a backward glance.

Nobody needed to tell Gren that he was now in Nomansland.

He could smell the smell of the sullen sea. He could hear the sound of the battle between the seaweeds and the land plants, though the noise was intermittent now, as both sides tired. He could sense a tension round him that never existed in the gentle middle layers of the forest where the human group had been born. Above all, he could see the sun glaring through the matted leaves over his head.

Underfoot, the ground was sour and pasty, a mixture of clay and sand with rock frequently outcropping. It was infertile stuff, and the trees growing from it showed their sickness. Their trunks were distorted, their foliage meagre. Many of them had intertwined in an attempt to support each other; and where this attempt had failed, they lay spilled over the ground in horrible distortions. Moreover, some of them through the long centuries had evolved such curious ways of defending themselves that they hardly resembled tree forms at all.

Gren decided that his best policy was to creep to the land end of the peninsula and try and pick up the tracks of Toy and the others from there. Once he got to the sea's edge, it should not be hard to see the peninsula; it would make a prominent landmark.

He had no doubt in which direction the sea lay, for he was able to look through the distorted trees and see the landward border of Nomansland. That was clearly designated.

Along a line that marked the end of good soil, the great banyan had established its outer perimeter. It stood unshakeably, though its boughs were scarred by innumerable assaults from bramble and claw. And to assist it, to help it repel the banished species of Nomansland, the creatures that used its shelter had gathered: trappersnappers, wiltmilts, berrywishes, pluggyrugs, and others, stood ready to scourge the slighest movement along its perimeter.

Keeping this formidable barrier at his back, Gren moved cautiously forward.

His progress was slow. Every sound made him jump. At one point he flung himself flat as a cloud of long deadly needles was launched at him from a thicket. Lifting his head, he saw a cactus shaking itself and rearranging its defences. He had never seen a cactus before; his stomach was like water to think of all the unknown perils about him.

A little later he met something stranger.

He stepped through a tree whose trunk had contorted itself into a loop. As he did so, the loop snapped together. Gren escaped constriction by the skin of his teeth and lost the skin of his legs. As he lay panting, an animal slid past almost near enough to touch.

66

It was a reptile, long and armoured, with a mirthless grin that revealed many teeth. Once (in the vanished days when humans had a name for everything) it had been called an alligator. It peered through goat's eyes at Gren, then scuttled under a log.

Almost all animals had died out millennia ago. The sheer weight of vegetable growth, as the sun favoured green things, had crushed and extinguished them. Yet as the last of the old trees were beaten back to the swamps and the fringes of the ocean, a few animals had retreated with them. Here they protracted their existence in Nomansland, enjoying the heat and the savour of life while life lasted.

Going more cautiously now, Gren moved forward again.

By now, the hubbub from the sea had abated and he travelled in dead quiet. Everything was silent, as if waiting, as if under a curse.

The ground began to shelve gradually towards the water. Shingle rasped underfoot. The trees which had grown more sparsely clustered together again to withstand possible attacks from the sea.

Gren halted. Anxiety still moved in his heart. He longed to be back with the others. Yet his feeling was not that he had behaved stubbornly in remaining behind on the termight castle, but that they had behaved foolishly in not offering to accept his lead.

Looking round him cautiously, he let out a whistle. No answer came. A sudden stillness settled, as if even those things that had no ears were listening.

Panic seized Gren.

"Toy!" he cried. "Veggy! Poyly! Where are you?"

As he was calling, a cage descended from the foliage above him and pinned him to the ground.

When Toy led her six fellows to the shore, they flung themselves into long grass and hid their eyes to recover from their fright. Their bodies were foam-drenched from the vegetable battle.

67

At last they sat up and discussed Gren's absence. Since he was a man child, he was valuable; though they could not go back for him, they could wait for him. It remained only to find a place where they could wait in comparative safety.

"We will not wait long," Veggy said. "Gren had no need to stay behind. Let us leave him and forget him."

"We need him for mating," Toy said simply.

"I will mate with you," Veggy said. "I am a man child with a big mater to stick into you. Look, you cannot wear this one out! I will mate with all you women before the figs come again! I am riper than the figs."

And in his excitement he stood up and danced, showing off his body to the women, who were not averse to it. He was now their only man child; was he not desirable therefore?

May jumped up to dance with him. Veggy ran at her. Ducking lithely, she shot away. He capered after. She was laughing, he shouting.

"Come back!" Toy and Poyly called furiously.

Unheeding, May and Veggy ran from the grass on to sloping sand and shingle. Almost at once a great arm shot up from the sand and grasped May's ankle. As she screamed, another arm came up, then another, fastening on her. May fell on her face, kicking in terror. Veggy flung himself savagely into the attack, pulling out his knife as he did so. Other arms came up from the sand and grasped him too.

When plant life had conquered the Earth, the animals least affected had been those of the sea. Theirs was an environment less susceptible to change than land. Nevertheless, alterations in size and distribution of the marine algae had forced many of them to change their habits or habitat.

The new monster seaweeds had proved expert at catching crabs, at wrapping them in a greedy frond as they scuttled over the ocean bed, or at trapping them beneath stones at that vulnerable time when the crabs were growing new shells. In a few million years, the brachyura were all but extinct.

Meanwhile, the octopuses were already in trouble with the seaweeds. The extinction of the crabs deprived them of a chief item in their diet. These factors and others forced them into an entirely new mode of life. Compelled both to avoid the seaweeds and to seek food, many of them left the oceans. They became shore-dwellers—and the sand octopus evolved.

Toy and the other humans ran to Veggy's rescue, terrified by this threat to their only remaining man child. Sand flew as they hurled themselves into the fight. But the sand octopus had arms enough to deal with all seven of them. Without raising its body from where it was hidden, it took them all in its tentacles, fight how they might.

Their knives were of little use against that rubbery embrace. One by one, their faces were pressed down into the slithering sand and their shouts stifled.

For all that they had finally triumphed, the vegetables had triumphed as much by weight of numbers as by inventiveness. Time and again, they succeeded simply by imitating some device used long since—perhaps on a smaller scale—in the animal kingdom, as the traverser, that mightiest of all plant-creatures, flourished simply by adopting the way of life chosen by the humble spider back in the Carboniferous Age.

In Nomansland, where the struggle to survive was at its most intense, this process of imitation was particularly noticeable. The willows were a living example of it; they had copied the sand octopus, and by so doing had become the most invincible beings along that dreadful coast.

Killerwillows now lived submerged under sand and shingle, only their foliage occasionally showing. Their roots had acquired a steely flexibility and become tentacles. To one of these brutes the group now owed its lives.

A sand octopus was obliged to stifle its prey as soon as possible. Too long a struggle attracted its rivals, the killerwillows; for those that imitated it had become its deadliest enemies. They moved up on it now, two of them, heaving themselves along under the sand with only their leaves showing like innocent bushes, and a furrow of disturbed dirt behind them.

They attacked without hesitation or warning.

Their roots were long and sinewy and fearfully tough. One from one side, one from the other, they took a hold on the tentacles of the sand octopus. It knew that deadly grip, it recognized that obscene strength. Relinquishing its hold on the humans, it turned to fight the killerwillows for its life.

With a heave that sent the group scattering, it emerged from the sand, its beak agape, its pale eyes round with fright. Giving a sudden twist, one of the killerwillows sent it sprawling upside down. The sand octopus twisted back into position, managing to free all its tentacles but one as it did so. Angrily, it pecked off the offending tentacle with one savage bite, as if its own flesh were the enemy.

Close at hand lay the sullen sea. Its impulse was to retreat there in an emergency. But even as it began its frantic scuttle, the tentacular roots of the killerwillows thrashed blindly about, seeking for it. They found it! The octopus whipped up a curtain of sand and pebble in its fury as its retreat was checked.

But the killerwillows had it—and between them they commanded some thirty-five knotty legs.

Forgetting themselves, the humans stared fascinated at this unequal duel. Then the blindly waving arms flashed in their direction.

"Run!" Toy cried, picking herself up as sand spurted near her.

"It's got Fay!" Driff screamed.

The smallest of the group had been caught. Searching for a hold, one of those thin white tentacles of roots had wrapped Fay round the chest. She could not even cry out. Her face and arms went purple. Next second she was lifted up and dashed brutally against the trunk of a nearby tree. They saw her half-severed body roll bloodily over into the sand.

"It is the way," Poyly said sickly. "Let's move!"

They fled into the nearest thicket and lay gasping there. As they mourned the loss of their youngest companion, the sounds came to them of the sand octopus being shredded to pieces.

9

For a long while after the horrible noises had stopped, the six members of the group lay where they were. At last Toy sat up and spoke to them.

"You see what has happened because you do not let me lead you," she said. "Gren is lost. Now Fay is dead. Soon we will all be dead and our souls rotting."

"We must get out of Nomansland," said Veggy sulkily. "This is all the suckerbird's fault." He was aware that he was to blame for the incident with the sand octopus.

"We shall get nowhere", Toy snapped, "until you obey me. Do you have to die before you know that? After this, you do what I say. Do you understand, Veggy?"

"Yes."

"May?"

"Yes."

"And you, Driff and Shree?"

"Yes," they said, and Shree added, "I'm hungry."

"Follow me quietly," Toy said, tucking her soul more securely into her belt.

She led them, testing every step she took.

By now, the din of the sea battle was abating. Several trees had been dragged down into the water. At the same time, much seaweed had been fished out of the sea. This was now being eagerly tossed among the victor trees, anxious as they were for nourishment in that barren soil.

As the group crept forward, a soft-pelted thing rushed past on four legs and was gone before they had their wits about them.

"We could have eaten that," Shree said grumpily. "Toy promised us the suckerbird to eat and we never got it."

The thing had scarcely disappeared before there was a scuffle in the direction it had taken, a squeal, a hasty gobbling sound, and then silence.

"Something else ate it," Toy whispered. "Spread out and we'll stalk it. Knives ready!"

They fanned out and slid through the long grass, happy to engage in positive action. This part of the business of living they understood.

To track down the source of that quick gobbling sound was easy. The source was in captivity and could not move away.

From a particularly gnarled tree a pole hung; attached to the bottom of the pole was a crude cage consisting of only a dozen wooden bars. The bars dug down into the ground. Contained in the cage, its snout protruding one way, its tail another, was a young alligator. Some scattered pieces of pelt lay by its jaws, the remains of the furry thing the group had seen alive five minutes before.

The alligator stared at the humans as they emerged from the long grass and they stared back at it.

"We can kill it. It cannot move," May said.

"We can eat it," Shree said. "Even my soul is hungry."

The alligator, thanks to its armour, proved difficult to kill Right at the onset, its tail sent Driff spinning into a pile of shingle, where she cut her face badly. But by stabbing at it from all sides, and by blinding it, they at last exhausted it enough for Toy to thrust her hand bravely into the cage and cut the creature's throat.

As the reptile threshed about in its death agony, a curious thing happened. The bars of the cage lifted upwards so that their pronged ends emerged from the ground, and the whole contraption clenched together like a hand. The straight pole above it twisted into several loops; it and the cage vanished up into the green boughs of the tree.

With exclamations of awe, the group seized their alligator and ran.

Winding their way through tight-packed tree trunks, they

came on a bare outcrop of rock. It looked like a safe refuge, particularly as it was fringed by a spiky local variant of the whistlethistle.

Crouching on the rock, they began their unlovely meal. Even Driff joined in, though her face still bled from where she had grazed it on the shingle.

Scarcely were their jaws in motion than they heard Gren calling for help near at hand.

"Wait here and guard the food," Toy commanded. "Poyly will come with me. We will go and find Gren and bring him back here."

Her command was a good one. To travel with food was never wise; travelling alone was dangerous enough.

As she and Poyly skirted the thistles, Gren's cry came again to guide them. The two girls moved round a bank of mauve cactus, and there he lay. He sprawled face downward under a tree similar to the one beneath which they had killed the alligator, penned in a cage similar to the alligator's.

"Oh Gren!" cried Poyly. "How we missed you!"

Even as they ran towards him, a trailer creeper swung at him from the limb of a nearby tree, a creeper with a wet red mouth at its extremity, bright as a flower, poisonous-looking as a dripper-lip. It swooped for Gren's head.

Poyly's feelings for Gren went deep. Without thought, she flung herself at the creeper, meeting it as it swung forward, catching it as high as possible to avoid those pulpy lips. Drawing a new knife, she severed the stem that pulsed beneath her fingers. Then she dropped back lightly to the ground. It was easy to avoid the mouth that now writhed there, ineffectually pursing and opening.

"Above you, Poyly!" Toy cried in warning, darting forward. The parasite, alerted now to danger, uncurled a full dozen of its trailing mouths. Gay and deadly, they swung about Poyly's head. But Toy was beside her. Expertly they lopped away, till milk spurted from the creeper's wounds, till the mouths lay gasping

73

at their feet. Vegetable reaction time is not the fastest thing in the universe, perhaps because it is rarely prompted by pain.

Breathing hard, the two girls turned their attention to Gren, who still lay pinned beneath the cage.

"Can you get me out?" he asked, looking up helplessly at them.

"I am leader. Of course I can get you out," Toy said. Using some of the knowledge she had gained from dealing with the alligator, she said, "This cage is a part of the tree. We will make it move and let you go."

She knelt down and began to saw at the bars of the cage with her knife.

Over the land where the banyan ruled, covering everything with its layers of green, the chief problem for lesser breeds was to propagate their kind. With plants like the whistlethistle that had developed the curious dumblers, and the burnurn that had turned its seedcases into weapons, the solution to this problem was ingenious.

No less ingenious were some of the solutions of the flora of Nomansland to their particular problem. Here the main problem was less one of propagation than of sustenance; this accounted for the radical difference between these outcasts of the beaches and their cousins inland.

Some trees like the mangroves waded into the sea and fished deadly seaweeds for mulch. Others like the killerwillows took on the habits of animals, hunting in the manner of carnivores and nourishing themselves on decomposed flesh. But the oak, as one million-year stretch of sunlight succeeded another, shaped some of its extremities into cages and caught animals alive, letting their dung feed its starved roots. Or if they eventually starved to death, in decomposing they would still feed the tree.

Nothing of this Toy knew. She knew only that Gren's cage should move, just as the one enclosing the alligator had done. Grimly, with Poyly helping, she hacked at the bars. The two girls worked at each of the twelve bars in turn. Perhaps the oak assumed the damage being done was greater in fact than it was;

74

the bars were suddenly pulled from the ground and the whole contraption sprang up into the boughs above them.

Ignoring tabu, the girls grabbed Gren and ran with him back to the rest of the party.

When they were reunited, they devoured the alligator meat, keeping guard as they did so.

Not without a certain amount of boasting, Gren told them what he had seen inside the termight's nest. They were unbelieving.

"Termights have not enough sense to do all that you say," Veggy said.

"You all saw the castle they made. You sat on it."

"In the forest, termights have not so much sense," May said, backing Veggy up as usual.

"This is not the forest," Gren said. "New things happen here. Terrible things."

"Only in your head they happen," May teased. "You tell us about these funny things so that we will forget you did wrong to disobey Toy. How could there be windows underground to look out on to the sea?"

"I tell you only what I saw," Gren said. He was angry now. "In Nomansland, things are different. It is the way. Many termights also had a bad fungus growth on them such as I have not seen before. I have seen this fungus again since then. It looks bad."

"Where did you see it?" Shree asked.

Gren threw a curiously-shaped piece of glass into the air and caught it, perhaps pausing to create suspense, perhaps because he was not keen to mention his recent fright.

"When I was caught by the snaptrap tree," he said, "I looked up into its branches. There among the leaves I saw a fearful thing. I could not make out what it was until the leaves stirred. Then I saw one of the fungi that grew on the termights, all shining like an eye and growing on the tree."

Toy stood up.

"Too many things bring death here," she said. "Now we must move back to the forest where we can live happily. Get up, all of you."

"Let me finish this bone off," Shree said.

"Let Gren finish his story," Veggy said.

"Get up, all of you. Tuck your souls in your belts, and do as I order."

Gren slipped his curious glass under his belt and jumped up first to show he was anxious to obey. As the others stood up too, a dark shadow passed overhead; two rayplanes fluttered by, locked in combat.

Over the disputed strip called Nomansland many sorts of vegbird passed, both those that fed at sea and those that fed on land. They passed without alighting, knowing well the dangers that lurked there. Their shadows sped and dappled over the outcast plants without pause.

The rayplanes were so mortally engaged they did not know where they went. With a crash they sprawled among the upper branches near the group.

At once Nomansland sprang to life.

The famished angry trees spread up and lashed their branches. Toothed briars uncurled. Gigantic nettles shook their bearded heads. Moving cactus crawled and launched its spikes. Climbers hurled sticky bolas at the enemy. Cat-like creatures, such as Gren had seen in the termights' nest, bounded past and swarmed up the trees to get to the attack. Everything that could move did so, prodded on by hunger. On the instant, Nomansland turned itself into a war machine.

Those plants that possessed no sort of mobility came alert for secondary spoils. The thicket of whistlethistles near which the group now lay trembling shook its thorns in anticipation. Harmless enough in its normal habitat, here the need to feed its roots had goaded the whistlethistle into a more offensive role. It would impale any passer-by it could. Similarly, a hundred other plants, small and stationary and armed, prepared to ignore the

76

doomed rayplanes but to feed on those who—returning carelessly from *their* feed—blundered into their path.

A great killerwillow appeared, heaving itself into view with root-tentacles waving. Sand and grit poured off its pollarded head as it struggled up. Soon it too was grappling with the luckless rayplanes, with the snaptrap trees, and indeed with any living thing whose existence offended it.

The scene was chaos. The rayplanes never had a chance.

"Look—there's some of the fungus!" Gren exclaimed, pointing.

In among the short snake-like branches that formed the head of the killerwillow grew the deadly fungus. Nor was this the first time Gren had seen it since the rayplanes crashed. Several of the plants lumbering past had borne traces of it. Gren shuddered at the sight, but the others were less impressed. Death, after all, had many shapes; everyone knew it: it was the way.

Twigs showered on them from the target area. The rayplanes were shredded by now; the fight was among the feasters.

"We are too close to the trouble," Poyly said. "Let's move."

"I was about to order it myself," Toy said stiffly.

They scrambled up and made their way as best they could. All were armed now with long poles which they thrust out before them to test the ground for danger. The fearful remorselessness of the killerwillows had struck caution into their hearts.

For a long while they moved, overcoming obstacle after obstacle and frequently avoiding death. Finally they were overcome—by sleep.

They found a fallen trunk of a tree that was hollow. They beat out the poisonous leafy creature that lived in it, and slept there, curled up together and feeling secure. When they awoke, they were prisoners. Both ends of the tree trunk were sealed.

Driff, who was the first to rouse and discover this, set up a howl that quickly brought the others to investigate. No doubt of it, they were now sealed in and liable to suffocation. The walls of

77

the tree that previously had felt dry and rotten were now tacky, dripping a sweetish syrup on to them. In fact, they were about to be digested!

The fallen trunk was nothing more than an abdomen into which they had thoughtlessly climbed.

After eons of time, the bellyelm had entirely abandoned its earlier attempts to draw nourishment from the inhospitable shores of Nomansland. Retracting all form of root structure, it had adopted its present horizontal mode of living. It camouflaged itself as a dead log. Its branch and leaf system had become separate, evolving into the symbiotic leafy creature the group had beaten off—a symbiotic creature that acted as a useful decoy to lure other beings into the open stomach of its partner.

Though the bellyelm normally attracted only vegetal creatures into its maw, flesh also satisfied its nutritive requirements. Seven little humans were very welcome.

The seven little humans fought savagely, slithering in the dirty dark as they attacked the strange plant with knives. Nothing they did had any effect. The syrupy rain came down faster, as the bellyelm worked up an appetite.

"It's no good," Toy gasped. "Rest for a little while and try to think what we can do."

Close together, they squatted on their haunches. Baffled, frightened, numbed by the dark, they could only squat.

Gren tried to make a useful picture come into his head. He concentrated, ignoring the muck trickling down his back.

He tried to remember what the trunk had looked like outside. They were seeking somewhere to sleep when they came on it. They had climbed up a slope, skirting a suspicious patch of bare sand, and found the bellyelm lying at the top of the incline in short grass. Externally, it had been smooth. . . .

"Ha!" he exclaimed in the dark.

"What is it?" Veggy asked. "What are you ha-ing about?" He was angry with them all; was he not a man, who should have been protected from this danger and indignity?

"We will all throw ourselves against this wall together," Gren said. "That way we may be able to make the tree roll."

Veggy snorted in the dark.

"How will that help us?" he asked.

"Do what he says, you little worm!" Toy's voice was savage. They all jumped at its lash. She, as much as Veggy, could not guess what Gren had in mind, but she had to keep authority. . . . "All push at this wall, quickly."

In the gummy mess they scrambled together, touching each other to discover whether they were all facing the same way.

"All ready?" Toy asked. "Push! And again! Push! Push!"

Their toes slithered in the tacky sap, but they pushed. Toy called encouragement.

The bellyelm rolled.

Now they were all caught in excitement. They heaved gladly, shouting in unison. And the bellyelm rolled again. And again. And then continuously.

Suddenly there was no further need to push. As Gren had hoped, the trunk began to roll down the slope of its own accord. Seven humans found themselves somersaulting at increasing speed.

"Get ready to run as soon as you get the chance," Gren called. "*If* you get the chance. The tree may split at the bottom of the slope."

When it hit sand, the bellyelm slowed its pace and, as the incline flattened out, it stopped. Its partner, the leafy creature, which had been pursuing it meanwhile, now caught up. It jumped on top of the trunk and plugged its lower appendages firmly into the runnels of the trunk; but it had no time to preen.

Something moved beneath the sand.

A white root-like tentacle appeared, then another. They waved blindly and grasped the bellyelm round the middle. As the leafy thing scuttled for its life, a killerwillow heaved itself up into view. Still trapped inside the trunk, the humans heard the bellyelm groan.

"Get ready to jump clear," Gren whispered.

Few things could resist the clutches of a killerwillow. Its present victim was utterly defenceless. Beneath the grip of those hawser-like tentacles, it cracked with a sound of snapping ribs. Hopelessly, tugged from more than one direction, it broke apart like a cracker.

As daylight splintered into being about them, the group jumped for safety.

Only Driff could not jump. She was trapped at one end of the trunk as it caved in. Frantically she cried and struggled, but could not get loose. The others—bounding for long grass—halted and looked back.

Toy and Poyly glanced at each other, then ran to the rescue.

"Come back, you fools!" Gren cried. "It will get you too!"

Unheeding, they ran back to Driff, plunging into the patch of sand. In a panic, Gren rushed after them.

"Come away!" he shouted.

Three yards from them rose the great body of the killerwillow. In its poll fungus glistened, the dark crinkled fungus they had seen before. It was terrible to behold—Gren could not understand how the others dared to stay. He pulled at Toy, hitting her and screaming at her to come away and save her soul.

Toy took no notice. Within inches of those strangulating white roots, she and Poyly struggled to set Driff free. The latter's leg was caught between two sandwiching slabs of wood. At last one of these shifted, so that she could be dragged away. Seizing her between them, Poyly and Toy ran for the long grass where the others crouched, and Gren ran with them.

For minutes they all lay panting. They were covered in stickiness and filth and nearly unrecognizable.

Toy was the first to sit up. She turned to Gren and said in a voice cold with rage, "Gren, I dismiss you from the group. You are an outcast from now on."

Gren jumped up, tears in his eyes, conscious of their stares.

80

Banishment was the most terrible punishment that could be used against anyone. It was rarely invoked against females; to invoke it against a male was almost unheard of.

"You can't do this!" he cried. "Why should you do this? You have no reason."

"You hit me," Toy said. "I am your leader but you hit me. You tried to stop Driff from being rescued, you would have let her die. And always you want your own way. I cannot lead you, so you must go."

The others, all but Driff, were standing now, open-mouthed and anxious.

"It's lies, lies!"

"No, it is true." Then she weakened and turned to the five faces anxiously regarding her. "Isn't it true?"

Driff, clutching her hurt leg, agreed heartily that it was. Shree, being Driff's friend, also agreed. Veggy and May merely nodded their heads without speaking; they were feeling guilty because they had not also gone to the rescue of Driff, and compensated for it by backing up Toy now. The only note of dissent came unexpectedly from Toy's dearest friend, Poyly.

"Never mind if what you say is true or not," Poyly declared. "But for Gren we would now be dead inside that bellyelm. He saved us there, and we should be grateful."

"No, the killerwillow saved us," Toy said.

"If it had not been for Gren——"

"Keep out of this, Poyly. You saw him hit me. He must go from the group. I say he must be outcast."

The two women faced each other angrily, hands on knives, their cheeks red.

"He is our man. We cannot let him go!" Poyly said. "You talk rubbish, Toy."

"We have Veggy still, or have you forgotten?"

"Veggy is only a man child, and you know it!"

Angrily Veggy jumped up.

"I'm old enough to do it to you, Poyly, you fat thing," he

81

cried, hopping about and exposing himself. "Look how I'm made—just as good as Gren!"

But they cuffed him down and went on quarrelling. Benefiting by this example, the others also began to quarrel. Only when Gren burst into angry tears did they fall silent.

"You are all fools," he cried between his sobs. "I know how to get out of Nomansland but you don't. How can you do it without me?"

"We can do anything without you," Toy said, but she added, "What is your plan?"

Gren laughed bitterly.

"You are a fine leader, Toy! You don't even know where we are. You don't even realize that we are on the edge of Nomansland. Look, you can see our forest from here."

He pointed dramatically with outstretched finger.

10

In their hurried escape from the bellyelm, they had hardly taken in their new surroundings. There was little room for doubt that Gren was right. As he said, they stood on the fringe of Nomansland.

Beyond them, the gnarled and stunted trees of the region grew more closely, as if tightening their ranks. Among them were spiky soldier trees, thorn and bamboo, as well as tall grasses with edges sharp enough to lop off a human arm. All were woven together by an absolute barricade of brambles. It was a thicket impossible to penetrate, suicide to enter. Every plant stood at guard like troops facing a common enemy.

Nor was the common enemy a reassuring sight.

The great banyan, pushing outwards as far as its nutritional requirements would allow, loomed high and black over the outcasts of Nomansland. Its outermost branches bore an abnormally dense thatch of leaves; they reached out as far as possible over the enemy like a wave ever about to break, cutting off as much sunlight as possible.

Aiding the banyan were the creatures that lived in its forest aisles, the trappersnappers, the jack-in-the-box wiltmilts, the berrywishes, the deadly dripperlips and others. They patrolled the perimeters of the mighty tree like eternal watchdogs.

The forest, so welcoming to the humans in theory, presented only its claws to them from where they now stood.

Gren watched their faces as the others regarded that double wall of hostile vegetation. Nothing moved; the lightest breeze slinking in from the sea hardly shifted one armoured leaf; only their bowels stirred in dread.

"You see," Gren said. "Leave me here! Let me watch you walk through that barrier! I want to see you do it."

He had the initiative now and gloried in it.

They looked at him, at the barrier, back at him.

"*You* don't know how to get through," Veggy said uneasily. Gren sneered.

"I know a way," he said flatly.

"Do you think the termights will help you?" Poyly asked him.

"No."

"What then?"

He stared at them defiantly. Then he faced Toy.

"I will show you the way if you follow me. Toy has no brains. I have brains. I will not be outcast. I will lead you instead of Toy. Make me leader and I will get you to safety."

"Pah, you man child," Toy said. "You talk too much. You boast all the time." But round her the others were muttering.

"Women are leaders, not men," Shree said, with doubt in her voice.

"Toy is a bad leader," Gren shouted.

"No, she's not," said Driff, "she's braver than you," and the others murmured agreement with this, even Poyly. Though their faith in Toy was not unbounded, their trust in Gren was small. Poyly went to him and said quietly, "You know the law and the way of humans. They will outcast you if you do not tell them a good way to safety."

"And if I do tell them?" His truculence faded, because Poyly was fair to look upon.

"Then you can stay with us as is right But you must not expect to lead in Toy's place. That is not right."

"I will say what is right or not."

"That is not right either."

He pulled a face at her.

"You are a right person, Poyly. Make no argument with me."

"I do not want to see you outcast. I am on your side."

"Look, then!" And Gren turned towards the rest of them. From his belt he produced the curiously-shaped piece of glass he had handled earlier. He held it out in his open palm.

"This I picked up when I was trapped by the snaptrap tree," he told them. "It is called mica or glass. Perhaps it came from the sea. Perhaps it is what the termights use for their windows on to the sea."

Toy made to examine it, but he pulled his hand back.

"Hold it in the sun and it makes a little sun beneath it. When I was trapped, I burned my hand with it. I could have burnt my way out of the trap if you had not come along. So we can burn our way out of Nomansland. Light some sticks and grass here and the flame will grow. The little breeze will tickle it towards the forest. Nothing likes fire—and where the fire has been we can follow, safely back into the forest."

They all stared at each other.

"Gren is very clever," Poyly said. "His idea can save us."

"It won't work," Toy said stubbornly.

In a sudden rage, Gren hurled the crude lens at her.

"You stupid girl! Your head is full of toads. You're the one who should be outcast! You should be driven off!"

She caught the lens and backed away.

"Gren, you are mad! You don't know what you say. Go away," she shouted, "before we have to kill you."

84

Gren turned savagely to Veggy.

"You see how she treats me, Veggy! We cannot have her for leader. We two must go or she must."

"Toy never hurt me," Veggy said sullenly, anxious to avoid quarrelling. "I'm not going to be outcast."

Toy caught their mood and used it quickly.

"There can be no arguing in the group or the group will die. It is the way. Gren or I must go, and you all must decide which it is to be. Cast your vote now. Speak, anyone who would turn me away rather than Gren."

"Unfair!" Poyly cried. Then an uneasy silence fell. Nobody spoke.

"Gren must go," Driff whispered.

Gren pulled out a knife. Veggy at once jumped up and drew his. May behind him did the same. Soon they all stood armed against Gren. Only Poyly did not move.

Gren's face was thin with bitterness.

"Give me back my glass," he said, holding out his hand to Toy.

"It is ours," Toy said. "We can make a small sun without your help. Go away before we kill you."

He scanned their faces for the last time. Then he turned on his heel and walked silently away.

He was blind with defeat. No possible future lay open to him. To be on one's own in the forest was dangerous; here it was doubly dangerous. If he could get back to the middle layers of the forest, he might be able to find other human groups; but those groups were scarce and shy; even supposing they accepted him, the idea of fitting in with strangers did not appeal to Gren.

Nomansland was not the best place in which to walk about blind with defeat. Within five minutes of being outcast, he had fallen victim to a hostile plant.

The ground beneath his feet shelved down raggedly to a small water course along which water no longer flowed. Boulders taller than Gren lay thickly about, with shingle and the littered small change of pebbles underfoot. Few plants grew here except razor-sharp grasses.

As Gren wandered regardlessly on, something fell on to his head—something light and painless.

Several times, Gren had seen and been worried by the dark brain-like fungus that attached itself to other creatures. This discomycete plant form was a mutated morel. Over the ages it had learnt new ways of nourishing and propagating itself.

For some while Gren stood quite still, trembling a little beneath the touch of the thing. Once he raised his hand only to drop it again. His head felt cool, almost numb.

At last he sat down by the nearest boulder, his backbone firm against it, staring in the direction he had come. He was in deep shade, in a clammy place; at the top of the watercourse bank lay a brilliant bar of sunlight, behind which a backdrop of foliage seemed painted in indifferent greens and whites. Gren stared at it listlessly, trying to bring meaning out of the pattern.

Dimly he knew that it would all be there when he was dead— that it would even be a little richer for his death, as the phosphates of his body were reabsorbed by other things: for it seemed unlikely he would Go Up in the manner approved and practised by his ancestors; he had no one to look after his soul. Life was short, and after all, what was he? Nothing!

"You are human," said a voice. It was the ghost of a voice, an unspoken voice, a voice that had no business with vocal chords. Like a dusty harp, it seemed to twang in some lost attic of his head.

In his present state, Gren felt no surprise. His back was against stone; the shade about him covered not only him; his body was of common material; why should there not be silent voices to match his thoughts?

"Who is that speaking?" he asked idly.

"You call me morel. I shall not leave you. I can help you."

He had a detached suspicion that morel had never used words before, so slowly did they come.

86

"I need help," he said. "I am an outcast."

"So I see. I have attached myself to you to help you. I shall always be with you."

Gren felt very dull, but he managed to ask, "How will you help me?"

"As I have helped other beings," said morel. "Once I am with them I never leave them. Many beings have no brain; I am brain. I collect thoughts. I and those of my kind act as brains, so that the creatures we attach ourselves to are more cunning and able than the others."

"Will I be more cunning than other humans?" Gren asked. The sunlight at the top of the watercourse never changed. Everything was mixed in his mind. It was as though he spoke with the gods.

"We have never caught a human before," said the voice, choosing its words more rapidly now. "We morels live only in the margins of Nomansland. You live only in the forests. You are a good find. I will make you powerful. You shall go everywhere, taking me with you."

Giving no answer, Gren rested against the cool stone. He was drained of energy and content to let time pass. At length the voice twanged in his head again.

"I know much about humans. Time has been terribly long on this world, and on the worlds in space. Once in a very distant time, before the sun was hot, your two-legged kind ruled this world. You were large beings then, five times as tall as you are now. You shrank to meet new conditions, to survive in whatever way you could. In those days, my ancestors were small, but change is always taking place, though so slowly as to go unnoticed. Now you are little creatures in the undergrowth, while I am capable of consuming you."

After listening and thinking, Gren asked, "How can you know all this, morel, if you have not met a human till now?"

"By exploring the structure of your mind. Many of your memories and thoughts are inherited from the far past and buried so that you cannot reach them. But I can reach them.

87

Through them I read the history of your kind's past. My kind could be as great as your kind was. . . ."

"Then would I be great too?"

"It would probably have to be that way. . . ."

All at once a wave of sleep came over Gren. The sleep was fathomless, but full of strange fish—dreams he could not afterwards grasp by their flickering tails.

He woke suddenly. Something had moved nearby.

On the top of the bank, where the bright sun would always shine, stood Poyly.

"Gren, my sweet!" she said, when his slight movement revealed him. "I have left the others to be with you and be your mate."

His brain was clear now, clear and sharp as spring water. Many things were plain to him that had been hidden before. He jumped up.

Poyly looked down at him in the shade. With horror she saw the dark fungus growing from him as it had from the snaptrap trees and the killerwillows. It protruded from his hair, it formed a ridge down the nape of his neck, it stood like a ruff half way round his collarbone. It glistened darkly in its intricate patterns.

"Gren! The fungus!" she cried in horror, backing away. "It's all over you!"

He climbed out rapidly and caught her by the hand.

"It's all right, Poyly, there's no cause for alarm. The fungus is called morel. It will not hurt us. It can help us."

At first Poyly did not answer. She knew the way in the forest, and in Nomansland. Things looked after themselves, not after others. Dimly she guessed that the real purpose of the morel was to feed on others and to propagate itself as widely as possible; and that to this end it might be clever enough to kill its hosts as slowly as possible.

"The fungus is bad, Gren," she said. "How can it be anything but bad?"

Gren fell on his knee and pulled her down with him, murmuring reassuring as he did so.

He stroked her russet hair.

"Morel can teach us many things," he said. "We can be so much better than we are. We are poor creatures; surely there's no harm in being better creatures?"

"How can a fungus make us better?"

In Gren's head, morel spoke.

"She surely shall not die. Two heads are better than one. Your eyes shall be opened. Why—you'll be like gods!"

Almost word for word, Gren repeated to Poyly what morel had said.

"Perhaps you know best, Gren," she said falteringly. "You were always very clever."

"You can be clever, too," he whispered.

Reluctantly she lay back in his arms, nestling against him.

A slab of the fungus fell from Gren's neck on to her forehead. She stirred and struggled, made as if to protest, then closed her eyes. When she opened them again, they were very clear.

Like another Eve, she drew Gren to her. They made love in the warm sunlight, letting their wooden souls fall as they undid their belts.

At last they stood up, smiling at each other.

Gren glanced down at their feet. "We've dropped our souls," he said.

She made a careless gesture. "Leave them, Gren. They're only a nuisance. We don't need them any more."

They kissed and stretched and began to think of other things, already completely accustomed to the crown of fungus on their heads.

"We don't have to worry about Toy and the others," Poyly said. "They have left us open a way back to the forest. Look!"

She led him round a tall tree. A wall of smoke drifted gently inland where flame had bitten a path back to the banyan. Hand in hand, they walked together towards that way out of Nomansland, their dangerous Eden.

PART 2

II

Little silent things without minds sped around the highway, appearing from and disappearing into the dark greens that surrounded it.

Two fruit cases moved along the highway. From under them, two pairs of eyes looked askance at the silent things, and flitted here and there like the things themselves in their search for danger.

The highway was a vertical one; the anxious eyes could see neither its beginning nor its end. Occasional branches forked horizontally from the highway; these were ignored in the slow but steady progress. The surface of the highway was rough, providing excellent holds for the moving fingers and toes that protruded from the fruit cases. Also, the surface was cylindrical, for the highway was one trunk of the mighty banyan tree.

The two fruit cases moved from its middle layers towards the ground below. Foliage gradually filtered out the light, so that they seemed to move in a green mist towards a tunnel of black.

At last the leading fruit case hesitated and turned aside on to one of the horizontal branches, pursuing a scarcely visible trail. The other case followed it. Together they sat up, half leaning against each other, and with their backs to their erstwhile highway.

"I fear going down towards the Ground," Poyly said, from under her case.

"We must go where the morel directs," Gren said with patience, explaining as he had explained before. "He has more wisdom than we have. Now that we are on the trail of another group, it would be foolish to disobey him. How can we live in the forest on our own?"

He knew that the morel in her head was soothing her with similar arguments. Yet ever since he and Poyly had left Nomansland several sleeps ago, she had been uneasy, her self-exile from the group having imposed on her a greater strain than she had expected.

"We should have made a stronger effort to pick up the trail of Toy and our other friends," Poyly said. "If we had waited till the fire died down, we might have found them."

"We had to move on because you were afraid of being burnt," Gren said. "Besides, you know Toy would not have taken us back. She had no mercy or understanding even for you, her friend."

At this, Poyly merely grunted, and silence fell between them. Then she began again.

"Need we go farther?" she asked in a tiny voice, taking hold of Gren's wrist.

Then they waited with a timorous patience for another voice that they knew would answer them.

"Yes, you shall go farther, Poyly and Gren, for I advise you to go and I am stronger than you." The voice was already familiar to them both. It was a voice made without lips and heard without ears, a voice born and dying within their heads like a jack-in-the-box eternally imprisoned in its little chest. It had the tone of a dusty harp.

"I have brought you so far in safety," the morel continued, "and I will take you farther in safety. I taught you to wear the fruit cases for camouflage and already we have come a long way in them unharmed. Go a little farther and there will be glory for you."

"We need a rest, morel," Gren said.

"Rest and then we will go on. We have found the traces of another human tribe—this is not the time to be faint of heart. We must find the tribe."

Obeying the voice, the two humans lay down to rest. The cumbersome skins, hacked from two of the oedematous fruits of the forest, crudely pierced with holes for their legs and arms, prevented them from lying flat. They crouched as they could, limbs sprawling upwards as if they had been crushed to death by the weight of the leafage above them.

Like a distracting background hum, the thoughts of the morel ran somewhere beyond their supervision. In this age of vegetables, plants specialized in size while remaining brainless; the morel fungus, however, had specialized in intelligence—the sharp and limited intelligence of the jungle. To further its own wider propagation, it could become parasitic on other species, adding its deductive powers to their mobility. The particular individual which had bisected itself to take over both Poyly and Gren, laboured under constant surprise as it discovered in their nervous centres something owned by no other creature—a memory that included dim racial memories hidden even from their possessors.

Although the morel remained unaware of the phrase "In the country of the blind the one-eyed man is king", it was nevertheless in the same position of power. The life forms of the great hothouse world lived out their days in ferocity or flight, pursuit or peace, before falling to the green and forming compost for the next generation. For them there was no past and no future; they were like figures woven into a tapestry, without depth. The morel, tapping human minds, was different. It had perspective.

It was the first creature in a billion years to be able to look back down the long avenues of time. Prospects emerged that frightened, dizzied, and nearly silenced the harp-like cadences of its voice.

"How can morel protect us from the terrors of the Ground?" Poyly asked after a spell. "How can he protect us from a wilt-milt or a dripperlip?"

"He knows things," Gren said simply. "He made us put on

these fruit skins to hide us from enemies. They have kept us safe. When we find this other tribe we will be still safer."

"My fruit skin chafes my thighs," Poyly said, with a womanly gift for irrelevance that eons of time had not quenched.

As she lay there, she felt her mate's hand grope for her thigh and rub it tenderly. But her eyes still wandered among the boughs overhead, alert for danger.

A vegetable thing as bright as a parakeet fluttered down and settled on a branch above them. Almost at once a jittermop fell from its concealment above, dropping smack on to the vegbird. Antipathetic liquids splashed. Then the broken vegbird was drawn up out of sight, only a smear of green juice marking where it had been.

"A jittermop, Gren! We should move on," Poyly said, "before it falls on us."

The morel too had seen this struggle—had in fact watched with approval, for vegbirds were great fanciers of a tasty morel.

"We will move, humans, if you are ready," it said. One pretext for moving on was as good as another; being parasitic, it needed no rest.

They were reluctant to move from their temporary comfort even to avoid a jittermop, so the morel prodded them. As yet it was gentle enough with them, not wishing to provoke a contest of wills and needing their co-operation. Its ultimate objective was vague, vain-glorious, and splendid. It saw itself reproducing again and again, until fungus covered the whole Earth, filling hill and valley with its convolutions.

Such an end could not be achieved without humans. They would be its means. Now—in its cold leisurely way—it needed as many humans under its sway as it could get. So it prodded. So Gren and Poyly obeyed.

They climbed back head downwards on to the trunk that was their highway, clinging to its rounded surface, and resumed their advance.

Other creatures used the same route, some harmless like the

leafabians, making their endless leafy caravanserais from the depths of the jungle to its heights, some far from harmless, green in tooth and claw. But one species had left minute distinguishing marks down the trunk: a stab mark here, a stain there, that to a trained eye meant that humanity was somewhere near at hand. It was this trail the two humans followed.

The great tree and the denizens of its shade went about their business in silence. So did Gren and Poyly. When the marks they pursued turned along a side branch, they turned too, without discussion.

So they continued, horizontally and vertically, until Poyly glimpsed movement. A flitting human form revealed itself. Ducking among the leaves, it plunged for safety into a clump of fuzzypuzzle on a branch ahead—just the mystery of it, then silence.

They had seen no more than a flash of shoulder and a glimpse of face alert under flying hair, yet it had an electrifying effect on Poyly.

"She'll escape if we don't catch her," she told Gren. "Let me go and try to get her! Keep watch in case her companions are near."

"Let me go."

"No, I'll get her. Make a noise to distract her attention when you think I'm ready to pounce."

Shucking off her fruit case and sliding forward on her belly, she edged over the curve of the branch until she hung upside down under it. As she began to work her way along, the morel, anxious for its own safety in an exposed position, invaded her mind. Her perceptions became extraordinarily sharp, her vision clearer, her skin more sensitive.

"Go in from behind. Capture it, don't kill it, and it will lead us to the rest of its tribe," twanged the voice in her head.

"Hush, or she'll hear," Poyly breathed.

"Only you and Gren can hear me, Poyly; you are my kingdom."

94

Poyly crawled beyond the fuzzypuzzle patch before climbing on to the upper side of the branch again, never rustling the leaves about her as she did so. Slowly she slid forward.

Above the soft lollipop buds of the fuzzypuzzle she spied her quarry's head. A fine young female was looking guardedly about, eyes dark and liquid under a sheltering hand and a crown of hair.

"She did not recognize you under your fruit cases as human, so she hides from you," said the morel.

That was silly, Poyly thought to herself. Whether this female recognized us or not, she would always hide from strangers. The morel sucked the thought from her brain and understood why his reasoning had been false; for all he had already learnt, the whole notion of a human being was still alien to him.

Tactfully he removed himself from Poyly's mind, leaving her free to tackle the stranger in her own way.

Poyly moved a step nearer, and another step, bent almost double. Head down, she waited for Gren to signal as instructed.

On the other side of the fuzzypuzzle patch, Gren shook a twig. The strange female peered in the direction of the noise, her tongue running over her open lips. Before she could pull the knife from her belt, Poyly jumped on her from behind.

They struggled in among the soft fibres, the stranger grappling for Poyly's throat. Poyly in return bit her in the shoulder. Bursting in, Gren gripped the stranger round her neck and tugged her backwards until her saffron hair fell about his face. The girl put up a savage struggle, but they had her. Soon she was bound and lay on the branch looking up at them.

"You have done well! Now she will lead us——" began the morel.

"Quiet!" Gren rasped, so that the fungus instantly obeyed.

Something was moving fast in the layers of the tree above them.

Gren knew the forest. He knew how predators were attracted by the sounds of struggle. Hardly had he spoken when a thinpin

95

came spiralling down the nearest trunk like a spring and launched itself at them. Gren was ready for it.

Swords were useless against thinpins. He caught it a blow with a stick, sending it spinning. It anchored itself by a springy tail before rearing to strike again—and a rayplane curved down from the foliage above, snapped up the thinpin, and swooped on.

Poyly and Gren flung themselves flat beside their captive and waited. The terrible silences of the forest came in again like a tide all round them, and it was safe once more.

12

Their captive was almost speechless. She pouted and tossed her head in answer to Poyly's questions. They elicited from her only the fact that she went by the name of Yattmur. Obviously she was alarmed by the sinister ruff about their necks and the glistening lumps on their heads.

"Morel, she is too fearful to speak," Gren said, moved by the beauty of the girl who sat bound at their feet. "She does not care for the look of you. Shall we leave her and go on? We'll find other humans."

"Hit her and then she may speak," twanged the silent voice of the morel.

"But that will make her more fearful."

"It may loosen her tongue. Hit her face, on that cheek you seem to admire——"

"Even though she is causing me no danger?"

"You silly creature, why can you never use all of your brain at once? She causes us all danger by delaying us."

"I suppose she does. I never thought of that. You think deep, morel, that I must admit."

"Then do as I say and hit her."

Gren raised his hand hesitantly. Morel twitched at his muscles. The hand came down violently across Yattmur's cheek, jerking her head. Poyly winced and looked questioningly at her mate.

"You foul creature! My tribe will kill you," Yattmur threatened, showing her teeth at them.

His eyes gleaming, Gren raised his hand again.

"Do you want another blow? Tell us where you live."

The girl struggled ineffectually.

"I am only a herder. You do wrong to harm me if you are of my kind. What harm did I do you? I was only gathering fruit."

"We need answers to questions. You will not be hurt if you answer our questions." Again his hand came up, and this time she surrendered.

"I am a herder—I herd the jumpvils. It is not my job to fight or to answer questions. I can take you to my tribe if you wish."

"Tell us where your tribe is."

"It lives on the Skirt of the Black Mouth, which is only a small way from here. We are peaceful people. We don't jump out of the sky on to other humans."

"The Skirt of the Black Mouth? Will you take us there?"

"Do you mean us harm?"

"We mean no harm to anyone. Besides you can see there are only two of us. Why should you be afraid?"

Yattmur put on a sullen face, as if she doubted his words.

"You must let me up then, and set my arms free. My people shall not see me with tied hands. I will not run away from you."

"My sword through your side if you do," Gren said.

"You are learning," the morel said with approval.

Poyly released Yattmur from her bonds. The girl smoothed her hair, rubbed her wrists, and began to climb among the silent leaves, her two captors following close. They exchanged no more words, but in Poyly's heart doubts rose, particularly when she saw that the nature of the jungle changed and that the endless uniformity of the banyan was breaking.

Following Yattmur, they descended the tree. One great mass of broken stone crowned with nettlemoss and berrywish thrust itself up beside their way, and then another. But although they descended, it grew lighter overhead; which meant the banyan was here far from its average height. Its branches twisted and thinned. A spear of sunlight pierced through to the travellers. The Tips were almost meeting the ground. What could it mean?

Poyly whispered the question in her mind, and the morel answered.

"The forest must fail somewhere. We are coming to a broken land where it cannot grow. Do not be alarmed."

"We must be coming to the Skirt of the Black Mouth. I fear the sound of it, morel. Let us go back before we meet fatal trouble."

"We have no back to go to, Poyly. We are wanderers. We can only go on. Have no fear. I will help you and I shall never leave you."

Now the branches grew too weak and narrow to bear them. With a flying leap, Yattmur threw herself on to a massive outcrop of rock. Poyly and Gren landed beside her. They lay there looking at each other questioningly. Then Yattmur raised a hand.

"Listen! Some jumpvils coming!" she exclaimed, as a sound came like rain through the forest. "These are the beasts my tribe catches."

Below their island of rock stretched the ground. It was not the foul quagmire of decay and death about which Gren and Poyly had so often been warned in their tribal days. It was curiously broken and pitted, like a frozen sea, and coloured red and black. Few plants grew in it. Instead, it seemed to have a frozen life of its own, so indented was it with holes that had stretched themselves into agonized navels, eye sockets, or leering mouths.

"The rocks have evil faces," Poyly whispered as she gazed down.

"Quiet! They're coming this way," Yattmur said.

As they looked and listened, a horde of strange creatures poured over the pitted ground, loping from the depths of the forest with a strange gait. They were fibrous creatures, plants that over an immensity of eons had roughly learnt to copy the hare family.

98

Their running was slow and clumsy by the standards of the animals they superseded. As they moved, their fibrous sinews cracked sharply; they lurched from side to side. Each jumpvil had a head all scoop jaw and enormous ears, while its body was without line and irregularly coloured. The front legs were more like poor stumps, small and clumsy, while the hind pair were much longer and captured at least something of the grace of an animal's leg.

Little of this was apparent to Gren and Poyly. To them, the jumpvils were merely a strange new species of creature with inexplicably ill-shaped legs. To Yattmur they meant something different.

Before they came into sight she pulled a weighted line from round her waist and balanced it between her hands. As the hordes thudded and clacked below the rock, she flung it dexterously. The line extended itself into a sort of elementary net, with the weights swinging at key points.

It tripped three of the queer-limbed creatures. At once Yattmur scrambled down, jumped at the jumpvils before they could right themselves, and secured them to the line.

All the rest of the herd parted, ran on, and disappeared. The three that had been captured stood submissively in vegetable defeat. Yattmur looked challengingly at Gren and Poyly as if relieved to have shown her mettle—but Poyly ignored her, pointing into the clearing ahead of them and shrinking against her companion.

"Gren! Look! A—monster, Gren!" she said in a strangled voice. "Did I not say this place was evil?"

Against a wide shoulder of rock, and near the path of the fleeing jumpvils, a silvery envelope was inflating. It stretched out into a great globe far higher than any human.

"It's a greenguts! Don't watch it!" Yattmur said. "It makes a bad thing for humans!"

But they stared fascinated, for the envelope was now a soggy sphere, and on that sphere grew one eye, a huge jelly-like eye with a green pupil. The eye swivelled until it appeared to be regarding the humans.

A vast gap appeared low down in the envelope. The last few retreating jumpvils saw it, paused, then staggered round on a new course. Six of them jumped through the gap, which at once closed over them like a mouth, while the envelope began to collapse.

"Living shadows!" Gren gasped. "What is it?"

"It is a greenguts," Yattmur said. "Have you never seen one before? Many of them live near here, stuck to the tall rocks. Come, I must take these jumpvils to the tribe."

The morel thought differently. It twanged in the heads of Gren and Poyly. Reluctantly they moved towards the shoulder of rock.

The greenguts had entirely collapsed. It was drawn in, adhering to the rock like so many folds of wet tissue. A still moving bulge near the ground marked its bag of jumpvils. As they surveyed it in horror, it surveyed them with its one striated green eye. Then the eye closed, and they seemed to be looking only at rock. The camouflage was perfect.

"It cannot hurt us," twanged the morel. "It is nothing but a stomach."

They moved away. Again they followed Yattmur, walking painfully on the broken ground, the three captive creatures humping along at their side as if this was something they did every day.

The ground sloped upwards. In their heads, the morel suggested that this was why the banyan was falling away overhead, and waited to see what they would answer.

Poyly said, "Perhaps these jumpvils have long back legs to help them get uphill."

"It must be so," said the morel.

But that's absurd, thought Gren, for what about when they want to run downhill again? The morel cannot know everything, or it would not agree to Poyly's silly idea.

"You are right that I do not know everything," twanged the morel, surprising him. "But I am capable of learning quickly, which you are not—for unlike some past members of your race, you work mainly by instinct."

"What is instinct?"

"Green thoughts," said the morel, and would not elaborate.

At length Yattmur halted. Her first sullenness had worn away, as if the journey had made them friends. She was almost gay.

"You are standing in the middle of my tribal area, where you wished to be," she said.

"Call them, then; tell them that we come with good desires and that I shall speak to them," Gren said, adding anxiously for the morel's benefit, "but I don't know what to say to them."

"I shall tell you," twanged the morel.

Yattmur raised a clenched hand to her lips and blew a piping note through it. Alertly, Poyly and her mate looked about them. . . . Leaves rustled, and they became surrounded by warriors who seemed to rise up from the ground. Glancing upwards, Poyly saw strange faces there regarding her from the branches overhead.

The three jumpvils shuffled uneasily.

Gren and Poyly stood absolutely still, allowing themselves to be inspected.

Slowly Yattmur's tribe came closer. Most of them, as was customary, were female, with flowers adorning their private parts. All were armed, many were as striking of feature as Yattmur. Several wore round their waists the same weighted trapping lines that Yattmur had carried.

"Herders," Yattmur said, "I have brought you two strangers, Poyly and Gren, who wish to join us."

Prompted by the morel, Poyly said, "We are wanderers who will do you no harm. Make us welcome if you wish to Go Up in peace. We need rest and shelter now, and later we can show you our skills."

One of the group, a stocky woman with braided hair in which

was inserted a gleaming shell, stood forward. She held out her hand palm upwards.

"Greetings, strangers. I am called Hutweer. I lead these herders. If you join us, you follow me. Do you consent to that?"

If we do not consent, they may kill us, thought Gren.

Right from the first we must show we are leaders, replied the morel.

Their knives point at us, Gren told it.

We must lead from the start or not at all, the morel returned.

As they stood wrapped in conflict, Hutweer clapped her hands impatiently.

"Answer, strangers! Will you follow Hutweer?"

We must agree, morel.

No, Gren, we cannot afford to.

But they will kill us!

You must kill her first then, Poyly!

No!

I say yes.

No. . . . No. . . . No. . . .

Their thoughts grew more fierce as a three-cornered argument grew up.

"Herders, alert!" Hutweer called. Dropping her hand to her sword belt, she came a pace nearer, her face stern. Obviously these strangers were not friends.

To the strangers something strange was happening. They began to writhe, as if in an unearthly dance. Poyly's hands twisted up to the darkly glistening ruff about her neck, and then fell away again. Gren's hands went down to his sword and then curved away as if dragged by force. Both of them twisted slowly and stamped their feet. Their faces stretched and wrinkled in an unknown pain. From their mouths came foam, and in their extremity they urinated upon the hard ground.

Slowly they moved, staggered, turned, arching their bodies, biting their lips, while their eyes glared madly at nothing.

The herders dropped back in awe.

"They fell on me from the sky! They must be spirits!" Yatt-mur cried, covering her face.

Hutweer dropped the sword she had drawn, her countenance pale. It was a sign to her followers. With frightened haste they dropped their weapons and sank to their knees. They groaned in their prostration, hiding their faces in their hands.

Directly the morel saw that it had inadvertently achieved what it had wished to do, it ceased trying to impose its will on Gren and Poyly. As the wrenching pressure on their minds relaxed, they would have fallen had the fungus not stiffened them again.

"We have won the victory we need, Poyly," it said in its harp-like voice. "Hutweer kneels before us. Now you must speak to them."

"I hate you, morel," she said sullenly. "Make Gren do your work—I won't."

Strongly prompted by the fungus, Gren went over to Hutweer and took her hand.

"Now you have acknowledged us," he said, "you need fear no more. Only never forget that we are spirits inhabited by spirits. We will work with you. Together we shall establish a mighty tribe where we can live in peace. Human beings will no longer be fugitives of the forest. We are going to lead you out of the forest to greatness."

"The way out of the forest is only just ahead," Yattmur ventured. She had handed the captive jumpvils to one of the other women, and now came forward to hear what Gren was saying.

"We will lead you farther than that," he told her.

"Will you free us from the great spirit of the Black Mouth?" Hutweer enquired boldly.

"You shall be led as you deserve," Gren declared. "First my fellow spirit Poyly and I desire food and sleep, then we will talk with you. Take us now to your place of safety."

Hutweer bowed—and disappeared into the ground beneath her feet.

13

The tortured lava bed on which they were standing was pierced by many holes. Under some of these, the earth had fallen away or had been scooped out by the herders to form a hideout below ground level. Here they lived in something like safety and something like darkness, in a cave provided with bolt-holes conveniently situated overhead.

With Yattmur helping them, Poyly and Gren were induced to go down into the gloom more gently than Hutweer had done. There they were seated on couches and a meal was brought to them almost at once.

They tasted jumpvil, which the herders had flavoured in a way unknown to the two travellers, with spices to make it tempting and peppers to make it hot. Jumpvil, Yattmur explained, was one of their chief dishes; but they had a speciality, and this was now set before Gren and Poyly with some deference.

"It is called fish," Yattmur said, when they expressed their satisfaction with it. "It comes from the Long Water that pours from the Black Mouth."

At this, the morel became attentive and made Gren ask, "How do you catch this fish if it lives in water?"

"We do not catch them. We do not go to the Long Water, for a tribe of strange men called Fishers live there. Sometimes we meet them, and as we are at peace with them we exchange our jumpvil for their fish."

The life of the herders sounded pleasant. Trying to work out exactly what their advantages were, Poyly asked Hutweer, "Are there not many enemies around you?"

Hutweer smiled.

"There are very few enemies here. Our big enemy, the Black Mouth, swallows them. We live near the Black Mouth because we believe one big enemy is easier to deal with than a lot of small ones."

At this the morel began to confer urgently with Gren. Gren

had now learnt to talk in his mind with the morel without speaking aloud, an art Poyly never mastered.

"We must examine this Mouth of which they talk so much," the morel twanged. "The sooner the better. And since you have lost face by eating with them like an ordinary human, you must also make them a stirring speech. The two must go together. Let us find out this Mouth and show them how little we fear it by speaking there."

"No, morel! You think clever but you don't think sense! If these fine herders fear the Black Mouth, I am prepared to do the same."

"If you think like that, we are lost."

"Poyly and I are tired. You do not know what tiredness is. Let us sleep as you promised us we could."

"You are always sleeping. First we must show how strong we are."

"How can we when we are weak from tiredness?" Poyly interposed.

"Do you want to be killed while you sleep?"

So the morel had its way, and Gren and Poyly demanded to be taken to look at the Black Mouth.

At this the herders were startled. Hutweer silenced their murmurs of apprehension.

"It shall be as you say, O Spirits. Come forth, Iccall," she cried, and at once a young male with a white fishbone in his hair jumped forward. He held his hand palm upwards in greeting to Poyly.

"Young Iccall is our best Singer," Hutweer said. "With him you will come to no harm. He will show you the Black Mouth and bring you back here. We will await your return."

They climbed up again in the broad and everlasting daylight. As they stood blinking, feeling the hot pumice beneath their feet, Iccall smiled brilliantly at Poyly and said, "I know you feel tired, but it is only a little way I have to take you."

"Oh, I'm not tired, thank you," Poyly said, smiling back, for Iccall had large dark eyes and a soft skin, and was as beautiful in his way as Yattmur. "That is a pretty bone in your hair, shaped like the veins of a leaf."

"They are very rare—perhaps I might get you one."

"Let's move if we are going," Gren said sharply to Iccall, thinking he had never seen a man grin so foolishly. "How can a mere singer—if that is what you are—be any use against this mighty enemy, the Black Mouth?"

"Because when the Mouth sings, I sing—and I sing better," said Iccall, not at all upset, and he led the way among the leaves and the broken pillars of rock, swaggering a little as he went.

As he foretold, they did not have far to go. The ground continued to rise gently and became more and more coated with the black and red igneous rock, so that nothing could grow there. Even the banyan, which had crossed a thousand miles of continent in its sinewy stride, was forced to draw back here. Its outmost trunks showed scars from the last lava flow, yet they dropped aerial roots which explored among the rock for nourishment with greedy fingers.

Iccall brushed past these roots and crouched behind a boulder, beckoning them to join him. He pointed ahead.

"There is Black Mouth," he whispered.

For Poyly and Gren it was a strange experience. The whole idea of open country was completely unknown to them; they were forest folk. Now their eyes stared ahead in wonder that a prospect could be so strange.

Broken and tumbled, the lava field stretched away from them into the distance. It tilted and shaped up towards the sky until it turned into a great ragged cone. The cone in its sad eminence dominated the scene, for all that it stood some distance away.

"That is the Black Mouth," whispered Iccall again, watching the awe on Poyly's face.

He stabbed his finger to a suspiration of smoke that rose from the lip of the cone and trickled up into the sky.

"The Mouth breathes," he said.

Gren pulled his eyes away from the cone to the forest beyond

106

it, the eternal forest reasserting itself. Then his eyes were drawn back to the cone as he felt the morel grope deep into his mind with a dizzying sensation that made him brush his hand over his forehead. His sight blurred as the morel expressed resentment f his gesture.

The morel bored down deeper into the sludge of Gren's unconscious memory like a drunken man pawing through the faded photographs of a legacy. Confusion overwhelmed Gren; he too glimpsed these brief pictures, some of them extremely poignant, without being able to grasp their content. Swooning, he pitched over on to the lava.

Poyly and Iccall lifted him up—but already the fit was over and the morel had what it needed.

Triumphantly it flashed a picture at Gren. As he revived, the morel explained to him.

"These herders fear shadows, Gren. We need not fear. Their mighty Mouth is only a volcano, and a small one at that. It will do no harm. Probably it is all but extinct." And he showed Gren and Poyly what a volcano was from the knowledge he had dredged out of their memory.

Reassured, they returned to the tribe's subterranean home, where Hutweer, Yattmur and the others awaited them.

"We have seen your Black Mouth and have no fear of it," Gren declared. "We shall sleep in peace with quiet dreams."

"When the Black Mouth calls, everyone must go to it," Hutweer said. "Though you may be mighty, you scoff because you have only seen the Mouth in its silence. When it sings, we will see how you dance, O spirits!"

Poyly asked the whereabouts of the Fishers, the tribe Yattmur had mentioned.

"From where we stood, we could not see their home trees," Iccall said. "From the belly of the Black Mouth comes the Long Water. That also we did not see for the rise of the land. Beside the Long Water stand the trees, and there live the Fishers, a strange people who worship their trees."

At this the morel entered into Poyly's thought, prompting her to ask, "If the Fishers live so much nearer to the Black Mouth than you, O Hutweer, by what magic do they survive when the Mouth calls?"

The herders muttered among themselves, keen to find an answer to her question. None presented itself to them. At length one of the women said, "The Fishers have long green tails, O spirit."

This reply satisfied neither her nor the others. Gren laughed, and the morel launched him into a speech.

"Oh you children of an empty mouth, you know too little and guess too much! Can you believe that people are able to grow long green tails? You are simple and helpless and we will lead you. We shall go down to the Long Water when we have slept and all of you will follow.

"There we will make a Great Tribe, at first uniting with the Fishers, and then with other tribes in the forests. No longer shall we run in fear. All other things will fear us."

In the reticulations of the morel's brain grew a picture of the plantation these humans would make for it. There it would propagate in peace, tended by its humans. At present—it felt the handicap strongly—it had not sufficient bulk to bisect itself again, and so to take over some of the herders. But as soon as it could manage it, the day would come when it would grow in peace in a well-tended plantation, there to take over control of all humanity. Eagerly it compelled Gren to speak again.

"We shall no longer be poor things of the undergrowth. We will kill the undergrowth. We will kill the jungle and all its bad things. We will allow only good things. We will have gardens and in them we will grow—strength and more strength, until the world is ours as it was once long ago."

Silence fell. The herders looked uneasily at each other, anxious yet half-defiant.

In her head, Poyly thought that the things Gren said were too big and without meaning. Gren himself was past caring. Though he looked on the morel as a strong friend, he hated the sensation of being forced to speak and act in a way often just beyond his comprehension.

Wearily, he flung himself down into a corner and dropped asleep almost immediately. Equally indifferent to what the others thought, Poyly too lay down and went to sleep.

At first the herders stood looking down in puzzlement at them. Then Hutweer clapped her hands for them to disperse.

"Let them sleep for now," she said.

"They are such strange people! I will stay by them," Yattmur said.

"There is no need for that; time enough to worry about them when they wake," said Hutweer, pushing Yattmur on ahead of her.

"We shall see how these spirits behave when the spirit of the Black Mouth sings," Iccall said, as he climbed outside.

14

While Poyly and Gren slept, the morel did not sleep. Sleep was not in its nature.

At present the morel was like a small boy who dashes into a cave only to find it full of jewels; he had staggered into wealth unsuspected even by its owner and was so constituted that he could not help examining it. His first predatory investigation merged into excited wonder.

That sleep which Gren and Poyly slept was disturbed by many strange fantasies. Whole blocks of past experience loomed up like cities in a fog, blazed on their dreaming eye, and were gone. Working with no preconceptions which might have provoked antagonism from the unconscious levels through which it sank, the morel burrowed back through the obscure corridors of memory where Gren's and Poyly's intuitive responses were stored.

The journey was long. Many of its signs, obnubilated by countless generations, were misleading. The morel worked down to records of the days before the sun had begun to radiate extra energy, to the days when man was a far more intelligent and aggressive being than his present arboreal counterpart. It surveyed the great civilizations in wonder and puzzlement—and then it plunged back still further, far back, into much the longest mistiest epoch of man's history, before history began, before he had so much as a fire to warm him at night, or a brain to guide his hand at hunting.

And there the morel, groping among the very shards of human memory, made its astonishing find. It lay inert for many heartbeats before it could digest something of the import of what it chanced on.

Twanging at their brains, it roused Gren and Poyly. Though they turned over exhaustedly, there was no escaping that inner voice.

"Gren! Poyly! I have made a great discovery! We are more nearly brothers than you know!"

Pulsing with an emotion they had never before known it to show, the morel forced on them pictures stored in their own limbos of unconscious memory.

It showed them first the great age of man, an age of fine cities and roads, an age of hazardous journeys to the nearer planets. The time was one of great organization and aspiration, of communities, communes, and committees. Yet the people were not noticeably happier than their predecessors. Like their predecessors, they lived in the shade of various pressures and antagonisms. All too easily they were crushed by the million under economic or total warfare.

Next, the morel showed, Earth's temperatures began to climb as the sun went into its destructive phase. Confident in their technology, the people prepared to meet this emergency.

"Show us no more," Poyly whimpered, for these scenes were very bright and painful. But the morel paid her no heed and continued to force knowledge upon her.

As their preparations were being made, people began to fall

sick. The sun was pouring out a new band of radiation, and gradually all mankind succumbed to the strange sickness. It affected their skin, their eyes—and their brains.

After a prolonged spell of suffering, they became immune to the radiations. They crawled forth from their beds. But something had changed. They no longer had the power to command and cogitate and fight.

They were like different creatures!

They crawled away from their great and beautiful towns, left their cities, deserted their houses—as if all that had once been home had suddenly become alien. Their social structures also collapsed, and all organization died overnight. From then on, the weeds began to flourish in the streets, and the pollen to blow over the cash registers; the advance of the jungle had begun.

The downfall of man happened not gradually but in one dreadful rush, like the collapse of a tall tower.

"It's enough," Gren told the morel, struggling against its power. "What is past is no concern of ours. Why should we care what happened so very long ago? You've worried us enough! Let us sleep."

A curious sensation took him, as if his inside were being rattled while his outside remained still. The morel was metaphorically shaking him by the shoulders.

"You are so indifferent," twanged the morel, still gripped by excitement. "You must attend. Look! We are going back now to very distant days, when man had no history or heritage, when he was not even Man. He was then a puny thing similar to what you are now. . . ."

And Poyly and Gren could do nothing but see the visions that followed. Though the glimpses were blurred and muddy, they watched tarsier-like people sliding down trees and running barefoot among the ferns. They were small people, nervous and without language. They squatted and pranced and hid in bushes. No detail was clear, for there had never been clear perception to record it. Scents and sounds were sharp—yet taunting as a riddle. The humans saw merely flashes of half-light, as in that primaeval world the little lives scampered and enjoyed and died.

For no reason that they recognized, nostalgia flooded them and Poyly wept.

A clearer picture came. A group of the little people paddled in marsh under giant ferns. From the ferns, things dropped and landed on their heads. The things that dropped were recognizable as morel fungi.

"In that early oligocene world, my kind was the first to develop intelligence," twanged the morel. "There's the proof of it! In ideal conditions of gloom and moisture we first discovered the power of thought. But thought needs limbs it can direct. So we became parasitic on those small creatures, your remote ancestors!"

And it pushed Poyly and Gren forward in time again, showing them the true history of the development of man, which was also the history of the morels. For the morels, which began as parasites, developed into symbiotes.

At first they clung to the outsides of the skulls of the tarsier-people. Then as those people prospered under the connection, as they were taught to organize and hunt, they were induced, generation by slow generation, to increase their skull capacity. At last the vulnerable morels were able to move inside, to become truly a part of the people, to improve their own abilities under a curving shelter of bone. . . .

"So the real race of men developed," intoned the morel, throwing up a storm of pictures. "They grew and conquered the world, forgetting the origins of their success, the morel brains which lived and died with them. . . . Without us, they would still have remained among the trees, even as your tribes live now without our aid."

To enforce its point, it again provoked their latent memories of the time when the sun had entered its latest phase and all mankind fell sick.

"Men were physically stronger than morels. Though they

survived the stepping-up of solar radiation, their symbiotic brains did not. *They* quietly died, boiled alive in the little bone shelters they had fashioned for themselves. Man was left . . . to fend for himself equipped only with his natural brains, which were no better than those of the higher animals. . . . Small wonder he lost his splendid cities and took again to the trees!"

"It means nothing to us . . . nothing at all," Gren whimpered. "Why do you haunt us now with this ancient disaster, which all finished uncounted millions of years ago?"

The morel gave a silent noise like laughter in his head.

"Because the drama may not yet be finished! I am a sturdier strain than those of my bygone ancestors; I can tolerate high radiation. So can your kind. Now is the historic moment for us to begin another symbiosis as great and profitable as the one which once tempered those tarsiers until they rode among the stars! Again the clocks of intelligence begin to chime. The clocks have hands again. . . ."

"Gren, he is mad and I do not understand!" Poyly cried, appalled by the turmoil behind her closed eyes.

"Hear the clocks chime!" twanged the morel. "They chime for us, children!"

"Oh, oh! I can hear them!" Gren moaned, twisting restlessly where he lay.

And in all their ears came a sound to drown all else, a chiming sound like diabolic music.

"Gren, we are all going mad!" Poyly cried. "The terrible noises!"

"The chimes, the chimes!" the morel twanged.

Then Poyly and Gren awoke, sitting up in a sweat with the morel afire about their heads and necks—and the terrible sound still came, more terrible still!

Through the disturbed race of their thoughts they perceived that they were now the sole occupants of the cavern under the lava bed. All the herders had gone.

The terrifying noises they could hear came from outside. Why they should be so frightening was hard to say. The main sound was almost a melody, though it gave no prospect of resolution. It sang not to the ear but to the blood, and the blood responded by alternately freezing and racing to its call.

"We must go!" Poyly said, struggling up. "It's singing for us to go."

"What have I done?" wailed the morel.

"What's gone wrong?" Gren asked. "Why do we have to go?"

They clung together in fear, yet the urge in their veins would not let them remain. Their limbs moved without obedience. Whatever the dreadful tune was, it had to be followed to its source. Even the morel had no thought but to do otherwise.

Regardless of their bodies, they scrambled up the rock fall that served as stairs and into the open, to find themselves in the midst of nightmare.

Now the awful melody blew about them like a wind, though not a leaf moved. Frenziedly it plucked and tugged at their limbs. Nor were they the only creatures answering that syren call. Flying things and running things and hopping things and things that slithered battered their way through the clearing, all heading in one direction—towards the Black Mouth.

"The Black Mouth!" the morel cried. "The Black Mouth sings to us and we must go!"

It tugged not only at their ears but at their eyes. Their very retinas were partially drained of sensation, so that all the world appeared in black and white and grey. White the sky glimpsed overhead, grey the foliage that dappled it, black and grey the rocks distorted beneath their running feet. With hands extended before them, Gren and Poyly began to run amid the running things.

Now through a maelstrom of dread and compulsion they saw the herders.

Like so many shadows, the herders stood against the last trunks of the banyan. They had strapped or tied themselves there with ropes. In the centre of them, also tied, stood Iccall the Singer. Now he sang! He sang in a peculiarly uncomfortable position, as if disfigured, as if his neck were broken, with his head hanging down and his eyes wildly fixed on the ground.

He sang with all his voice and all his heart's blood. The song came valiantly out, flinging itself against the might of the Black Mouth's song. It had a power of its own, a power to counteract the evil that would otherwise have drawn all the herders out towards the source of that other melody.

The herders listened with grim intensity to what he sang. Yet they were not idle. Lashed to the tree trunks, they cast their line nets before them, trapping the creatures that poured past them to the undeniable call.

Poyly and Gren could not make out the words of Iccall's song. They had not been trained to it. Its message was over-ridden by the emanations from the mighty Mouth.

Wildly, they fought against that emanation—wildly but fruitlessly. Despite themselves, they stumbled on. Fluttering things struck them on the cheeks. The whole black and white world heaved and crawled in one direction alone! Only the herders were immune while they listened to Iccall's song.

When Gren stumbled, galloping vegetable creatures hopped over him.

Then the jumpvils poured by, teeming through the jungle. Still desperately listening to Iccall's song, the herders snared them as they flocked past, staying them and slaying them in the middle of the mêlée.

Poyly and Gren were passing the last of the herders. They were moving faster as the dreadful melody grew stronger. The open lay ahead of them. Framed in a canopy of foreground branches stood the distant Black Mouth! A strangled cry of—what? admiration? horror?—was torn from their lips at that spectacle.

Terror now had forms and legs and feelings, animated by the Black Mouth's song.

Towards it—they saw with their drained eyes—poured a

stream of life, answering that accursed call, making as fast as it could go over the lava field, and up the volcanic slopes, and finally throwing itself in triumph over the lip and into that great aperture!

Another chilling detail struck their eyes. Over the edge of the Mouth appeared three great long chitinous fingers which waved and enticed and kept time to the fateful tune.

Both the humans screamed at the sight—yet they redoubled their speed, for the grey fingers beckoned them.

"O Poyly! O Gren! Gren!"

The cry came as a will o' the wisp. They did not pause. Gren managed a quick glance back, towards the jolting blacks and greys of the forest.

The last herder they had passed was Yattmur; regardless of Iccall's song, she threw off the thong that tied her to the tree. Her hair flying wild, she was plunging knee deep through the tide of life to join them. Her arms stretched out to him like those of a lover in a dream.

In the weird light her face was grey, but bravely she sang as she ran, a song like Iccall's to counteract that other evil melody.

Gren faced ahead again, looking towards the Black Mouth, and instantly forgot about her. The long beckoning fingers beckoned him alone.

He had hold of Poyly's hand, but as they dashed past one of the outcrops of rock, Yattmur snatched his free hand.

For a saving moment they paid her attention. For a saving moment her brave song rose uppermost in their attention. Like a flash the morel seized this chance to break from bondage.

"Swerve aside!" it twanged. "Swerve aside if you wish to live!"

A peculiar-looking copse of young shoots stood just by their path. Labouring hand in hand, they turned into its doubtful refuge. A jumpvil hurtled in ahead of them, no doubt looking for a short cut in its stampede. They plunged into the grey gloom.

At once the Black Mouth's monstrous tune lost much of its

power. Yattmur fell against Gren's breast and sobbed—but all was still far from well.

Poyly touched one of the slender rods near her and screamed. A glutinous mass slid from the rod and over her head. She waved it and clutched it, hardly knowing what she did.

In despair they stared about, realizing they were in some kind of small enclosure. Their faulty vision had deceived them into entering a trap. Already the jumpvil that had entered before them was inextricably caught by the mess extruded from the rods.

Yattmur grasped the truth first.

"A greenguts!" she cried. "We've been swallowed by a greenguts!"

"Cut our way out, quickly!" twanged the morel. "Your sword, Gren—fast, fast! It's closing on us."

The gap had shut behind them. They were totally enclosed. The "ceiling" started to crumble and come down on them. The illusion of being in a copse faded. They were in a greenguts's stomach.

Wrenching out their swords, they began to defend their lives. As the rods about them—rods growing so cunningly to suggest the trunks of saplings—buckled and telescoped, so the ceiling lowered, its folds oozing a suffocating jelly. Jumping high, Gren slashed mightily with his sword. A great split appeared in the greenguts's envelope.

The two girls helped him enlarge it. As the bag crumpled down, they managed to get their heads through the rent, thus avoiding certain death.

But now the older menace reasserted itself. Again the death wail from the Mouth seized them by their bloodstreams. They hacked with redoubled energy at the greenguts, to get loose and and answer that chilling call.

They were free now but for their feet and ankles, which were stuck in the jelly. The greenguts was firmly anchored to a shoulder of rock so that it could not obey the call of the Black Mouth. It had collapsed entirely now, its solitary eye mournfully, helplessly, regarding their attempts to cut it to pieces.

"We must go!" Poyly cried, and at last managed to drag herself free. With her aid, Gren and Yattmur also broke away from the ruined creature. It closed its eye as they hurried off.

The delay had been longer than they knew. The ooze on their feet impeded them. They made their way over the lava as well as they could, still jostled by other creatures. Yattmur was too exhausted to sing again. Their wills were blotted out by the strength of the Black Mouth's song.

They started to scramble up the slopes of the cone, surrounded by a galloping phantasmagoria of life. Above them the three long fingers waved in sinister invitation. A fourth finger appeared, and then a fifth, as if whatever it was in the volcano was working itself up to a climax.

Their eyes saw everything in a fuzz of grey as the melody swelled to an unbearable intensity and their hearts laboured. The jumpvils really showed their paces, their long back legs enabling them to bound up the steeper slopes. They poured by, jumped on to the lip of the crater and then took their final leap to whatever lured them.

The humans were filled with longing to meet the dread singer. . . . Panting, impeded by the mess about their feet, they scrambled across the last few yards that separated them from the Black lip.

The dreadful melody ceased in mid-note. So unexpected was it, they fell flat on their faces. Exhaustion and relief washed over them. They lay with closed eyes, sobbing together. The melody had stopped, had stopped, entirely stopped.

After many pulses of his blood had gone by, Gren opened one eye.

The colours of the world were returning to normal again, white flooding with pink again, grey turning to blue and green and yellow, black dissolving into the sombre hues of the forest. By the same token, the overmastering desire in him turned to a revulsion for what they had been about to do.

The creatures round about that were too late to suffer the privilege of being swallowed by the Black Mouth evidently felt as he did. They turned and limped back towards the shelter of the forest, slowly at first and then faster, until their earlier stampede was reversed.

Soon the landscape was deserted.

Above the humans, five terrible long fingers came to rest precisely together on the lip of the Black Mouth. Then one by one they were withdrawn, leaving Gren with a vision of some unimaginable monster picking its teeth after an obscene repast.

"But for the greenguts we'd be dead by now," he said. "Are you all right, Poyly?"

"Let me alone," she said. Her face remained buried in her hands.

"Are you strong enough to walk? For the gods' sake let's get back to the herders," he said.

"Wait!" Yattmur exclaimed. "You deceived Hutweer and the others into thinking you were great spirits. By your running to the Black Mouth, they will know now you are not great spirits. Because you deceived them, they will surely kill you if you return."

Gren and Poyly looked at each other hopelessly. Despite the manœuvres of the morel, they had been pleased to be with a tribe again; the prospect of having to wander alone once more did not please them.

"Fear not," twanged the morel, reading their thought. "There are other tribes! What of these Fishers of which we heard? They sounded a more docile tribe than the herders. Ask Yattmur to lead us there."

"Are the Fishers far away?" Gren asked the girl herder.

She smiled at him and pressed his hand. "It will be pleasant to take you to them. You can see where they live from here."

Yattmur pointed down the flanks of the volcano. In the opposite direction to that from which they had come, an opening was apparent at the base of the Black Mouth. From the opening came a swift broad stream.

"There runs Long Water," Yattmur said. "Do you see the strange bulb-shaped trees, three of them in number, growing on the bank? That is where the Fishers live."

She smiled, looking Gren in the face. The beauty of her stole over his senses like a tangible thing.

"Let's get off this crater, Poyly," he said.

"That dreadful singing monster . . .," she said, stretching out a hand. Taking it, Gren pulled her to her feet.

Yattmur regarded them both without speaking.

"Off we go, then," she said sharply.

She took the lead and they began sliding down towards the water, ever and anon glancing back fearfully over their shoulders to make sure that nothing came climbing out of the volcano after them.

15

At the foot of the Black Mouth they came to the stream called Long Water. Once they had escaped from the shadow of the volcano, they lay in the warmth by the river bank. The waters ran dark and fast and smooth. On the opposite bank, the jungle began again, presenting a colonnade of trunks to the onlookers. On the near bank, lava checked that luxuriant growth for some yards.

Poyly dipped her hand into the water. So fast was it running that a bow wave formed against her palm. She splashed her forehead and rubbed her wet hand over her face.

"I am so tired," she said, "tired and sick. I want to go no farther. All these parts here are so strange—not like the happy middle layers of jungle where we lived with Lily-yo. What happens to the world here? Does it go mad here, or fall apart? Does it end here?"

"The world has to end somewhere," Yattmur said.

"Where it ends may be a good place for us to start it going again," twanged the morel.

"We shall feel better when we are rested," Gren said. "And then you must return to your herders, Yattmur."

As he looked at her, a movement behind him caught his eye. He spun round, sword in hand, jumping up to confront three hairy men who seemed to have materialized out of the ground.

The girls jumped up too.

"Don't hurt them, Gren," Yattmur cried. "These are Fishers and they will be perfectly harmless."

And indeed the newcomers looked harmless. At second glance, Gren was less sure that they were human. All three were plump and their flesh beneath the abundant hair was spongy, almost like rotting vegetable matter. Though they wore knives in their belts, they carried no weapon in their hands, and their hands hung aimlessly by their sides. Their belts, plaited out of jungle creepers, were their only adornments. On their three faces, their three expressions of mild stupidity were so similar as to represent almost a uniform.

Gren took in one other noteworthy fact about them before they spoke: each had a long green tail, even as the herders had said.

"Do you bring us food for eating?" the first of them asked.

"Have you brought us food for our tummies?" asked the second.

"Can we eat any food you have brought?" asked the third.

"They think you are of my tribe, which is the only tribe they know," Yattmur said. Turning to the Fishers, she replied, "We have no food for your bellies, O Fishers. We did not come to see you, only to travel."

"We have no fish for you," replied the first Fisher, and the three of them added almost in chorus, "Very soon the time for fishing will be here."

"We have nothing to exchange for food, but we should be glad of some fish to eat," Gren said.

121

"We have no fish for you. We have no fish for us. The time for fishing will soon be here," the Fishers said.

"Yes. I heard you the first time," Gren said. "What I mean is, will you give us fish when you have it?"

"Fish is fine to eat. There is fish for everyone when it comes."

"Good," Gren said, adding for the benefit of Poyly, Yattmur and the morel, "these seem very simple people."

"Simple or not, they didn't go chasing up the Black Mouth trying to kill themselves," the morel said. "We must ask them about that. How did they resist its beastly song? Let's go to their place, as they seem harmless enough."

"We will come with you," Gren told the Fishers.

"We are going to catch fish when the fish come soon. You people do not know how to catch."

"Then we will come and watch you catch fish."

The three Fishers looked at each other, a slight uneasiness ruffling the surface of their stupidity. Without saying a word more, they turned and walked away along the river bank. Given no option, the others followed.

"How much do you know of these people, Yattmur?" Poyly asked.

"Very little. We trade sometimes, as you know, but my people fear the Fishers because they are so strange, as if they were dead. They never leave this little strip of river bank."

"They can't be complete fools, for they know enough to eat well," Gren said, regarding the plump flanks of the men ahead.

"Look at the way they carry their tails!" Poyly exclaimed. "These are curious folk. I never saw the like."

"They would be simple for me to command," thought the morel.

As they walked, the Fishers reeled in their tails, holding them in neat coils in their right hands; the action, done so easily, was clearly automatic. For the first time, the others saw that these tails were extraordinarily long; in fact, the ends of them were not visible. Where they joined the Fishers' bodies, a sort of soft green pad formed at the base of their spines.

Suddenly and in unison the Fishers stopped and turned.

"You can come no farther now," they said. "We are near our trees and you must not come with us. Stop here and soon we will bring you fish."

"Why can't we come any farther?" Gren asked.

One of the Fishers laughed unexpectedly.

"Because you have no tail! Now wait here and soon we will bring you fish." And he walked on with his companion, not even bothering to look back and see if his order was being obeyed.

"These are curious folk," Poyly said again. "I don't like them, Gren. They are not like people at all. Let us leave them; we can easily find our own food."

"Nonsense! They may be very useful to us," twanged the morel. "You see they have a boat of some kind down there."

Farther down the bank, several of the people with long green tails were working. They laboured under the trees, dragging what looked like some sort of a net into their boat. This boat, a heavy barge-like craft, rode tight in against the near bank, plunging occasionally in the stiff currents of Long Water.

The first three Fishers rejoined the main party and helped them with the net. Their movements were languid, although they appeared to be working with haste.

Poyly's gaze wandered from them to the three trees in the shade of which they worked. She had never seen trees like them before, and their unusual aspect made her more uneasy.

Standing apart from all other vegetation, the trees bore a resemblance to giant pineapples. A collar of spiny leaves projected outwards direct from the ground, protecting the central fleshy trunk, which in each of the three cases was swollen into a massive knobbly ovoid. From the knobs of the ovoid sprouted long trailers; from the top of the ovoid sprouted more leaves, spiny and sharp, extending some two hundred feet into the air, or hanging stiffly out over Long Water.

"Poyly, let us go and look more closely at those trees," the morel twanged urgently. "Gren and Yattmur will wait here and watch us."

"I do not like these people or this place, morel," Poyly said. "And I will not leave Gren here with this woman, do what you will."

"I shall not touch your mate," Yattmur said indignantly. "What makes you think such a silly thing?"

Poyly staggered forward under a sudden compulsion from the morel. She looked appealingly at Gren; but Gren was tired and did not meet her eye. Reluctantly she moved forward and soon was under the bloated trees. They towered above her, casting a spiked shade. Their swollen trunks stuck out like diseased stomachs.

The morel seemed not to feel their menace.

"Just as I had assumed!" it exclaimed after a long inspection. "Here is where the tails of our Fishers end. They are joined to the trees by their rumps—our simple friends belong to the trees."

"Humans do not grow from trees, morel. Did you not know——" She paused, for a hand had fallen on her shoulder.

She turned. One of the Fishers confronted her, looking her closely in the face with his blank eyes and puffing out his cheeks.

"You must not come under the trees," he said. "Their shade is sacred. We said you must not come under our trees and you did not remember we said it. I will take you back to your friends who have not come with you."

Poyly's eye travelled down his tail. Even as the morel had claimed, it joined on to the swelling of the nearest spiky tree. She felt a shiver of dread and moved away from him.

"Obey him!" twanged the morel. "There is evil here, Poyly. We must fight it. Let him walk with us back to the others and then we will capture him and ask him a few questions."

This will cause trouble, she thought, but at once the morel filled her mind saying, "We need these people and perhaps we need their boat."

So she yielded to the Fisher as he grasped her arm and

walked her slowly back to Gren and Yattmur, who watched this performance intently. As they went, the Fisher solemnly paid out his tail.

"Now!" cried the morel, when they reached the others.

Forced on by his will, Poyly flung herself on the Fisher's back. The move was so sudden that he staggered and fell forward.

"Help me!" Poyly called. Before she had spoken, Gren was springing forward with his knife ready. And at the same moment a cry came from all the other Fishers. They dropped their great net and began in unison to run towards Gren and his party, their feet padding heavily over the ground.

"Quickly, Gren, cut this creature's tail off," Poyly said, prompted by the morel, as she struggled in the dust to keep her opponent down.

Without questioning her, for the morel's orders were in his mind too, Gren reached forward and slashed once.

The green tail was severed a foot from the Fisher's rump. At once the man ceased struggling. The tail that had been attached to him commenced a writhing motion, lashing the ground like an injured snake, and catching Gren in its coils. He slashed at it again. Leaking sap, it curled up and went looping back to the tree. As if this were a signal, the other Fishers came to a standstill *en masse*; they milled about aimlessly and then turned and went indifferently back to loading their net into the boat.

"Praise the gods for that!" Yattmur exclaimed, brushing her hair back. "What made you attack this poor fellow, Poyly, jumping on him from behind as you did with me?"

"All these Fishers are not like us, Yattmur. They can't be human at all—their tails attach them to the three trees." Not meeting the other girl's eyes, Poyly stared down at the stump of tail on the fellow weeping at her feet.

"These fat Fisher people are slaves of the trees," twanged the morel. "It is disgusting. The trailers from the trees grow into their backbones and compel the men to guard them. Look at this poor wretch grovelling here—a slave!"

125

"Is it worse than what you do with us, morel?" Poyly asked, showing signs of tears. "Is it any different? Why don't you let us go? I had no wish to attack this fellow."

"I help you—I save your lives. Now, attend to this poor Fisher and let's have no more silly talk from you."

The poor Fisher was attending to himself, sitting up and examining a knee that had been grazed in his fall on to the rock. He gazed at them with an anxiety that still did not remove the simplicity from his countenance. Huddled there, he looked like a roughly rounded lump of dough.

"You can get up," Gren told him gently, extending his hand to help the fellow to his feet. "You're shaking. There's nothing to be afraid of. We won't hurt you if you answer our questions."

The Fisher broke in a torrent of words, most of it incomprehensible, gesturing with his broad hands as he talked.

"Speak slowly. You're talking about the trees? What are you saying?"

"Please. . . . The tummy-trees, yes. I and them all one part, all tummy or tummy-hands. Tummy-head to think for me where I serve Tummy-trees. You kill my tummy-cord, I feel no good in my veins, no good sap. You wild lost people with no Tummy-tree, not have the sap to see what I say. . . ."

"Stop it! Talk sense, you great tummy! You're human, aren't you? You call those big swollen plants Tummy-trees? And you have to serve them? When did they catch you? How long ago?"

The Fisher put his hand to the height of his knee, rolled his head stupidly and burst into speech again.

"No-high the Tummy-trees take us, cuddle, bed, save snugly like mothers. Babies go in the soft folds, just legs to see, keep on sucking at the tummy, get put on a tummy-cord to walk. Please you let me go back, try find a new tummy-cord or I'm a poor baby too without one."

Poyly, Gren and Yattmur stared at him as he chattered, not taking in half he said.

"I don't understand," Yattmur whispered. "He talked more sense before his tail was cut off."

"We've set you free—we'll set all your friends free," Gren said, the morel prompting him. "We'll take you all away from these filthy Tummy-trees. You'll be free, free to work with us and start a new life, slaves no longer."

"No, no, please. . . . Tummy-trees grow us like flowers! We have no want to be wild men like you, no lovely Tummy-trees——"

"Shut up about the trees!" Gren raised his hand and at once the other fell silent, biting his lips and scratching his fat thighs in anguish. "We are your liberators and you should be grateful to us. Now, tell us quickly, what is this fishing we've heard about? When does it start? Soon?"

"Soon now, so soon, please," the Fisher said, trying to catch Gren's hand in entreaty. "Most times, no fishy swim in Long Water, cut too sharply on out the hole of Black Mouth, so no fish swim. And if no fish means no fishing, see? Then the Black Mouth sing to all things to be a meal for him in his mouth, and so Tummy-trees make us big mummy noise, cuddle us up, not let us be any meal in his mouth. Then short time Mouth make rest, no sing, no eat, no noise. Then Mouth drop away what he eat not need not eat not have, drop away in Long Water under his self. Then up come big fish big hunger big eat all drop-away pieces, we quick Tummy-men Fishers go out catch big fish big hunger in big net, feed big glad Tummy-tree, feed Tummy-men, all feed——"

"All right, that'll do," Gren said, and the Fishers subsided wretchedly, standing on one foot with the other. As they began an excited discussion, he sank down to the ground, holding his head dolorously in his hands.

With the morel, Gren and Poyly quickly came to a plan of action.

"We can save them all from this humiliating way of life," Gren said.

"They don't want to be saved," Yattmur said. "They're happy."

"They're horrible," Poyly said.

While they were talking, the Long Water changed colour. A myriad bits and pieces erupted on to its surface, dappling it as they were swept along in the direction of the Tummy-trees.

"The remains of the Mouth's feast!" Gren exclaimed. "Come on, before the boat casts off and the Fishers start to fish. Out with your knives."

Impelled by the morel, he bounded off, Poyly and Yattmur following. Only the latter cast a backward glance at the Fisher. He was rolling on the ground in a bout of misery, indifferent to everything but his own wretchedness.

The rest of the Fishers had by now loaded their net into the boat. On seeing the refuse in the stream they gave a cheer and climbed into the vessel, each paying out his tail over the stern as he went. The last one was scrambling aboard as Gren and the women rushed up.

"Jump for it!" Gren shouted, and the three of them jumped, landing on the crude and creaking deck close together. In unison, the nearer Fishers turned to face them.

Unwieldy though it was, built under the direction of the pseudo-aware Tummy-trees, the boat was made to serve a particular purpose: to catch the big scavenger fish of Long Water. It boasted neither oars nor sail, since its only function was to drag a heavy net across the stream from one bank to the other. Accordingly, a stoutly woven rope had been stretched across the water and anchored to trees on either side. To this rope the boat was loosely secured through a series of eyes, thus preventing its being swept away on the flood. It was manœuvred across the river by simple brute force, half the Fishers pulling on the guide rope while the others lowered the net into place. So it had been from dimmest times.

Routine governed the Fishers' lives. When the three intruders landed in their midst, neither they nor the Tummy-trees knew clearly what action to take. Divided in purpose, the Fishers were made half to continue hauling the boat into mid-stream and half to defend their position.

With one uniform rush, the defence force charged at Gren and the girls.

Yattmur glanced over her shoulder. It was too late to jump ashore again; they were away from the bank. She drew her knife and stood by Gren and Poyly. As the Fishers fell at them, she plunged it into the stomach of the nearest man. He stumbled, but others bore her down. Her knife went skidding over the deck and her hands were pinned before she could draw her sword.

The fat men flung themselves at Poyly and Gren. Though they fought desperately, they too were borne down.

Evidently the Fishers and their pot-bellied masters ashore had not thought to use knives until they saw Yattmur's. Now— as one man—they all produced knives.

Through Gren's brain, amid his panic and fury, scared the angry jangle of the morel's thought.

"You brainless tarsiers! Waste no time on these dolls of men Cut their umbilical cords, their tails, their tails, you fools! Hack their tails off and they'll not harm you!"

Cursing, ramming a knee into a groin and knuckles into an attacker's face, Gren knocked aside a down-curving knife and twisted over on to his knees. Impelled by the morel, he grasped another Fisher by the neck, wrenching it savagely and then flinging the man aside. Now his way was clear. With a leap he was up on the stern.

The green tails lay there, thirty of them together, stretching over to the shore.

Gren let out a shout of triumph. Then he brought his blade down.

Half a dozen slashes in cold anger and the thing was done!

The boat rocked violently. The Fishers jerked and fell. All their activity stopped. They moaned and cried, picking themselves up to stand helplessly together in a knot, their severed tails dangling. Shorn of its motive power, the boat rested in mid-stream.

"You see," remarked the morel, "the fight is over."

As Poyly picked herself up, a flailing movement caught her eye, and she looked at the bank they had left. A low cry of horror was wrenched from her lips. Gren and Yattmur turned to stare where she did. They stood transfixed, their knives still grasped in their hands.

"Get down!" Poyly shouted.

Scintillant leaves like toothed swords whirled above them. The three Tummy-trees heaved in wrath. Bereft of their willing slaves, they were lashing the tall leaves that formed their poll into action. Their whole bulk trembled as the dark green blades flashed above the vessel.

As Poyly flung herself flat, the first leaf struck, throwing a great raw weal across the rough wood of the deck. Splinters flew. A second and a third blow fell. Such a terrible bombard-ment, she knew, would kill them all in no time.

The unnatural anger of these trees was fearful to see. Poyly did not let it paralyse her. As Gren and Yattmur crouched under the frail shelter of the stern, she jumped up. Without needing the morel to guide her, she leant over the side and hacked at the tough fibres that kept the boat square across the river.

Armoured leaves flayed near her. The Fishers were struck once and then again. Parabolas of blood patterned the deck. Crying, the poor creatures tumbled together while their limbs bled and they staggered from the centre of the deck. Still the trees struck out mercilessly.

Tough though the securing rope was, it parted at last under Poyly's attack. She gave a shout of triumph as the boat freed itself and swayed round under the force of the water.

She was still climbing to cover as the next leaf crashed down. The spines along one fleshy edge of it raked her with full force across the chest.

130

"Poyly!" Gren and Yattmur cried with one voice, springing up.

They never reached her. The blow caught her off balance. She doubled up as the blood came weeping from her wound. As her knees buckled she fell backwards. Momentarily her eyes caught Gren's in tender appeal, and then she disappeared over the side and hit the waters.

They rushed to the side and peered down. An extra turbidity marked where she had sunk. One hand appeared on the surface, its fingers outspread, severed from its arm. It vanished almost at once in a welter of smooth fish bodies and then there was no more sign of Poyly.

Falling on to the deck, beating his fists on it in sorrow, Gren cried to the morel.

"Could you not have saved her, you miserable fungus, you useless growth? Could you not have done something? What did you ever bring her but trouble?"

A long silence followed. Gren called at it again—in grief and hatred. At length the morel spoke in a small voice.

"Half of me is dead," it whispered.

16

By this time the boat had begun to whirl away down the flood. Already they were safe from the Tummy-trees, which fell rapidly behind, their murderous polls still beating the water into lines of spray.

Seeing that they were being carried off, the Fishers began a chorus of groans. Yattmur paraded before them with her knife out, allowing herself to show no pity for their wounds.

"You Tummy-belly men! You long-tailed sons of swollen plants! Cease your noise! Someone real has died and you shall mourn her or I'll throw you all overboard with my own two hands."

At that the Fishers fell into abject silence. Grouped humbly together, they comforted each other and licked each other's wounds. Running over to Gren, Yattmur put her arm round him and pressed her cheek against his. Only for a moment did he try to resist her.

"Don't mourn too much for Poyly. She was fine in life—but a time comes for all of us to fall to the green. I am here now, and I will be your mate."

"You will want to get back to your tribe, to the herders," Gren said miserably.

"Ha! They lie far behind us. How shall I get back? Stand up and see how fast we are being swept along! I can hardly see the Black Mouth now—it's no bigger than one of my nipples. We are in danger, O Gren. Rouse yourself! Ask your magical friend the morel where we are going."

"I don't care what happens to us now."

"Look Gren——"

A shout rose from the Fishers. They showed a sort of apathetic interest, pointing ahead and calling, which was enough to pull Yattmur and Gren up at once.

Their boat was rapidly being swept towards another. More than one Fishers' colony grew by the banks of the Long Water. Another loomed ahead. Two bulging Tummy-trees marked its position. This colony's net was out across the stream, its boat resting against the far bank, full of Fishers. Their tails hung over the river along the top of the net.

"We're going to hit them!" Gren said. "What are we going to do?"

"No, we shall miss their boat. Perhaps their net will stop us. Then we can get safely ashore."

"Look at these fools climbing on to the sides of the boat. They'll be jerked overboard." He called to the Fishers in question, who were swarming over the bows. "Hey, you Short-tails! Get down there, or you'll be flung into the water."

His cry was drowned by their shouts and the roar of the water. They were rushing irresistibly towards the other boat. Next moment they struck the net that stretched across their path.

The cumbersome boat squealed and lurched. Several Fishers were flung down into the water by the impact. One of them managed to jump the narrowing distance into the other boat. The two vessels struck glancingly, cannoned off each other—and then the securing rope across the river broke.

They whirled free again, to go racing on down the flood. The other boat, being already against the bank, stayed there, bumping uncomfortably. Many of its crew were scampering about the bank; some had been flung into the stream, some had had their tails lopped off. But their misadventures remained hidden for ever more as Gren's boat swept round a grand curve, and jungle closed in on both sides.

"Now what do we do?" Yattmur asked, trembling.

Gren shrugged his shoulders. He had no ideas. The world had revealed itself as too big and too terrible for him.

"Wake up, morel," he said. "What happens to us now? You got us into this trouble—now get us out of it."

For answer the morel started turning his mind upside down. Dizzied, Gren sat down heavily. Yattmur clasped his hands while phantoms of memory and thought fluttered before his mental gaze. The morel was studying navigation.

Finally it said, "We need to steer this boat to get it to obey us. But there is nothing to steer it with. We must wait and see what happens."

It was an admission of defeat. Gren sat on the deck with an arm round Yattmur, properly indifferent to everything external. His thoughts went back to the time when he and Poyly were careless children in the tribe of Lily-yo. Life had been so easy, so sweet then, and little had they realized it! Why, it had even been warmer; the sun had shone almost directly overhead.

He opened one eye. The sun was quite far down in the sky.

"I'm cold," he said.

"Huddle against me," Yattmur coaxed.

Some freshly plucked leaves lay near them; perhaps they had

133

been plucked to wrap the Fishers' expected catch of fish in. Yattmur pulled them over Gren and lay close against him, letting her arms steal round him.

He relaxed in her warmth. As interest in her awoke, he began instinctively to explore her body. She was as warm and sweet as childhood dreams, and pressed ardently against his touch. Her hands too began a journey of exploration. Lost in delight of each other they forgot the world. When he took her, she was also taking him.

Even the morel was soothed by the pleasure of their actions under the warm leaves. The boat sped on down the river, occasionally bumping a bank, but never ceasing its progress.

After a while, it joined a much wider river and spun hopelessly in an eddy for some time, making them all dizzy. One of the wounded Fishers died here; he was thrown overboard; this might have been a signal, for at once the boat was released from the eddy and floated off again on the broad bosom of the waters. Now the river was very wide, and spreading still farther, so that in time they could see neither shore.

For the humans, especially for Gren to whom the idea of long empty distances was foreign, it was an unknown world. They stared out at the expanse only to turn away shivering and hide their eyes. Everywhere was motion!—and not only beneath them in the restless water. A cool wind had sprung up, a wind that would have lost its way in the measureless miles of the forest but was here master of all it passed over. It scuffed the water with its invisible footsteps, it jostled the boat and made it creak, it splashed spray in the troubled faces of the Fishers, it ruffled their hair and blew it across their ears. Gaining strength, it chilled their skins and drew a gauze of cloud over the sky, obscuring the traversers that drifted there.

Two dozen Fishers remained in the boat, six of them suffering badly from the attack of the Tummy-trees. They made no attempt to approach Gren and Yattmur at first, lying together like a living monument to despair. First one and then another

134

of the wounded died and was cast overboard, amid desultory mourning.

So they were carried out into the ocean.

The great width of the river prevented them from being attacked by the giant seaweeds which fringed the coasts. Nothing, indeed, marked their transition from river to estuary or from estuary to sea; the broad brown roll of fresh water continued far into the surrounding salt waves.

Gradually the brown faded into green and blue depths, and the wind stiffened, taking them in a different direction, parallel with the coast. The mighty forest looked no bigger than a leaf.

One of the Fishers, urged by his companions, came humbly over to Gren and Yattmur where they lay resting among the leaves. He bowed to them.

"O great herders, hear us speak when we speak if you let me start talking," he said.

Gren said sharply, "We will do you no harm, fat fellow. We are in trouble just as you are. Can't you understand that? We meant to help you, and that we shall do if the world turns dry again. But try to gather your thoughts together so that you talk sense. What do you want?"

The man bowed low. Behind him, his companions bowed low in heart-sick imitation.

"Great herder, we see you since you come. We clever Tummy-tree chaps are seeing your size. So we know you will soon love to kill us when you jump up from playing the sandwich game along with your lady in the leaves. We clever chaps are not fools, and not fools are clever to make glad dying for you. All the same sadness makes us not clever to die with no feeding. All we poor sad clever Tummy-men have no feeding and pray you give us feeding because we have no mummy Tummy-feeding——"

Gren gestured impatiently.

"We've no food either," he said. "We are humans like you. We too must fend for ourselves.

"Alas, we did not dare to have any hopes you would share

your food with us, for your food is sacred and you wish to see us starve. You are very clever to hide from us the jumpvil food we know you always carry. We are glad, great herder, that you make us starve if our dying makes you have a laugh and a gay song and another sandwich game. Because we are humble, we do not need food to die with. . . ."

"I really will kill these creatures," Gren said savagely, releasing Yattmur and sitting up. "Morel, what do we do with them? You got us into this trouble. Help us get out of it."

"Make them throw their net over the side and catch fish," twanged the morel.

"Good!" Gren said. He jumped up, pulling Yattmur with him, and began to shout orders at the Fishers.

Miserably, incompetently, fawningly, they arranged their net and cast it over the side of the vessel. The sea here teemed with life. No sooner was the net down than something big tugged at it—tugged and began unfalteringly to climb it.

The boat listed over to one side. With a cry, the Fishers fell away as a great pair of claws rattled over the gunwales. Gren was beneath them. Without thought, he pulled out his knife and smote.

A lobster head bigger than his own loomed up before him. An eyestalk went flying—and another, as he smote again.

Soundlessly, the marine monster released its hold and fell back into the depths, leaving a frightened band of Fishers moaning in the scuppers. Almost as frightened himself—for he sensed the morel's fear in his mind—Gren rounded on them, kicking and shouting.

"Get up, you flabby tummy-bellies! Would you lie there and die? Well I won't let you. Get up and haul the net in again before we get any more monsters in on us. Come on, move! Get this net in! Jump to it, you blubbering brutes!"

"O great herder, you may throw us to the wonders of the wet world and we will not complain. We may not complain! You see we praise you even when you fetch up the beasts of the wet

136

world upon us and we are too lowly to complain, so be merciful——"

"Merciful! I'll flay you alive if you don't get that net in at
once. Move!" he yelled, and they moved, the hair on their
flanks fluttering in the breeze.

The line came over the side laden with creatures that splashed
and flapped about their ankles.

"Wonderful!" Yattmur cried, squeezing Gren. "I am so
hungry, my love. Now we shall live! Soon there will be an end to
this Long Water, I know."

But the boat drifted as it would. They went to sleep once
more and then a second time, and the weather grew no warmer—
and then they woke to find the deck motionless beneath them.

Gren opened his eyes. A stretch of sand and bushes met his
gaze. He and Yattmur were alone in the boat.

"Morel!" he cried, leaping to his feet. "You never sleep—
why did you not wake me and tell us that the water had stopped?
And the flabby-bellies have escaped!"

He looked round at the ocean that had brought them here.
Yattmur stood up silently, hugging her breasts and regarding
with wonder a great peak that rose sheer from the nearby bushes.

The morel made something like a ghostly chuckle in Gren's
mind. "The Fishers will not get far—let them find out the
dangers for us first. I let you and Yattmur sleep on so that you
would feel fresh. You will need all your energies. This may be
the place where we build our new kingdom, my friend!"

Gren made a doubtful move. No traversers were visible overhead, and he took it as a bad omen. All there was to be seen,
apart from the forbidding island and the wastes of ocean, was a
speedseed bird, sailing along under the ceiling of high cloud.

"I suppose we'd better get ashore," Gren said.

"I'd rather stay in the boat," Yattmur said, eyeing the great
cliff of rock with apprehension. But when he put out a hand to
her, she took it and climbed over the side without fuss.

He could hear her teeth chattering.

They stood on the unwelcoming beach, testing it for menace.

The speedseed still flew alone in the sky. It changed direction by a degree or so without interrupting the pulse of its flight. High over the ocean it soared, its wooden wings creaking like a fully rigged sailing ship.

The two humans heard its noise and looked up. The speedseed had sighted land. Slowing, it circled and began to lose height.

"Is it after us?" Yattmur asked.

A choice of cover presented itself. They could hide under their boat, or they could dive into the fringe of jungle that curled over the low forehead of the beach. The boat was flimsy shelter from a large bird, should it choose to attack; together, man and woman slid into the foliage.

Now the speedseed was plunging steeply. Its wings did not retract. Stiffly outspread, they jarred and vibrated through the air under increased momentum.

Formidable though it was, the speedseed remained but a crude imitation of the true birds which had once filled the skies of Earth. The last of the true birds had perished many eons ago, when the sun had begun to pour out increased energy as it moved into the last phase of its existence. Speedseeds imitated the form of an extinct avian class with a lordly inefficiency in keeping with the supremacy of the vegetable world. The vibratory racket of its wings filled the heavens.

"Has it seen us, Gren?" Yattmur asked, peering from under the leaves. It was cold in the shadow of the towering cliff.

For answer Gren merely clutched her arm tightly, staring up with slitted eyes. Because he was both frightened and angry, he did not trust himself to speak. The morel offered him no comfort, withdrawing itself to await events.

It now became obvious that the clumsy bird could not straighten out in time to avoid hitting the land. Down it came, its shadow swept black over the bush, the leaves stirred as it shot past behind a nearby tree—and silence fell. No sound of impact reached the humans, though the bird must have hit the ground not more than fifty yards from them.

"Living shades!" Gren exclaimed. "Did something swallow it?"

His mind backed hurriedly away from trying to visualize something big enough to swallow a speedseed bird.

17

They stood waiting, but nothing interrupted the silence.

"It vanished like a ghost!" Gren said. "Let's go and see what happened to it."

She clung to him to hold him back.

"This is an unknown place, full of unknown perils," she said. "Let us not seek trouble when trouble is ready enough to seek us. We know nothing of where we are. First we must find what kind of place this is, and if we can live here."

"I would rather find trouble than let it find me," Gren said. "But perhaps you are right, Yattmur. My bones tell me that this is not a good place. What has happened to those stupid tummy-belly men?"

They emerged on to the beach and started to walk slowly along it, the whole time looking watchfully about them, keeping an eye open for signs of their pitiful companions, moving between the flatness of the sea and the steepness of the great cliff.

The signs they looked for were not far to seek.

"They've been here," said Gren, running along the strand.

Scuffed footprints and droppings marked the place where the tummy-belly men had paddled ashore. Many of the prints were imprecise and pointed this way and that; handprints also were not uncommon, marking where the creatures had stumbled into one another and fallen. The marks clearly betrayed the lumpish and uncertain way in which the tummy-bellies had progressed. After a short distance they led into a narrow belt of trees with leathery and sad leaves that stood between beach and cliff. As

139

Gren and Yattmur followed the prints into the gloom, a low sound made them stop. Moans came from near at hand.

Drawing out his knife, Gren spoke. Looking into the grove that drew nourishment what it could from the sandy soil, he called, "Whoever you are, come out before I haul you out squealing!"

The moans redoubled, a low threnody in which babbled words were distinguishable.

"It's a tummy-belly!" Yattmur exclaimed. "Don't be angry with him if he's hurt." Her eyes had adjusted to the shade, and now she ran forward as she spoke and knelt on the sandy ground among the sharp grasses.

One of the fat Fishers lay there with three of his companions huddled against him. He shuddered violently away, half-rolling over, as Yattmur appeared.

"I shan't hurt you," Yattmur said. "We were searching to find where you had gone."

"It is too late, for our hearts are broken by your not coming before," the man cried, tears rolling down his cheeks. Dried blood from a long scratch across one shoulder had matted his hair at that point, but Yattmur could see the wound was only superficial.

"It's a good thing we found you," she said. "There's nothing much wrong with you. You must all get up now and return to the boat."

At this the tummy-belly burst into fresh complaint; his fellows joined in the chorus, speaking in their peculiarly jumbled dialect.

"O great herders, the sight of you adds to our miseries. How very much we rejoice to see you again, though we know you will kill us, poor helpless loveable tummy-fellows that we are."

"We are, we are, we are, and though our love is loving you, you cannot love us, for we are only miserable dirt and you are cruel murderers who are cruel to dirt."

"You will kill us though we are dying! O how we admire your bravery, you clever tail-less heroes!"

"Stop this filthy babbling," Gren ordered. "We are not murderers and we have never desired to harm you."

"How clever you are, master, to be pretending that cutting us off our lovely tails is no harm! O we thought you were dead and finished with making sandwiches in the boat when the watery world turned solid, so we crept away in good grief, crept away on all our feet because your snores were loud. Now you have caught us again and because you do not snore we know you will kill us!"

Gren slapped the cheek of the nearest creature, who wailed and writhed as if in mortal agony.

"Be silent, blubbering fools! We shall not hurt you if you trust us. Stand up and tell us where the rest of your number is."

His order only brought forth fresh lamentation.

"You can see we four sad sufferers are fatally dying of the death that comes to all green and pink things, so you tell us to stand up, because to make any standing position will kill us badly, so that you kick us when our souls are gone and we can only be dead at you and not crying with our harmless mouths. O we fall down from our lying flat at such a sly idea, great herder!"

As they cried out, they tried blindly to grasp Yattmur and Gren's ankles and kiss their feet, making the two humans skip about to avoid this embrace.

"There's very little wrong with the foolish creatures," said Yattmur, who had been trying to examine them during this orgy of lamentation. "They are scratched and bruised, nothing more."

"I'll soon heal them," Gren said. His ankle had been caught; he kicked out into a podgy face. Impelled by loathing, he grasped one of the other prone tummy-bellies and dragged the creature to its feet by force.

"How wonderfully strong you are, master," it groaned, trying at once to kiss and bite his hands. "Your muscles and your cruelty are huge to poor little dying chaps like us whose blood is going bad inside them because of bad things and other bad things, alas!"

"I'll push your teeth down your throat if you don't keep quiet," Gren promised.

With Yattmur's help, he got the other three weeping tummy-bellies to their feet; as she had said, there was little wrong with them apart from self-pity. Silencing them, he asked them whither their sixteen companions had gone.

"O wonderful no-tail, you spare this poor tiny number four to enjoy killing the big number sixteen. What self-sacrifice you sacrifice! We happily tell you of the happiness we feel in telling you which way went our jolly sad sixteen number, so we can be spared to go on living and enjoying your smacks and blows and cruel kicks in the noses of our tender face. The sixteen number laid us down here to die in peace before they ran on that way for you to catch them and play killing."

And they pointed dejectedly along the shore.

"Stay here and keep quiet," Gren ordered. "We will come back for you when we've found your fellows. Don't go away or something may eat you."

"We will wait in fear even if we die first."

"See that you do."

Gren and Yattmur set off along the beach. Silence descended; even the ocean made hardly a murmur as it nuzzled against the land; and they felt again a huge unease, as if a million eyes watched them unseen.

As they walked, they surveyed their surroundings. Creatures of the jungle, they would never face anything more alien than the sea; yet the land here held a strangeness. It was not simply that the trees—with leathery leaves that seemed suitable for the colder climate—were of an unknown variety; nor that behind the trees there rose the steep cliff, so steep, so grey, so pitted, rising to a spire so far above their heads, that it dwarfed everything and seemed to cast a gloom over the whole scene.

Beside all these elements of visual strangeness was another, one to which they could give no name, but which seemed all the more obtrusive after their brush with the tummy-bellies. The murmuring silence of the beach contributed to their unease.

Taking a nervous glance across her shoulder, Yattmur looked up towards the towering cliff again. Gathering cloud scudding across the sky made that great wall look as if it were toppling.

Yattmur fell on her face and covered her eyes.

"The mighty cliffs are crashing down on us!" she cried, pulling Gren down with her.

He looked up once. The illusion caught him too: that grand and high tower was coming grandly down on top of them! Together they squeezed their soft bodies among the hard rocks, seeking safety by pressing their faces into damp shingly sand. They were creatures who belonged to the jungles of the hothouse world; so many things here were alien to them, they could respond only with fear.

Instinctively, Gren called the fungus that draped his head and neck.

"Morel, save us! We trusted you and you brought us to this dreadful place. Now you must get us away from it, quickly before the cliff comes down on us."

"If you die, I die," said the morel, sending its twanging harmonics through Gren's head. It added more helpfully, "You can both get up. The clouds move; the cliff does not."

A moment or two passed—an interval of waiting filled with the dirge of the ocean—before Gren dared to test the truth of this observation. At length, finding that no rocks cascaded down on to his naked body, he peered up. Feeling him move, Yattmur whimpered.

Still the cliff seemed to fall. He braced himself to look at it more thoroughly.

The cliff appeared to be sailing out of the heavens on to him, yet at last he assured himself that it did not move. He dared to look away from its pitted face and nudge Yattmur.

"The cliff is not harming us yet," he said. "We can go on."

She raised a woebegone face, its cheeks patterned redly

where they had pressed against the tiny stones of the shore, some of which still clung there.

"It is a magic cliff. It always falls yet it never falls," she said at last, after regarding the rock carefully. "I don't like it. It has eyes to watch us."

They scrambled on, Yattmur looking nervously up from time to time. Clouds were gathering, their shadows moving in from the sea.

The shore curved sharply and continuously, its sands often buried under great masses of rock on which the jungle encroached at one end and the sea at the other. Over these masses they had laboriously to climb, moving as quietly as possible.

"We shall soon be back where we started from," Gren said, looking back and finding that their boat was now concealed behind the central cliff.

"Correct," twanged the morel. "We are on a small island, Gren."

"We can't live here then, morel?"

"I think not."

"How do we get away?"

"As we arrived—in the boat. Some of these giant leaves would serve us as sails."

"We hate the boat, morel, and the watery world."

"But you prefer them to death. How can we live here, Gren? It is merely a great round tower of rock skirted by a strip of sand."

Gren lapsed into confused thought without reporting this unspoken conversation to Yattmur. The wise thing, he concluded, would be to postpone a decision until they had found the rest of the tummy-belly men.

He became aware of Yattmur looking more and more frequently over her shoulder at the high tower of rock. Bursting with nerves, he said, "What's the matter with you? Look where you are going or you will break your neck."

She took his hand.

144

"Hush! It will hear you," she said. "This terrible big tower of cliff has a million eyes that watch us all the time."

As he began to turn his head she seized his face, pulling him down with her behind a protruding rock.

"Don't let it see that we know," she whispered. "Peep at it from here."

So he did, his mouth dry, his gaze going over that large and watchful surface of grey. Cloud had obscured the sun, rendering the rock in the dull light more forbidding than ever. Already he had noticed that it was pitted; now he saw how evenly spaced those pits were, how much they resembled sockets, how uncannily they seemed to stare down at him from the rock face.

"You see!" Yattmur said. "What terrible thing broods over this place? The place is haunted, Gren! What life have we seen since we came here? Nothing moving in the trees, nothing scampering on the beach, nothing climbing on that rock face. Only the speedseed, that something swallowed. Only *we* are alive, and for how much longer will that be?"

Even as she moaned, something moved on the tower of rock. The bleak eyes—now there was no mistaking them for anything else—rolled; countless numbers of them rolled in unison, and turned in a new direction as if to stare at something out to sea.

Compelled by the intensity of that stone gaze, Gren and Yattmur also turned. From where they crouched, only a section of the sea was visible, framed among the nearby broken rock lying on the beach. It was view enough for them to observe, far out on the grey waters, a commotion marking where a large swimming thing laboured towards the island.

"O shades! That creature's heading towards us! Do we run back to the boat?" Yattmur asked.

"Let's lie still. It cannot have seen us between these rocks."

"The magic tower with eyes is calling it to come and devour us!"

"Nonsense," said Gren, speaking also to his secret fears.

Hypnotized, they watched the sea thing. Spray made it difficult to distinguish its shape. Only two great flippers that flailed the water like crazy paddlewheels could be seen clearly at intervals. Occasionally they thought they could see a head poised as though straining towards the shore; but visibility was still failing.

The broad sheet of sea puckered. A rain curtain blew in from the heavy skies, cutting off sight of the sea creature and sousing everything with cold stinging droplets.

Obeying a common impulse, Gren and Yattmur dived for the trees, to stand dripping against one of the trunks. The rain redoubled its strength. For a moment they could see no farther than the tattered frill of whiteness that marked the margin of the sea.

From out of the wetness came a forlorn chord, a warning note as if the world were falling away. The sea creature was signalling for guidance. Almost at once it received answer. The island or the rock tower itself gave voice in return.

One hollow jarring note was wrenched from its very foundations. Not that it was a loud note; but it filled all things, spilling down on to land and sea like the rain itself, as though every decibel was a drop that had to make itself individually felt. Shaken by the sound, Yattmur clung to Gren and cried.

Above her weeping, above the noise of the rain and sea, above the reverberations of the voice of the tower, another voice rose in a ragged intensity of fright and then died. It was a composite voice containing elements of supplication and reproach, and Gren recognized it.

"The missing tummy-belly men!" he exclaimed. "They must be near at hand."

He looked hopelessly about, dashing rain from his eyes as he did so. The great leathery leaves sagged and sprang up again under varying loads of water pouring off the cliff. Nothing but forest could be seen, forest bowing in submission to the downpour. Gren did not move; the tummy-bellies would have to wait till the rain abated. He stood where he was with an arm round Yattmur.

146

As they peered out towards the sea, the greyness before them was broken in a flurry of waves.

"Oh living shades, that creature has come to get us," Yattmur breathed.

The vast marine creature had entered shallow water and was heaving itself from the sea. They saw the rain sizzling in cataracts off a great flat head. A mouth as narrow and heavy as a grave creaked open—and Yattmur broke from Gren's arms and ran off along the beach in the direction from which they had come, shrieking with fright.

"Yattmur!" His muscles strained to follow her, but the full dead weight of the morel's will fought unexpectedly against him. Gren stayed locked, momentarily immobile in a sprinter's stance. Caught off balance, he fell sideways into the streaming sand.

"Stay where you are," twanged the morel. "Since the creature is obviously not after us, we must stay to see what it is doing. It will do us no harm if you keep quiet."

"But Yattmur——"

"Let the silly child go. We can find her later."

Through the violence of the rain came an irregular and protracted groaning. The vast creature was out of breath. Laboriously it dragged itself up the shelving beach some few yards from where Gren lay. The rain folded it in grey curtains, so that with its anguished breathing and pained movements it took on the aspect, lumbering there in surroundings as unlikely as itself, of a grotesque symbol of pain conjured up in a dream.

Its head became hidden from Gren by the trees. Only its body could be seen, moved forward by jerks from its unwieldy flippers, before that too was concealed. The tail slithered up the beach; then it also was swallowed by the jungle.

"Go and see where it has gone," ordered the morel.

"No," said Gren. He knelt, and his body ran brown where rain and sand mingled.

"Do as I tell you," twanged the morel. Always at the back of its mind lay its basic purpose, to propagate as widely as possible.

147

Although this human had at first seemed by reason of its intelligence to hold promise as a useful host, it had hardly come up to expectations; a brute of mindless power such as they had just seen was worth investigation. The morel propelled Gren forward.

Walking by the fringe of the trees, they came to the sea creature's tracks. It had churned up a trench as deep as a man's height in its progress up the beach.

Gren dropped on to hands and knees, his blood racing. The creature could be only a short distance away; a distinct rotten briny smell hung in the air. He peered round a bole of a tree, following the tracks with his eye.

Here the strip of jungle stopped unexpectedly, to resume some paces farther along the shore. In the gap, the sand led right to the base of the cliff—and in the cliff was a large cave. Through the driving rain the monster's tracks could be seen leading right into the cave. Yet although the limits of the cave were visible—it was large enough to contain the creature, but no more—it stood silent and empty, like a mouth caught in a perpetual yawn of rock.

Perplexed, forgetting his fright, Gren came out into the open to observe better, and at once saw some of the sixteen tummy-belly men.

They crouched together under the farther trees fringing the avenue of sand, pressing against the cliff very near the cave. Characteristically, they had sought shelter under an outcrop of rock that now sent a continuous spout of rainwater down upon them. With the long hairs of their bodies washed out flat, they looked very wet indeed, wet and frightened. When Gren appeared, they gave a wail of panic, clutching their genitals in apprehension.

"Come out here!" Gren called, still looking round to try to account for the disappearance of the sea monster.

With the rain spurting into their faces, the tummy-belly men were thoroughly demoralized; Gren recalled their idiot cry of fear when they had glimpsed the monster. Now they showed an inclination to run from him, milling round in tight circles like sheep and uttering meaningless sounds. Fury for their stupidity filled Gren's veins. He picked up a heavy stone.

"Come out here to me, you blubbering belly babies!" he called. "Quickly before the monster finds you!"

"O terror! O master! All things hate poor lovely tummy-belly men!" they cried, blundering into each other and turning their fat backs on him.

Infuriated, Gren flung his stone. It hit one of the men on the buttock, a good shot that had a bad effect. The stricken one jumped squealing into the avenue of sand, whirled about, and began to run away from Gren towards the cave. Taking up the cry, the others bounded and tumbled after him, all clasping their behinds in imitation.

"Come back!" Gren cried, running after them down the centre of the sea monster's tracks. "Stay out of that cave."

They paid him no heed. Yelping like curs, they burst into the cave, their noise echoing sharply back from its walls. Gren followed them.

The briny reek of the sea monster was heavy in the air.

"Get out of here as quickly as you can," the morel advised in Gren's mind, sending a twinge through his whole body.

All over the walls and roof of the cave were protruding rods of rock, pointing inwards and ending in eye sockets similar to those on the outside of the cliff. These eye sockets too were watchful; as the tummy-belly men bumped into them, they rolled back lids and began to stare, one by one, more and more.

Finding they were cornered, the men began to sprawl in the sand at Gren's feet and set up a hullaballoo for mercy.

"O mighty big killing lord with strong skin, O king of running and chasing, look how we ran to you when we saw you! How glad we are to honour our poor old tummy-eyes with a sight of you. We ran straight to you, though our poor running was confused and somehow our legs sent us the wrong way instead of happy right ways because the rain confused us."

149

More eyes were opening round the cave now, directing a stony stare at the group. Gren seized one of the tummy-bellies roughly by his hair and pulled him into a standing position; at this the others fell quiet, glad perhaps that they had been momentarily spared.

"Now you listen to me," Gren said, through clenched teeth. He had come to hate these people with a fierce aversion, for they drew out all the latent bullying instincts in him. "I wish none of you harm, as I've told you before. But you have all got to get out of here at once. Danger waits here. Back on to the beach, quick, the lot of you!"

"You will stone us——"

"Never mind what I'll do! Do what I say. Move!" And as he spoke he sent the fellow reeling towards the cave mouth.

Then what Gren thought of afterwards as the Mirage began.

A critical number of eyes in the cave walls had opened.

Time stopped. The world turned green. The tummy-belly man by the cave mouth, perched on one leg in a flying attitude, turned green, petrified in his absurd position. The rain behind him turned green. Everything: green and immobile.

And shrinking. To dwindle. To shrivel and contract. To become a drop of rain falling forever down the lungs of the heavens. Or to be a grain of sand marking an eternal tumble through hourglasses of endless time. To be a proton speeding inexhaustibly through its own pocket-sized version of limitless space. Finally to reach the infinite immensity of being nothing . . . the infinite richness of non-existence . . . and thus of becoming God . . . and thus of being the top and tail of one's own creation. . . .

. . . of summoning up a billion worlds to rattle along the green links of every second . . . of flying through uncreated stacks of green matter that waited in a vast ante-chamber of being for its hour or eon of use. . . .

For he *was* flying, wasn't he? And these happier notes alongside (weren't they?), were the beings that he or someone else,

150

someone on another plane of memory, had once called "tummy-bellies". And if it was flight, then it was happening in this impossible green universe of delight, in some element other than air and in some flux apart from time. And they were flying in light, emitting light.

And they were not alone.

Everything was with them. Life had replaced time, that was it; death had gone, for the clocks here would tick off fertilities only. But two of the everythings were familiar. . . .

In that vague other existence—oh it was so hard to recall, a dream within a dream—that existence connected with a beach of sand and grey rain (grey? that could be nothing like green, for green had no likenesses), in that existence there had been a great bird diving and a great beast emerging from the sea . . . and they had come through the . . . mirage and were here in this same sappy delight. The element about them was full of the assurance that here there was room for everything to grow and develop without conflict, to develop for ever if needed, tummy-belly, bird, or monster.

And he knew that the others had been directed to the mirage in a way he had not. Not that it mattered, for here was the sugar of being, of just being in this effortless eternal flight/dance/song, without time or scale or worry.

With only the fulfilment of growing green and good.

—Yet he was somehow falling behind the others! His first impetus was dying. There was worry, even here, and dimension had some meaning even here, or he would not be behind them. They would not be looking back, smiling, beckoning, the bird, the beast, the tummy-bellies. Spores, seeds, happy sappy things, would not be whirling, filling the growing distance between him and his companions. He would not be following, crying, losing it all. . . . Oh, losing all this suddenly dear and bright unimaginable natured place.

He would not be aware again of fear, of a last hopeless attempt to regain paradise, of the green going, of vertigo taking him, and eyes, a million eyes all saying "No" and spitting him back where he belonged . . .

He was back in the cave, sprawled on the trampled sand in a posture crudely aping flight. He was alone. About him, a million stone eyes closed in disdain, and a green music died from his brain. He was doubly alone as the tower of rock removed its presence from the cave.

The rain still rained. He knew that that measureless eternity during which he had been away had lasted only for a flicker of time. Time . . . whatever it was . . . perhaps it was just a subjective phenomenon, a mechanism in a human bloodstream from which vegetables did not suffer.

Gren sat up, startled by his thoughts.

"Morel!" he whispered.

"I'm here. . . ."

A long silence fell.

At last without prompting the brain fungus spoke.

"You have a mind, Gren," it twanged. "So the tower would not accept you—us. The tummy-bellies were almost as mindless as the sea creature or the bird; they were accepted. What is now mirage to us is now reality to them. They were accepted."

Another silence.

"Accepted where?" Gren asked. It had been so beautiful. . . .

The morel did not answer directly.

"This age is the long age of the vegetable," it said. "It has grown green upon the earth, it has rooted and proliferated without thought. It has taken many forms and exploited many environments, so that every possible ecological nook has long since been filled.

"The earth is more impossibly overcrowded than it ever was in any earlier age. Plants everywhere . . . all ingeniously, mindlessly, seeding and propagating, doubling the confusion, adding to the pressing problem of how one more blade of grass can find a niche in which to grow.

152

"When your distant predecessor, man, was ruler of this planet, he had a way with the overcrowded bed in his garden. He transplanted or weeded out. Now, somehow, nature has invented her own gardener. The rocks have shaped themselves into transmitters. Probably there are stations like this all round the coasts . . . stations where any near-mindless thing can be accepted for onward transmission . . . stations where plants can be transplanted. . . ."

"Transplanted *where*?" Gren asked. "Where was that place?"

Something like a sigh floated down the aisles of his mind.

"Can't you see I'm guessing, Gren? Since I have joined forces with you, I have become part human. Who knows the worlds available to different forms of life? The sun means one thing to you and another to a flower. To us the sea is terrible; to that great creature we saw. . . . There would be neither words nor thoughts to describe where we went; how could there be, when it was so patently the product of . . . non-ratiocinactive processes. . . ."

Gren got unsteadily to his feet.

"I want to be sick," he said.

He staggered out of the cave.

"To conceive of other dimensions, other modes of being——" continued the morel.

"For soul's sake, shut up!" Gren cried. "What does it matter to me that there are places—states—I can't . . . can't attain. I can't, and that's that. It was all a beastly mirage, so leave me alone, will you? I want to be sick."

The rain was abating a little. It pattered lightly on his backbone as he arched it to lean a head forward against a tree. His head throbbed, his eyes watered, his stomach heaved.

They would have to make sails from the big leaves and sail away from here, he and Yattmur and the four surviving tummy-belly men. They must get away. As it had become colder, they might have to make coverings for themselves out of those same leaves. This world was no paradise, but in some respects it was manageable.

He was still throwing up the contents of his stomach when he heard Yattmur calling.

He looked up, grinning feebly. She was coming back to him along the rainy beach.

<h1 style="text-align:center">18</h1>

They stood hand in hand, as confusedly he tried to tell her of his experiences in the cave.

"I'm glad you came back," she said gently.

He shook his guilty head, thinking how beautiful and strange the experience had been. Weariness filled him. He dreaded the thought of their having to put to sea again, yet obviously they could not remain on this island.

"Get moving, then," said the morel inside his head. "You're as slow as a tummy-belly."

Still holding Yattmur's hand, he turned and they trudged slowly back down the beach. A chilly wind blew up, carrying the rain out to sea. The four tummy-belly men stood huddling together where Gren had told them to wait. They fell on the sand in self-abasement as Gren and Yattmur came up.

"You can stop that," he told them without humour. "We've all got work to do, and you are going to do your share."

Slapping their fat flanks, he drove them before him towards the boat.

A breeze blew over the ocean as bright and sharp as glass.

To the occasional traverser that soared far overhead, the boat with its six passengers looked like nothing more than a drifting log. It floated now far beyond the island of the tall cliff.

The sail of large and crudely stitched leaves hung from an improvised mast; but adverse winds had long since torn it, robbing it of usefulness. In consequence the boat now moved without control and was carried eastwards on a strong thermal current.

The humans watched with either apathy or anxiety, according to their natures, as they were swept along. They had eaten several times and slept much since sailing away from the island of the tall cliff.

Much lay on either side for them to see when they cared to look. To port ran a long coastline, presenting from this distance an unbroken aspect of forest on its cliffs. Throughout uncounted watches it had remained the same; when hills appeared inland, as they did with increasing frequency, they too were clothed in forest.

Between coast and boat, small islands sometimes interposed themselves. On these grew a variety of foliage the mainland lacked, some being crowned by trees, some being covered in strange blossoms, some remaining mere barren humps of rock. Sometimes it appeared that the boat would be dashed against the shoals that fringed these islands: but so far it had always been carried clear at the last moment.

To starboard stretched the infinite ocean. This was now punctuated by evil-looking shapes of whose nature Gren and Yattmur had as yet no clue.

The helplessness of their position, as well as the mystery of it, bore down on the humans, though they were used to a subordinate place in the world. Now to add to their troubles a mist came up, closing round their boat and hiding all landmarks from them.

"It's the thickest mist I have ever seen," Yattmur said, as she stood with her mate staring over the side of the boat.

"And the coldest," Gren said. "Have you noticed what is happening to the sun?"

In the gathering mist, nothing now could be seen except the sea immediately about the boat and a great red sun which hung low over the water in the direction from which they had come, dangling a sword of light across the waves.

Yattmur pressed more tightly to Gren.

"The sun used to be high above us," she said. "Now the watery world threatens to swallow it."

"Morel, what happens when the sun goes?" Gren asked.

"When the sun goes, there is darkness," twanged the morel, adding with gentle irony, "as you might have deduced for yourself. We have entered the realm of eternal sunset and the stream carries us deeper and deeper into it."

It spoke reservedly, yet a tremor ran through Gren at the fear of the unknown. He held more tightly to Yattmur as they stared fixedly at the sun, dull and huge through the moisture-laden air. As they watched, one of the phantom shapes they had observed to starboard intervened between them and the sun, taking a great jagged bite out of it. Almost at the same time, the mist thickened and the sun was lost to view.

"Ohhh! Ahhh!" At the sun's disappearance, a cry of dismay rose from the tummy-bellies. They had been cuddled together on a pile of dead leaves in the stern. Now they came scampering forward, seizing Gren's and Yattmur's hands.

"O mighty master and sandwich-makers!" they cried. "All this mighty watery world sailing is too much badness, too much badness, for we have sailed away and lost all the world. The world has gone by bad sailing and we must quickly good-sail to get it back."

Their long hair glistened with moisture, their eyes were in a fine frenzy rolling. They bounced up and down, crying their woes.

"Some creature has eaten the sun, O great herder!"

"Stop your silly noise," Yattmur said. "We are as frightened as you are."

"No we are not," Gren exclaimed angrily, dashing their clammy hands from his flesh. "Nobody could be as frightened as they are, for they are always frightened. Stand back, you blubbering tummy-bellies! The sun will come again when the mist clears."

"You brave cruel herder," one of the creatures cried. "You have hidden the sun to scare us because you love us no more, though we happily enjoy your lovely blows and happy good bad words! You——"

Gren struck out at the man, glad to relieve his tensions in action. The poor fellow reeled backwards squealing. His companions fell on him instantly, cuffing him for not enjoying the mighty hurts with which his master honoured him. Savagely, Gren pulled them away.

As Yattmur came to his aid, a shock sent them all reeling. The deck canted sharply, and they sprawled together, six of them in a heap. Splinters of a jagged transparent stuff showered on to them.

Unhurt, Yattmur picked up one of the splinters and looked at it. As she watched it, the shard changed, dwindled, and left only a tiny puddle of water in her hand. She stared in surprise. A wall of the same glassy substance loomed over the front of the boat.

"Oh!" she said dully, realizing they had struck one of the phantom shapes they had noticed riding along on the sea. "A mountain of fog has caught us."

Gren jumped up, silencing the loud protestations of the tummy-belly men. A gash was visible in the bows of their boat, through which only a trickle of water ran. He climbed on to the side and peered about.

The warm current had carried them into a great glassy mountain that appeared to float on the sea. The mountain had been eroded at water level, forming a sloping shelf there; it was up this icy beach that they had been driven, and this that kept their broken bow partly above the water.

"We shan't sink," Gren said to Yattmur, "for there is a ledge under us. But the boat is useless now; off the ledge, it would sink."

It was indeed filling steadily with water, as the wails of the tummy-bellies testified.

"What can we do?" Yattmur asked. "Perhaps we should have stayed at the island of the tall cliff."

157

Doubtfully, Gren looked about. A great row of what resembled long sharp teeth hung over the deck as if about to bite the ship in two. Icy droplets of saliva fell from them, splashing the humans. They had sailed straight into this glass monster's mouth!

Near at hand, its entrails were dimly visible, filling their vision with an array of blue and green lines and planes, some of which—with a dull murderous beauty—glowed orange from a sun still hidden from the humans.

"This ice beast prepares to eat us!" yelped the tummy-bellies, scampering round the deck. "Oh, oh, our death moment come hot upons us, ice cold in these nasty freezing jaws."

"Ice!" exclaimed Yattmur. "Yes! How strange that these foolish belly-boy fishers should give us knowledge. Gren, this stuff is called ice. In the marsh grounds near Long Water where the tummies lived grew little flowers called colderpolders. At certain times these flowers, which flourish in the shade, made this cold ice to keep their seed in. When I was a girl-child I went into the marshes to get these ice drops and suck them."

"Now this big ice drop sucks us," Gren said, as cold water soused down on his face from the vault overhead. "What do we do, morel?"

"There is no safety here, so we must look for some," twanged the morel. "If the boat slips back off the ice shelf, all will drown but you: for the boat will sink and you alone can swim. You must get off the boat at once, and take the tummy-fishers with you."

"Right! Yattmur, sweet, climb out on to the ice while I drive these four fools after you."

The four fools were loath to leave the boat, though half of its deck was now shallowly under water. When Gren shouted at them, they leapt away, scattering as he approached, dashing away as he rushed to seize them, dodging and squealing as they went.

"Save us! Spare us, O herder! What have we four poor filthy lumps of compost done that you should wish to throw us to the ice beast? Help, help! Alas, that we should be so nasty you love to treat us in this way!"

Gren dived at the nearest and hairiest, who skipped away screaming, his bosoms flopping up and down as he went.

"Not me, great beastly spirit! Kill the other three that don't love you, but not me who loves you——"

Gren tripped him as he fled. The tummy-belly man sprawled, his sentence turning into a squeal before he pitched at full length head first into the water. Quickly Gren was on him; they splashed in the icy water until Gren got a firm hold and dragged the spluttering creature up by the flesh and hair of his neck, to pull him by sheer force to the side of the boat. With a heave, he sent him sprawling over, collapsing crying in the shallows at Yattmur's feet.

Thoroughly cowed by this display of force, the other three tummy-bellies climbed meekly out of their refuge and into the maw of the ice beast, teeth chattering with fear and cold. Gren followed them. For a moment the six stood together, looking into a grotto which to four of them at least was a gigantic throat. A ringing noise from behind made them turn back.

One of the ice fangs hanging overhead had cracked and fallen. It stuck upright in the wood of the deck like a dagger before slipping sideways and shattering into bits. Almost as if this were a signal, a much louder noise came from under the boat. The whole shelf on which the vessel rested gave way. Momentarily, the edge of a thin tongue of ice slid into view. Before it slumped back into the water, their boat was borne away on the dark flood. They watched it filling rapidly as it disappeared.

They were able to follow its progress for some while; the mist had lifted slightly and the sun once again painted a streak of cold fire down the back of the ocean.

For all that, it was with profound gloom that Gren and Yattmur turned away. With their boat gone, they were stranded on the iceberg. In silence the four tummy-bellies followed them as they took the only course possible and climbed along the cylindrical tunnel in the ice.

Splashing through chill puddles, they were hemmed in by

ribs of ice, against which every sound threw itself in a frenzy of echoes. With each step they took, the noise grew louder and the tunnel smaller.

"O spirits, I hate this place! Better if we had perished with the boat. How much farther can we go?" Yattmur asked, as Gren paused.

"No farther," he said grimly. "We've come to a dead end. We're trapped here."

Hanging nearly to the floor, several magnificent icicles barred their way almost as effectively as a portcullis. Beyond the portcullis, a flat pane of ice faced them.

"Always trouble, always difficulty, always some fresh trouble to living!" Gren said. "Man was an accident on this world or it would have been made better for him!"

"I have already told you that your kind was an accident," twanged the morel.

"We were happy till you started interfering," Gren said sharply.

"You were a vegetable till then!"

Infuriated by this thrust, Gren grasped one of the great icicles and pulled. It snapped off some way above his head. Holding it like a spear, he hurled it at the wall of ice before him.

Painful carillons sparked down the tunnel as the entire wall shattered under the blow. Ice fell, broke, skidded past their ankles, as a whole half-melted curtain celebrated its downfall in swift disintegration. The humans crouched, holding their hands over their heads while it seemed as if the entire iceberg was collapsing round them.

When the din died, they looked up, to find through the gap ahead a whole new world awaiting them. The iceberg, caught in an eddy to the coastward side of the current, had come to rest against an islet where, held in the arms of a small bay, it was now weeping down into water again.

Though the isle looked far from hospitable, the humans drank in with relief the sight of the sparse green on it, at flowers clinging to it, and at seed pods towering in the air at the top of tall stalks. Here they could enjoy the feeling of ground that did not heave perpetually.

Even the tummy-bellies momentarily took heart. With small happy cries they followed Yattmur and Gren round a ledge of ice, eager to be beneath those flowers. Without too much protest, they jumped over a narrow gulf of deep blue water, to land on protruding rock and thus scramble safely ashore.

The islet was certainly no paradise. Broken rock and stone covered the crown of it. But in its smallness lay advantage: it was too tiny to support the larger sort of vegetable menaces that flourished on the mainland; with the smaller menaces, Gren and Yattmur could cope. To the disappointment of the tummy-bellies, no tummy-belly tree grew here to which they could attach themselves. To the morel's disappointment, none of his kind grew here; much though he wished to take control of Yattmur and the tummy-bellies, as well as Gren, his bulk was as yet too small to allow him to do this, and he was counting on allies to help him. To the disappointment of Gren and Yattmur, no humans lived here with whom they could join forces.

As compensation, a spring of pure water surged out of the rock, larking among the big tumbled stones which covered much of the islet. First they heard its music, then they saw it. The little stream cascaded down on to a strip of beach and so into the sea. With one rush, they ran along the sand to it, drinking there without waiting to gain a less brackish draught higher up.

Like children, they forgot their cares. When they had drunk too much and belched sufficiently, they plunged into the water to bathe their limbs, although the chill of it did not tempt them to stay there for long. Then they began to make themselves at home.

For a time they lived on the islet and were content. In this realm of eternal sunset, the air was cool. They devised themselves better body covering from leaves or trailing moss, binding the latter tightly round their bodies. Mists and fogs swallowed them from time to time; then the sun would shine again, low over the sea. Sometimes they would sleep, sometimes would lie on the sunward-facing rocks idly eating fruit while listening to the icebergs groan as they sailed by.

The four tummy-belly men built themselves a crude shelter a distance apart from Gren and Yattmur. During one sleep it collapsed on top of them. After that they slept in the open, huddled together under leaves as close to their masters as Gren would allow.

Being happy again was good. When Yattmur and Gren made love together, the tummy-bellies would jump about and hug each other with excitement, praising the agility of their clever clutching master and his sandwich lady.

Huge seed pods grew and clattered overhead. Underfoot ran vegetable equivalents of lizards. In the air fluttered cordate butterflies with wide wings that lived by photosynthesis. Life continued without the punctuation of nightfall or sunrise. Sloth ruled; peace reigned.

The humans would have merged contentedly into this general pattern had it not been for the morel.

"We cannot stay here, Gren," it said on one occasion, when Gren and Yattmur woke from a comfortable sleep. "You have rested enough and been well refreshed. Now we must move again, to find more humans and establish our own kingdom."

"You speak nonsense, morel. Our boat is lost. We must always remain on this island. Chilly it may be, yet we have seen worse places. Let us stay here in content."

He and the girl were splashing naked through a series of pools which had formed among the big square blocks of stone on the crown of the islet. Life was sweet and idle, Yattmur kicked her pretty legs and sang one of her herder's songs: he was loath to listen to that dreary voice in his head. More and more it came to represent something he disliked.

Their silent conversation was interrupted by a squeal from Yattmur.

Something like a hand with six bloated fingers had seized her ankle. Gren dived for it and pulled it away without difficulty. It struggled in his grasp as he examined it.

"I'm silly to make a noise," Yattmur said. "It is just another of those creatures that the tummy-bellies have named crawl-paws. They swim out of the sea on to land. If the tummy-bellies catch them, they split them open and eat them. They are tough but sweet to taste."

The fingers were grey and bulbous, wrinkled in texture and extremely cold. They flexed slowly as Gren held them. Finally he dropped it on to the bank, where it scuttled off into the grass.

"Crawlpaws swim out of the sea and burrow into the ground. I've watched them," Yattmur said. Gren made no answer.

"Does anything trouble you?" she asked.

"No," he said flatly, not wishing to tell her that the morel desired them to move again. He sank stiffly to the ground, almost like an old man. Though she was uneasy, she stifled her apprehensions and returned to the bathing place. Yet from that time on she was aware of Gren drawing away from her and becoming more closed in on himself; and she knew the morel was to blame for it.

Gren woke from their next communal sleep to find the morel already restless in his mind.

"You wallow in sloth. We must *do* something."

"We are content here," replied Gren sulkily. "Besides, as I have said, we have no boats to get us to the big land."

"Boats are not the only way of crossing seas," said the fungus.

"Oh morel, cease being clever before you kill us with it. Leave us in peace! We're happy here."

"Happy, yes! You would grow roots and leaves if you could. Gren, you do not know what life is for! I tell you that great pleasures and powers await you if you only let me help you stretch out for them."

"Go away! I don't know what you mean."

He jumped up as if to run away from the morel. It gripped him tightly, rooting him to the spot. Gathering strength, he concentrated on sending waves of hatred at the morel—uselessly, for its voice continued in his head.

"Since it is impossible for you to be my partner, you must suffer being my slave. The spirit of enquiry is all but dead in you; you will respond to orders but not to observation."

"I don't know what you are saying!" He cried the words aloud, waking Yattmur, who sat up and gazed mutely at him.

"You neglect so much!" said the morel. "I can only see things through your senses, yet I take the trouble to analyse and find what is behind them. You can make nothing from your data, whereas I can make a lot. Mine is the way to power. Look about you again! Look at the stones over which you climb so regardlessly."

"Go away!" Gren cried again. Instantly he doubled up in anguish. Yattmur came running over to him, holding his head and soothing him. She peered into his eyes. The tummy-bellies came up silently to stand behind her.

"It's the magic fungus, isn't it?" she said.

Dumbly he nodded. Phantoms of fire chased themselves over his nerve centres, burning a tune of pain through his body. While the tune continued he could scarcely move. At length it passed. Limply he said, "We must help the morel. He wishes us to explore these rocks more carefully."

Trembling in every limb, he rose to do what was commanded of him. Yattmur stood with him, sympathetically touching his arm.

"When we've explored, we will catch fish in the pool and eat them with fruit," she said, with a woman's talent for producing comfort when it was needed.

He flashed her a humble look of gratitude.

The big stones had long been part of the natural landscape. Where the brook ran among them they were buried in mud and

164

pebbles. Grass and sedge grew on them, deep earth covered them in many places. In particular, here prospered a crop of the flowers that bore their seed pods aloft on tall stalks, which the humans had seen from the iceberg; these Yattmur had casually named the Stalkers, without realizing until much later how appropriate the title was.

Over the stones ran the roots of the Stalkers, like so many lengths of petrified snake.

"What a nuisance these roots are," grumbled Yattmur. "They grow everywhere!"

"The funny thing is the way the roots from one plant grow into another as well as into the ground," Gren said, answering abstractedly. He was squatting by a branch of two roots, one of which ran back to one plant, one to another. After they had joined, they curled over a block of stone and down into an irregular gap between other stones to the earth.

"You can get down there. You will come to no harm," said the morel. "Scramble down between the stones and see what you can see."

A hint of that painful tune sprang again over Gren's nerves.

He scrambled down between the blocks as he was directed, nimble as a lizard for all his reluctance. Feeling cautiously, he discovered that they rested on other blocks below, and those on other blocks below that. They lay loosely; by twisting his body he was able to slide himself down between their cool planes.

Yattmur climbed after him, showering down a gentle rain of dirt on to his shoulders.

After crawling down the depth of five blocks, Gren reached solid ground. Yattmur arrived beside him. Now they were able to move horizontally, half squashed between the walls of stone. Attracted by a lessening in the darkness, they squeezed along to a large space, large enough for them to stretch out their arms.

"The smell of cold and dark is in my nostrils and I am afraid," Yattmur said. "What has your morel made us come down here for? What has he to tell of this place?"

"He is excited," Gren replied, unwilling to admit that the morel was not communicating with him.

Gradually they began to see more clearly. The ground above had fallen away to one side, for the source of light was the sun, shining in horizontally between the piled stone, sending a thin ray probing there. It revealed twisted metal among the blocks, and an aperture ahead of them. In the collapse of these stones long ago, this gap had remained. Now the only living things here beside themselves were stalker roots, twisting down into the soil like petrified serpents.

Obeying the morel, Gren scrabbled in the grit at his feet. Here was more metal and more stone and brick, most of it immoveable. Fumbling and tugging, he managed to pull out some broken bits of guttering; then came a long metal strip as tall as himself. One end of it was shattered; on the rest of it was a series of separate marks arranged to form a pattern:

ƎƎHƆNIᴚWO

"That is writing," wheezed the morel, "a sign of man when he had power in the world, uncounted ages ago. We are on his tracks. These must once have been his buildings. Gren, climb forward into the dark aperture and see what else you can find."

"It is dark! I cannot go in there."

"Climb forward, I tell you."

Shards of glass glinted dully by the aperture. Rotted wood fell away all round it as Gren put a hand forward to steady himself. Plaster showered down on his head as he climbed through. On the other side of the aperture was a drop; Gren slid down a slope of rubble into a room, cutting himself on glass as he went.

From outside, Yattmur gave a squeak of alarm. He called back softly to reassure her, pressing a hand to his heart to steady it. Anxiously he stared about in the all-but-blackness. Nothing moved. The silence of the centuries, thick and cloying, lay here, lived here, more sinister than sound, more terrible than fear.

For a spell he stood frozen, until the morel nudged him.

Half the roof had collapsed. Metal beams and brick made a maze of the room. To Gren's untutored eye, everything was indistinguishable. The ancient smell of the place choked him.

"In the corner. A square thing. Go there," ordered the morel, using his eyesight to advantage.

Reluctantly, Gren picked his way across to the corner. Something scuttled from under his feet and out the way he had come; he saw six thick fingers, and recognized a crawlpaw like the one that had seized Yattmur's ankle. A square box three times his height loomed over him, its front surface marked by three protruding semi-circles of metal. He could reach only the lowest of these semi-circles, which, the morel instructed him, were handles. He tugged at it obediently.

It opened the width of a hand, then stuck.

"Pull, pull, pull!" twanged the morel.

Growing savage, Gren pulled till the whole box rattled, but what the morel termed the drawer would come no farther. Still he pulled, while the tall box shook. Something was dislodged from the top of it. From high above Gren's head, an oblong thing came crashing down. As he ducked, it fell to the floor behind him, sending up a cloud of dust.

"Gren! Are you all right? What are you having to do down there? Come out!"

"Yes, yes, I'm coming! Morel, we'll never open this stupid box thing."

"What's this object that nearly hit us? Examine it and let me see. Perhaps it is a weapon. If we could only find something to help us. . . ."

The thing that had fallen was thin, long, and tapered, like a flattened burnurn seed. It seemed to be composed of a material with a soft surface, not cold like metal. The morel pronounced it to be a container. When it found that Gren could lift it with comparative ease, it became excited.

"We must carry this container to the surface," it said. "You can pull it up between the stones. We will examine it in daylight and find what it contains."

"But how can the thing help us? Will it get us to the mainland?"

"I didn't expect to find a boat down here. Have you no curiosity? This is a sign of power. Come on, move! You are as stupid as a tummy-belly."

Smarting under this gross insult, Gren scrambled back up the debris to Yattmur. She clutched him, but would not touch the yellow case he carried. For a moment they whispered together, pressing each others' genitals to gain strength; then they struggled up between the layers of tumbled stone back to daylight, dragging and pushing the container with them.

"Phooo! Daylight tastes sweet!" Gren muttered as he levered himself up the last block. As they emerged bruised and cut into the misty air, up came the tummy-bellies scampering, their tongues lolling out in relief. Dancing round their masters, they raised a hullabaloo of complaint and reproach at their absence.

"Kill us please, pretty cruel master, before you jump again into the lips of the earth! Stab us with wicked killing before you leave us alone to fight unknown fights alone!"

"Your bellies are too fat for you to have squeezed down that crevice with us," Gren said, ruefully examining his wounds. "If you're so pleased to see us, why not get us some food?"

When Yattmur and he had bathed their cuts and bruises in the stream, he turned his attention to the container. Squatting over it carefully, he turned it over several times. There was a strangeness about its symmetry that alarmed him. Evidently the tummy-bellies felt the same.

"That very bad strange shape for touching is a strange bad touching shape," one of them wailed, dancing up and down. "Please only do a touching for throwing it into the splashing watery world." He clung to his companions, and they peered down in silly excitement.

"They offer you sensible advice," Yattmur said, but with the

168

morel urging him, Gren sat down and took the container between feet and fingers. While he examined it, he felt the fungus snatch at his impressions as soon as they arrived in his brain; shivers ran along his spine.

On the top of the container was one of the patterns that the morel called writing. This one resembled

HECKLER or ᴚƎ⅃ꓘƆƎH

depending on which way you looked at it, and was followed by several lines of similar but smaller patterns.

He began to tug and push at the container. It did not open. The tummy-bellies quickly lost interest and wandered away. Gren himself would have flung the thing aside, had the morel not kept him at it, poking and pressing. As he ran his fingers along one of the longer sides, a lid flipped open. He and Yattmur looked askance at one another, then peered down at the object in the container, squatting in the dirt and gaping with awe.

The object was of the same silky yellow material as its container. Reverently, Gren lifted it out and placed it on the ground. Releasing it from the box activated a spring; the object, which had been wedge-shaped to conform to the dimensions of its resting place, suddenly sprouted yellow wings. It stood between them, warm, unique, perplexing. The tummy-bellies crept back to stare.

"It's like a bird," Gren breathed. "Can it really have been made by men like us and not grown?"

"It's so smooth, so. . . ." Words failing, Yattmur put out a hand to stroke it. "We will call it Beauty."

Age and the endless seasons had puckered its container; the winged thing remained as new. As the girl's hand ran over its upper surface, a lid clicked back, revealing its insides. Four tummy-belly men dived for the nearest bush. Fashioned of strange materials, of metals and plastics, the insides of the yellow bird were marvellous to behold. Here were small spools, a line of knobs, a glimpse of amplifying circuits, a maze of

169

cunning intestines. Full of curiosity, the two humans leant forward to touch. Full of wonder, they let their fingers—those four fingers with opposed thumb that had taken their ancestors so far—enjoy the delight of toggle switches.

The tuning knobs could be twiddled, the switches clicked!

With scarcely a murmur, Beauty rose from the ground, hovered before their eyes, rose above their heads. They cried with astonishment, they fell backwards, breaking the yellow container. It made no difference to Beauty. Superb in powered flight, it wheeled above them, glowing richly in the sun.

When it had gained sufficient altitude, it spoke.

"Make the world safe for democracy!" it cried. Its voice was not loud but piercing.

"Oh, it speaks!" cried Yattmur, gazing in delight at the flashing wings.

Up came the tummy-bellies, running to join in the excitement, falling back in apprehension when Beauty flew over them, standing baffled as it circled round their heads.

"Who rigged the disastrous dock strike of '31?" Beauty demanded rhetorically. "The same men who would put a ring through your noses today. Think for yourselves, friends, and vote for SRH—vote for freedom!"

"It—what is it saying, morel?" Gren asked.

"It is talking of men with rings through their noses," said the morel, who was as baffled as Gren. "That is what men wore when they were civilized. You must try to learn from what it is saying."

Beauty circled round one of the tall stalkers and remained overhead, buzzing slightly and emitting an occasional slogan. The humans, feeling they had gained an ally, were greatly cheered; for a long while they stood with their heads back, watching and listening. The tummy-bellies beat their stomachs in delight at its antics.

"Let us go back and try to unearth another toy," Yattmur suggested.

After a moment's silence, Gren replied, "The morel says not. He wants us to go down when we do not want to; when we want to go, he does not. I do not understand."

"Then you are foolish," grumbled the morel. "This circling Beauty will not get us ashore. I want to think. We must help ourselves; especially I wish to observe these stalker plants. Keep quiet and don't bother me."

It did not communicate with Gren for a long while. He and Yattmur were free to bathe again in the pool, and wash the underground dirt from their bodies and hair, while the tummy-bellies lolled near at hand, scarcely complaining, hypnotized by the yellow bird that circled tirelessly above them. Afterwards, they hunted over the ridge of the islet, away from the tumbled stones; Beauty wheeled above them following, occasionally crying "The SRH and a two-day working week!"

20

Bearing in mind what the morel had said, Gren took more notice than before of the stalker plants. Despite their strong and interlinked root structure, the actual flowers were of a lowly order, though, canted towards the sun, they attracted the cordate butterflies. Beneath five bright and simple petals grew a dis-proportionately large seed pod, a sexfid drum, from each face of which protruded gummy and fringed bosses resembling sea anemones.

All this Gren observed without interest. What happened to the flowers on fertilization was more sensational. Yattmur was passing one of them when a treebee bumbled past her and landed on the blossom, crawling over its pistil. The plant responded to pollination with violence. With an odd shrilling noise, flower and seed drum rocked up skywards on a spring that unravelled itself from the drum.

Yattmur dived into the nearest bush in startlement, Gren close behind. Cautiously they watched; they watched the spring unwind more slowly now. Warmed by the sun, it straightened and dried into a tall stalk. The six-sided drum nodded in sunlight, far above their heads.

For the humans, the vegetable kingdom offered no wonders. Anything that held no menace held little interest. They had already seen these stalkers, waving high in the air.

"Statistics prove that you are better off than your bosses," Beauty said, flying round the new pole and returning. "Be warned by what happened to the Bombay Interplanetary Freight Handlers' Union! Stand up for your rights while you still have them."

Only a few bushes away, another stalker rattled up into the air, its stalk straightening and gaining rigidity.

"Let's get back," Gren said. "Let's go and have a swim."

As he spoke, the morel clamped down on him. He staggered and fought, then fell over into a bush, sprawling in pain.

"Gren! Gren! What is it?" Yattmur gasped, running to him, grasping his shoulders.

"I-I-I——" He could not get the words out of his mouth. A blue tinge spread from his lips outward. His limbs went rigid. Within his head, the morel was punishing him, paralysing his nervous system.

"I've been too gentle with you, Gren. You're a vegetable! I gave you a warning. In future I will do more commanding and you will do more obeying. Though I do not expect you to think, you can at least observe and let me do the thinking. Here we are on the fringe of finding something valuable about these plants, and you turn stupidly away. Do you want to rot forever on this rock? Now lie still and watch, or I'll visit you with cramps, like *this*!"

Painfully, Gren rolled over, burrowing his face in grass and dirt. She lifted him up, crying his name in sorrow at his hurt.

"It's this magic fungus!" she said, looking with distaste at the hard glistening crust that ringed his neck. Her eyes filled with tears. "Gren, my love, come along. Another mist is blowing up. We must get back to the others."

172

He shook his head. Again his body was his own—for the present at least—and the cramps died from it, leaving his limbs as weak as jelly.

"The morel wants me to remain here," he said faintly. Tears of weakness stood in his eyes. "You go back to the others."

Distressed, she stood up. She twisted her hands in anger at their helplessness.

"I'll be back soon," she said. The tummy-bellies had to be looked after. They were almost too stupid even to eat by themselves unless directed. As she picked her way back down the slope, she whispered aloud, "O spirits of the sun, banish that magic fungus of cruelty and guile before he kills my dear lover."

Unfortunately the spirits of the sun looked particularly weak. A chill wind blew from the waters, carrying with it a fog that obscured the light. Close by the island sailed an iceberg; its creaking and cracking could be heard even when it had disappeared phantom-like into the fog.

Half hidden by bushes, Gren lay where he was, watching. Beauty hovered overhead, faint in the gathering mist, calling out its slogan at intervals.

A third stalker had rocked upwards, squealing as it went. He watched it straighten out, more slowly than its partners now the sun was hidden. The mainland was lost to view. A butterfly fluttered past and was gone; he remained alone on an uncharted mound, rolled up in a universe of watery obscurity.

Distantly, the iceberg groaned, its voice echoing drably across the ocean. He was alone, isolated from his kind by the morel fungus. Once it had filled him with hopes and dreams of conquest; now it gave him only a feeling of sickness; but he knew no way of ridding himself of it.

"There goes another," the morel said, deliberately breaking into his thought. A fourth stalker had sprung up from the rock nearby. Its case loomed above them, hanging like a decapitated head on the dirty wall of fog. A breeze caught it, bumping it against its neighbour. The anemone-like protuberances stuck against each other, so that the two cases remained locked, swaying quietly on their long legs.

"Ha!" said the morel. "Keep watch, man, and don't worry. These blooms are not separate plants. Six of them with their communal root structure go to make up one plant. They have grown from the six-pronged tubers we have seen, the crawlpaws. You watch and you'll see the other two flowers of this particular group will be pollinated in a short while."

Something of his excitement passed to Gren, warming him as he lay hunched among cold stones; staring and waiting because he could do nothing else, he let an age go by. Yattmur returned to him, threw over him a mat the tummy-bellies had plaited, and lay beside him almost without speaking.

At last a fifth stalker flower was pollinated and rattled startlingly upward. As its stalk straightened, it swayed against one or its neighbours; they joined, nodded on to the other pair as they did so, and then locked, so that a single case and a bundle of four now stood high above the humans' heads.

"What's it mean?" Yattmur asked.

"Wait," Gren whispered. Scarcely had he spoken when the sixth and last fertilized drum headed up towards its brothers. Quivering, it hung in the mist awaiting a breeze; the breeze came; with hardly a sound, all six drums locked into one solid body. In the shrouded air, it resembled a hovering creature.

"Can we go now?" Yattmur asked.

Gren was shivering.

"Tell the girl to fetch you some food," twanged the morel. "You are not leaving here yet."

"Are you going to have to stay here forever?" she asked impatiently, when Gren passed on the message.

He shook his head. He didn't know. Impatiently she vanished into the mist. A long while passed before she returned, and by then the stalker had taken the next step in its development.

The fog parted slightly. Horizontal rays of sun struck the stalker's body, staining it bronze. As if encouraged by the slight

174

additional warmth, the stalker moved one of its six stalks. The bottom of it snapped free from the root system and became a leg. The movement was repeated in each of the other legs. One by one they came free. As the last one was liberated, the stalker turned and began—oh, it was unmistakeable, the seed cases on stilts began to walk downhill, slowly but sturdily.

"Follow it," the morel twanged.

Climbing to his feet, Gren began to move in the wake of the thing, walking as stiffly as it did. Yattmur followed quietly by his side. Overhead, the yellow machine also followed.

The stalker happened to take their usual route to the beach. When the tummy-bellies saw it coming, they ran squealing into the bush for safety. Unperturbed, the stalker kept straight on, jabbed its way delicately through their camp, and headed for the sand.

Nor did it pause there. It stalked into the sea until little but its lumpy six-part body was above the water. It was slowly swallowed by mist as it waded in the direction of the coast. Beauty flew after it, uttering slogans, only to return in silence.

"You see!" exclaimed the morel, sounding so noisily inside Gren's skull that he clutched his head. "There lies our escape route, Gren! These stalkers grow here, where there is room for their full development, then go back on to the mainland to seed themselves. And if these migratory vegetables can get ashore, they can take us with them!"

The stalker seemed to sag a little at its metaphorical knees. Slowly, as if rheumatism had it tight by those long joints, it moved its six legs, one by one, and with long vegetable pauses between each move.

Gren had had trouble getting the tummy-belly men into position. To them, the islet was something to be clung to even in the face of blows, rather than exchange it for some imagined future bliss.

175

"We can't stay here: the food will probably give out," Gren told them, as they cowered before him.

"O herder man, gladly we obey you with yesses. If food is all gone here, *then* we go away with you on a stalk-walker over the watery world. Now we eat lovely food with many teeth and do not go away till it is all gone."

"It will be too late then. We must go now, while the stalkers are leaving."

Fresh protests at this, with much slapping of buttocks in anguish.

"Never before have we seen the stalker-walkers to take a walk with them when they go stalking-walking? Where were they then when we never saw them? Terrible herder man and sandwich lady, now you two people without tails find this care to go with them. We don't find the care. We don't mind ever not to see the stalker-walkers stalky-walking."

Gren did not confine himself to verbal argument for long; when he resorted to a stick, the tummy-bellies were quickly persuaded to acknowledge the truth of his reasoning and move accordingly. Snuffling and snorting, they were driven towards a group of six stalker flowers, the buds of which had just opened. They grew together on the edge of a low cliff overlooking the sea.

Under the morel's direction, Yattmur and Gren had spent some while collecting food, wrapping it in leaves and attaching it with brambles to the stalker seed drums. Everything was ready for their journey.

The four tummy-bellies were forced to climb on to four drums. Telling them to hold on tightly, Gren went among them one by one, pressing his hand into the floury centre of each blossom. One by one, the seed cases shrilled into the air, noisily accompanied by a passenger hanging on for his life.

Only with the fourth case did anything go wrong. That particular flower was tilted towards the edge of the cliff. As the spring uncurled, the extra weight on the pod bore it sideways

176

rather than upwards. It sagged over, an ostrich with a broken neck, and the tummy-belly yelled and kicked as his heels swung in mid-air.

"O mummy! O tummy! Help your fat lovely son!" he cried, but no help came. He lost his grip. Amid a shower of provisions he fell, still protesting, an ignoble Icarus into the sea. The current carried him away. They saw his head go down below the swift water.

Freed of its burden, the stalker drum swayed upright, buffeted the three already erect, and joined with them into a solid unit.

"Our turn!" Gren said, turning to Yattmur.

Yattmur was still gazing out to sea. He grasped her arm and pushed her over to the two unsprouted flowers. Without showing anger, she freed herself from his grip.

"Do I have to beat you like a tummy-belly?" he asked her.

She did not laugh. He still held his stick.

When she did not laugh, his hold on the stick tightened. Obediently, she climbed on to the big green stalker drum.

They clutched the ribs of the plant, churning a hand about the pistil of the flower. Next minute, they too were spiralling up into the air. Beauty flew about them, begging them not to let vested interests prosper. Yattmur was most horribly afraid. She fell face forward among polleny stamens, almost unable to breathe for the scent of the flower, but incapable of moving. Dizziness filled her.

A timid hand touched her shoulder.

"If you have a making hungry by the fear, do not eat of the nasty stalker flower but taste good fish without walking legs we clever menchaps catch in a pool!"

She looked up at the tummy-belly, his mouth moving nervously, his eyes large and soft, a dust of pollen making his hair ludicrously fair. He had no dignity. With one hand he scratched his crutch, with the other offered her fish.

Yattmur burst into tears.

177

Dismayed, the tummy-belly crawled forward, putting a hairy arm over her shoulder.

"Do not make too many wet tears to fish when fish will not hurt you," he said.

"It's not that," she said. "It's just that we have brought so much trouble to you poor fellows——"

"O we poor tummy men all lost!" he began, and his two companions joined in a dirge of sorrow. "It is true you cruelly bring us so much trouble."

Gren had been watching as the six cases joined into one lumpy unit. He looked anxiously down to catch the first signs of the stalker detaching its legs from its root system. The chorus of lament made him switch his attention.

His stick landed loudly across plump shoulders. The tummy-belly who had been comforting Yattmur drew back crying. His companions also shrank away.

"Leave her alone!" Gren cried savagely, rising to his knees. "You filthy hairy tummy-tails, if you touch her again I'll throw you down to the rocks!"

Yattmur peered at him with her lips drawn back so that her teeth showed. She said nothing.

Nobody spoke again until at last the stalker began to stir with a purposeful movement.

Gren felt the morel's combination of excitement and triumph as the tall-legged creature took its first step. One by one its six legs moved. It paused, gaining its balance. It moved again. It halted. Then again it moved, this time with less hesitation. Slowly it began to stalk away from the cliff, across the islet, down to the gently shelving beach where its kin had gone, where the ocean current was less strong. Beauty followed, flying overhead.

Without hesitation, it waded into the sea. Soon its legs were almost entirely immersed, and the sea slid by on all sides.

"Wonderful!" Gren exclaimed. "Free of that hateful island at last."

"It did us no harm. We had no enemies there," Yattmur replied. "You said you wanted to stay there."

"We couldn't stay there for ever." Contemptuously, he offered her only what he had said to the tummy-bellies.

"Your magic morel is too glib. He thinks only of how he can make use of things—of the tummies, of you and me, of the stalkers. But the stalkers did not grow for him. They were not on the island for him. They were on the island before we came. They grow for themselves, Gren. Now they do not go ashore for us but for themselves. We ride on one, thinking ourselves clever. How clever are we? These poor fisher-bellies call themselves clever, but we see they are foolish. What if we are also foolish?"

He had not heard her speak like this. He stared at her, not knowing how to answer her until irritation helped him.

"You hate me, Yattmur, or you would not speak like that. Have I hurt you? Don't I protect you and love you? We know the tummy-bellies are stupid, and we are different from them, so we cannot be stupid. You say these things to hurt me."

Yattmur ignored all these irrelevancies. She said sombrely, as if he had not spoken. "We ride on this stalker but we do not know where it is going. We muddle its wishes with our own."

"It is going to the mainland of course," Gren said angrily.

"Is it? Why don't you look about you?"

She gestured with a hand and he did look.

The mainland was visible. They had started towards it. Then the stalker had entered a current of water and was now moving directly up it, travelling parallel with the coast. For a long while, Gren stared angrily, until it was impossible to doubt what was happening.

"You are pleased!" he hissed.

Yattmur made no reply. She leant over and dabbled her hand in the water, quickly withdrawing it. A warm current had carried them to the island. This was a cold current the stalker waded in, and they moved towards its source. Something of that chill found its way up to her heart.

PART 3

21

The icy water flowed by, bearing icebergs. The stalker kept steadily on its course. Once it became partially submerged and its five passengers were soaked; even then its pace did not alter.

It was not alone. Other stalkers joined it from other islands off the coast, all heading in the same direction. This was their migratory time when they made for unknown seed beds. Some of them were bowled over and broken by icebergs; the others continued.

From time to time the humans were joined on their raft-like perch by crawlpaws similar to the ones they had encountered on the island. Grey with cold, the tuberous hands hauled themselves up out of the water, fumbling about for a warm place, scuttling furtively from one nook to another. One climbed on to Gren's shoulder. He flung it disgustedly far out to sea.

The tummy-bellies complained little about these visitors climbing coldly over them. Gren had rationed their food as soon as he realized they would not be getting ashore so quickly as expected, and they had withdrawn into apathy. Nor did the cold improve matters for them. The sun seemed about to sink into the sea, while a chill wind blew almost continuously. Once hail deluged down on them out of a black sky, almost skinning them as they lay defenceless.

To the least imaginative among them it must have seemed that they were taking a journey into nowhere. The frequent fog banks that rolled up round them increased that impression; and when the fogs lifted they saw on the horizon ahead a line of darkness that threatened and threatened and never blew away. But the time came when at last the stalker swerved from its course.

Huddled together in the centre of the seed cases, Gren and Yattmur were roused from sleep by the chatter of the three tummy-bellies.

"The watery wetness of the watery world leaves us cold tummy-belly men by going dripping down long legs! We sing great happy cries, for we must be dry or die. Nothing is so lovely as to be a warm dry tummy-chummy chap, and the warm dry world is coming to us."

Irritably, Gren opened his eyes to see what the excitement was about.

Truly enough, the stalker's legs were visible again. It had turned aside from the cold current and was wading ashore, never altering its inflexible pace. The coast, covered thickly with the great forest, was near now.

"Yattmur! We're saved! We're going ashore at last!" It was the first time he had spoken to her in a long while.

She stood up. The tummy-bellies stood. The five of them, for once united, clasped each other in relief. Beauty flew overhead crying, "Remember what happened to the Dumb Resistance League in '45! Speak out for your rights. Don't listen to what the other side are saying—it's all lies, propaganda. Don't get caught between Delhi bureaucracy and Communist intrigues. Ban Monkey Labour now!"

"Soon we will be dry good chaps!" cried the tummy-bellies.

"We'll start a fire going when we get there," said Gren.

Yattmur rejoiced to see him in better spirits, yet a sudden wave of misgiving urged her to ask, "How do we get down off here?"

Anger burnt in his eyes as he stared at her, anger at having his elation punctured. When he did not immediately reply, she guessed he was consulting the morel for an answer.

"The stalker is going to find a place to seed itself," he said. "When it finds a place, it will sink to the ground. Then we shall get off. You do not need to worry; I am in command."

She could not understand the hardness of his tone. "But you

aren't in command, Gren. This thing goes where it will and we are helpless. That is why I worry."

"You worry because you are stupid," he said.

Although she was hurt, she determined to find all the possible comfort she could in the circumstances.

"We can all worry less when we get ashore. Then perhaps you will be less unkind to me."

The shore, however, did not extend them a particularly warm invitation. As they looked towards it hopefully, a pair of large black birds rose from the forest. Spreading their wings, they sailed upwards, hovered, and then began to beat their way heavily through the air towards the stalker.

"Lie flat!" Gren called, drawing his knife.

"Boycott chimp goods!" Beauty cried. "Don't allow Monkey Labour in your factory. Support Imbroglio's Anti-Tripartite scheme!"

The stalker was trampling through shallow water now.

Black wings flashed low overhead, thundering with a whiff of decay across the stalker. Next moment, Beauty had been snatched from its placid circling and was being carried coastwards in mighty talons. As it was borne off, its cry came back pathetically, "Fight today to save tomorrow. Make the world safe for democracy!" Then the birds had it down among the branches.

With water draining from its slender shanks, the stalker was now wading ashore. Four or five of its kind could be seen doing or about to do the same thing. Their animation, their human-like appearance of purpose, set them apart from the dreariness of their surroundings. The brooding sense of life that impregnated the world Gren and Yattmur had previously known was lacking entirely in these regions. Of that hothouse world, only a shade remained. With the sun lolling on the horizon like a bloody and raped eye upon a slab, twilight prevailed everywhere. In the sky ahead, darkness gathered.

From the sea, life seemed to have died. No monstrous seaweeds fringed the shore, no fish stirred in the rock pools. This desolation was emphasized by the shuddering calm of the ocean, for the stalkers—prompted by instinct—had chosen for their migration a season without storms.

On the land, a similar quietude reigned. The forest still grew, yet it was a forest stunned by shadow and cold, a forest half alive, smothered in the blues and greys of perpetual evening. As they moved above its stunted trunks, the humans looked down to see mildew speckling its foliage. Only at one point did a touch of yellow show brightly. A voice called to them, "Vote SRH today, the democratic way!" The heckler machine lay like a broken toy where the birds had left it, with one wing visible amid the tree tops; it called still as they trudged inland, out of earshot.

"When do we stop?" Yattmur whispered.

Gren did not answer; nor did she expect an answer. His face was cold and fixed; he did not even glance towards her. She dug her nails into her palm to keep her anger back, knowing the fault was not his.

Picking their way with care, the stalkers moved above the forest, leaves brushing against their legs or occasionally sweeping their bodies. Always the stalkers marched with the sun behind them, leaving it half-hidden beneath a wilderness of sour foliage. Always they marched towards the darkness that marked the end of the world of light. Once a flock of the black vegbirds rose from the treetops and clattered away towards the sun; but the stalkers never faltered.

Despite their fascination, their growing apprehension, the humans eventually had to resign themselves to eating more of their rations. Eventually, too, they had to settle to sleep, huddling up closely at the centre of their perch. And still Gren would not speak.

They slept, and when they woke, coming reluctantly back to the consciousness that was now associated with cold, the view about them had changed—though hardly for the better.

Their stalker was crossing a shallow valley. Darkness stretched beneath them, though one ray of sun lit the vegetable body on which they rode. Forest still covered the ground, a distorted forest that now resembled the newly blind who stagger forward with arms and fingers extended, fright apparent in every feature. Here and there a leaf hung, otherwise the limbs were naked, contorting themselves into grotesque forms as the great solitary tree that had over the ages turned itself into a whole jungle fought to grow where it had never been intended to grow.

The three tummy-bellies shuddered with alarm. They were looking not down but ahead.

"O tummies and tails! Here comes the swallowing-up place of all night for ever. Why did we not sadly happily die long long ago, when we were all together and sweating together was juicily nice so long ago?"

"Be quiet, the pack of you!" Gren shouted, grasping his stick. His voice rang hollow and confused to his ears as it was thrown back by the valley.

"O big little tailless herder, you should have been kind and killed us with killing cruelly long when we could sweat, in the time when we still grew on happy long tails. Now here comes the black old end of the world to chop its jaws over us without tails. Alas the happy sunshine, O poor us!"

He could not stop their cries. Ahead lay the darkness, piled up like layers of slate.

Emphasizing that mottled blackness stood one small hill. It stuck up uncompromisingly before them, bearing the weight of the night on its shattered shoulders. Where the sun struck its upper levels it had a golden touch, the world's last colour of defiance. Beyond it lay obscurity. Already they were climbing its lower slopes. The stalker toiled upwards into light; stretched out across the valley, five more stalkers could be seen, one near, four more half lost in murk.

The stalker was labouring. Yet it climbed up into the sunshine and continued on without pause.

The forest too had come through the valley of shadow. For this it had fought its way through that gloom: to be able to fling its last wave of greenery up the last strip of lit ground. Here, on slopes looking back towards the ever-setting sun, it threw off its blights to grow in something like its old exuberance.

"Perhaps the stalker will stop here," Yattmur said. "Do you think it will, Gren?"

"I don't know. Why should I know?"

"It *must* stop here. How can it go any farther?"

"I don't know, I tell you. I don't know."

"And your morel?"

"He does not know either. Leave me alone. Wait to see what happens."

Even the tummy-bellies fell silent, staring about them at the weird scene in mingled fear and hope.

Without giving any indication that it ever meant to stop, the stalker climbed on, creaking up the hill. Its long legs continued to pick a safe course through the foliage, until it dawned on them that wherever it intended to go it was not stopping here on this last bastion of light and warmth. Now they were at the brow of the hill, yet still it marched, an automatic vegetable thing they suddenly hated.

"I'm going to jump off!" Gren cried, standing up. Yattmur, catching the wildness in his eyes, wondered whether it was he or the morel that spoke. She wrapped her arms round his thighs, crying that he would kill himself. With his stick half lifted to strike her, he paused—the stalker, unpausing, had commenced to climb down the unlit side of the hill.

Just for a moment the sun still shone on them. They had a last glimpse of a world with gold in the dull air, a floor of black foliage, and another stalker looming up on their left flank. Then the shoulder of the hill shrugged upwards, and down they jolted into the world of night. With one voice they gave forth a cry: a cry that echoed into the unseen wastes about them, dying as it fled.

For Yattmur only one interpretation of events was possible. They had stepped out of the world into death.

Dumbly she buried her face into the soft hairy flank of the nearest tummy-belly, until the steadily continued jolting of the stalker persuaded her that she had not entirely lost company with the things that were.

Gren said, grasping at what the morel told him, "This world is fixed with one half always turned towards the sun . . . we are moving into the night side, across the terminator . . . into perpetual dark. . . ."

His teeth were chattering. She clasped him, opening her eyes for the first time to search for sight of his face.

In the darkness it floated, a ghost of a face from which she nevertheless drew comfort. Gren put his arms round the girl, so that they crouched there together with cheeks touching. The posture gave her warmth and courage enough to peer furtively around.

She had visualized in her terror a place of reeling emptiness, imagining that perhaps they had fallen into some cosmic sea shell washed up on the mythical beaches of the sky. Reality was less impressive and more nasty. Directly overhead, a memory of sunlight lingered, illumining the vale into which they plodded. This light was split by a shadow that grew and grew across the sky and was projected by the black ogre's shoulder down which they were still climbing.

Their descent was marked by thudding sounds. Peering down, Yattmur saw that they travelled through a bed of writhing worms. The worms were lashing themselves against the stilt legs of the stalker, which now moved with great care to avoid being thrown off balance. Glistening yellow in the stramineous light, the worms boiled and reared and thudded in fury. Some of them were tall enough to reach almost to where the humans crouched, so that as their heads flickered up on a level with Yattmur's, she saw they had bowl-like receptors at their tips. Whether these receptors were mouths, or eyes, or organs to catch what heat there was, she could not say. But her moan of horror roused Gren from his trance; almost cheerfully he set about tackling terrors which he could comprehend, lopping off the squidgy yellow tips as they flicked out of the murk.

The stalker over to their left was also in trouble. Though they could see it only dimly, it had walked into a stretch where the worms grew taller. Silhouetted against a bright strip of land to the far side of the hill, it had been reduced to immobility, while a forest of boneless fingers boiled all round it. It toppled. Without a sound it fell, the end of its long journey marked by worms.

Unaffected by the catastrophe, the stalker on which the humans rode continued to edge downwards.

Already it was through the thickest patch of opposition. The worms were rooted to the ground and could not follow. They fell away, grew shorter, more widely spaced, finally sprouted only in bunches, which the stalker avoided.

Relaxing slightly, Gren took the opportunity to look more searchingly at their surroundings. Yattmur hid her face in his shoulder; sickness stirred in her stomach and she wanted to see no more.

22

Rock and stones lay thick on the ground below the stalker's legs. This detritus had been shed by an ancient river which no longer flowed; the old river bed marked the bottom of a valley; when they crossed it, they began to climb, over ground free of any form of growth.

"Let us die!" moaned one of the tummy-belly men. "It is too awful to be alive in the land of death. Turn all things the same, great herder, give us the benefit of the cutting of your cosy and cruel little cutting sword. Let tummy-bellies men have a quick short cutting to leave this long land of death! O, O, O, the cold burns us, ayeee, the long cold cold!"

In chorus they cried their woe.

Gren let them moan. At last, growing weary of their noise,

which echoed so strangely across the valley, he lifted his stick to strike them. Yattmur restrained him.

"Are they not right to moan?" she asked. "I would rather moan with them than strike them, for soon it must be that we shall die with them. We have gone beyond the world, Gren. Only death can live here."

"We may not be free, but the stalkers are free. They would not walk to their death. You are turning into a tummy-belly, woman!"

For a moment she was silent. Then she said, "I need comfort, not reproach. Sickness stirs like death in my stomach."

She spoke without knowing that the sickness in her stomach was not death but life.

Gren made no answer. The stalker moved steadily over rising ground. Lulled by the threnody of the tummy-bellies, Yattmur fell asleep. Once the cold woke her. The chant had ceased; all her companions were sleeping. A second time she woke, to hear Gren weeping; but lethargy had her, so that she succumbed again to tiring dreams.

When she roused once more, she came fully awake with a start. The dreary twilight was broken by a shapeless red mass apparently suspended in the air. Gasping between fright and hope, she shook Gren.

"Look, Gren!" she cried, pointing up ahead. "Something burns there! What are we coming to?"

The stalker quickened its pace, almost as if it had scented its destination.

In the near-dark, seeing ahead was baffling. They had to stare for a long while before they could make out what lay in front of them. A ridge stretched immediately above them; as the stalker made its way up to the ridge, they saw more and more of what it had hitherto obscured. Some way behind the ridge loomed a mountain with a triple peak. It was this mountain that glowed so redly.

They gained the ridge, the stalker hauled itself stiffly over the lip, and the mountain was in full view.

No sight could have been more splendid.

All about, night or a pale brother of night reigned supreme. Nothing stirred; only the chilly breeze moved with stealth through the valleys unseen below them, like a stranger in a ruined town at midnight. If they were not beyond the world, as Yattmur thought, they were beyond the world of vegetation. Utter emptiness obscured utter darkness beneath their feet, magnifying their least whisper to a stammering shriek.

From all this desolation rose the mountain, high and sublime; its base was lost in blackness; its peaks soared tall enough to woo the sun, to fume in rosy warmth, to throw a reflection of that glow into the wide trough of obscurity at its foot.

Taking Yattmur's arm, Gren pointed silently. Other stalkers had crossed the darkness they had crossed; three of them could be seen steadily mounting the slopes ahead. Even their aloof and eerie figures mitigated the loneliness.

Yattmur woke the tummy-bellies, keen to let them see the prospect. The three plump creatures kept their arms round each other as they gazed up at the mountain.

"O the eyes make a good sight!" they gasped.

"Very good," Yattmur agreed.

"O very good, sandwich lady! This big chunk of ripe day makes a hill of a hill shape to grow in this night-and-death place for us. It is a lovely sun slice for us to live in as a happy home."

"Perhaps so," she agreed, though already she foresaw difficulties beyond their simpler comprehensions.

They climbed. It grew lighter. Finally they emerged from the margin of shadow. The blessed sun shone on them again. They drank the sight of it until their eyes were blinded and the sombre valleys beneath them danced with orange and green spots. Compressed to lemon shape and parboiled crimson by atmosphere, it simmered at them from the ragged lip of the world, its rays beating outwards over a panorama of shadow. Broken into a confusing array of searchlights by a score of peaks thrusting up from the blackness, the lowest strata of sunlight made a pattern of gilt wonderful to behold.

Unmoved by these vistas, the stalker continued immutably to climb, its legs creaking at every step. Beneath it scuttled an occasional crawlpaw, heading down towards the shrouded valley and ignoring their progress upward. At last the stalker came to a position almost in the dip between two of the three peaks. It halted.

"By the spirits!" Gren exclaimed. "I think it means to carry us no farther."

The tummy-bellies set up a hullabaloo of excitement, but Yattmur looked round doubtfully.

"How do we get down if the stalker is not going to sink as the morel said?" she asked.

"We must climb down," Gren said, after some thought, when the stalker showed no further sign of moving.

"Let me see you climb down first. With the cold, and with crouching here too long, my limbs are as stiff as sticks."

Looking defiantly at her, Gren stood up and stretched himself. He surveyed the situation. Since they had no rope, they had no means of getting down. The smoothly bulging skins of the seed drums prevented the possibility of their climbing down on to the stalker's legs. Gren sat again, lapsing into blankness.

"The morel advises us to wait," he said. He put an arm about Yattmur's shoulders, ashamed of his own helplessness.

There they waited. There they ate a morsel more of their food, which had begun to sprout mould. There they had perforce to fall asleep; and when they woke the scene had changed hardly at all, except that a few more stalkers now stood silent farther down the slopes, and that thick clouds were drawing across the sky.

Helpless, the humans lay there while nature continued inflexibly to work about them, like a huge machine in which they were the most idle cog.

The clouds came rumbling up from behind the mountain, big and black and pompous. They curdled through the passes, turning to sour milk where the sun lit them. Presently they obscured the sun. The whole mountainside was swallowed. It began to snow sluggish wet flakes like sick kisses.

Five humans burrowed together, turning their backs upwards to the drift. Underneath them, the stalker trembled.

Soon this trembling turned to a steady sway. The stalker's legs sank a little into the moistened ground; then, as they too became softened by wet, they began to buckle. The stalker became increasingly bow-legged. In the mists of the mountainside, other stalkers—lacking the assistance of weight on top of them—began slowly to copy it. Now its legs quivered farther and farther apart; its body sank lower.

Suddenly, frayed by the countless miles of travel and subverted by wet, its joints reached breaking point and split. The stalker's six legs fell outwards, its body dropped to the muddy ground. As it hit, the six drums that comprised it burst, scattering notchy seeds all about.

This sodden ruin in the middle of snow was at once the end and the beginning of the stalker plant's journey. Forced like all plants to solve the terrible problem of overcrowding in a hothouse world, it had done so by venturing into those chilly realms beyond the timberline where the jungle could not grow. On this slope, and a few similar ones within the twilight zone, the stalkers played out one phase of their unending cycle of life. Many of the seeds dispersed now would germinate, where they had plenty of space and some warmth, growing into the hardy little crawlpaws; and some of those crawlpaws, triumphing over a thousand obstacles, would eventually find their way to the realms of true warmth and light, there to root and flower and continue the endless vegetable mode of being.

When the seed drums split, the humans were flung aside into mud. Painfully they stood up, their limbs creaking with stiffness.

So thickly swirled the snow and cloud about them that they could hardly see each other: their bodies became white pillars, illusory.

Yattmur was anxious to gather the tummy-belly men together before they became lost. Seeing a figure glistening in the thick dim light, she ran to it and grasped it. A face turned snarling towards her, yellow teeth and hot eyes flared into her face. She cowered from attack, but the creature was gone in a bound.

This was their first intimation that they were not alone on the mountain.

"Yattmur!" Gren called. "The tummy-bellies are here. Where are you?"

She went running to him, her stiffness forgotten in fright.

"Somthing else is here," she said. "A white creature, wild and with teeth and big ears!"

The three tummy-bellies set up a cry to the spirits of death and darkness as Yattmur and Gren stared about.

"In this filthy mess, it's impossible to see anywhere," Gren said, dashing snow from his face.

They stood huddled together, knives ready. The snow slackened abruptly, turned to rain, cut off. Through the last shower they saw a line of a dozen white creatures bounding over a brow of the mountain towards the dark side. Behind them they pulled a sort of sledge loaded with sacks, from one of which a trail of stalker seeds bounced.

A ray of sun pierced across the melancholy hillsides. As if they feared it, the white creatures hurried into a pass and disappeared from view.

Gren and Yattmur looked at each other.

"Where they human?" Gren asked.

She shrugged. She did not know. She did not know what human meant. The tummy-bellies, now lying in the mud and groaning: were they human? And Gren, so impenetrable now that it seemed as if the morel had taken him over: could it be said he was still human?

192

So many riddles, some she could not even formulate in words, never mind answer. . . . But once more the sun shone warm on her limbs. The sky was lined with crumpled lead and gilt. Above them on the mountain were caves. They could go there and build a fire. They could survive and sleep warmly again. . . .

Brushing her hair off her face, she began to walk slowly uphill. Although she felt heavy and troubled, she knew enough to know that the others would follow her.

23

Life on the big slope was endurable, and sometimes more than just endurable, for the human spirit has a genius for making mountains out of molehills of happiness.

In the great and awful landscape in which they found themselves, the humans were dwarfed almost to insignificance. The pastoral of Earth and the drama of the weather unrolled without taking cognisance of them. Between slope and cloud, amid mud and snow, they lived their humble lives.

Though night and day no longer marked the passage of time, there were other incidents to tell of its passing. The storms increased, while the temperature fell; sometimes the rain that fell was icy; sometimes it was scalding hot, so that they ran screaming for the shelter of their caves.

Gren became more morose as the morel took a firmer hold over his will. Aware of how its own cleverness had brought them to a dead end, it brooded increasingly; oppressed by its need to procreate, it cut Gren off from communication with his fellows.

A third event marked the unceasing progression of time. During a storm, Yattmur gave birth to a son.

It became the reason for her existence. She called it Laren and was content.

On a remote mountainside of Earth, Yattmur cradled her baby in her arms, singing to him though he slept.

The upper slopes of the mountain were bathed in the rays of the ever-setting sun, while the lower slopes were lost in night. This whole tumbled area was one of darkness, lit occasionally by ruddy beacons where mountains thrust themselves up in stony imitation of living things to reach the light.

Even where darkness lay thickest, it was not absolute. Just as death is not absolute—the chemicals of life later reforming to create more life—so the darkness was often to be reckoned merely a lesser degree of light, a realm where lurked creatures that had been forced out of the brighter and more populous regions.

Among these exiles were the leatherfeathers, a pair of which skimmed over the mother's head, enjoying an acrobatic flight, storming downwards with their wings closed or spreading them to float upwards on a current of warmer air. The baby awoke and the mother pointed the flying creatures out to him.

"There they go, Laren, wheeee, down into the valley and—look, there they are!—back into the sun again, up so high."

Her baby wrinkled its nose, indulging her. The leathery fliers dived and turned, flashing in the light before they sank into a mesh of shadows, only to rise again as if out of a sea, sweeping upwards occasionally almost as far as the low canopy of cloud. The clouds held a bronze aura; they were as much a feature of the landscape as the mountains themselves, reflecting light over the obscure world below, scattering it from their contours like showers, until the barren countrysides were dappled with yellow and fugitive gold.

Amid this cross-hatching of brightness and dusk the leatherfeathers sped, feeding on the spores which even here floated thick, wafted from the vast propagating machine that covered the sunlit face of the planet. The infant Laren gurgled in delight, stretching out his hands; Yattmur the mother gurgled too, filled with pleasure at every movement of her child.

One of the fliers was diving steeply now. Yattmur watched with sudden surprise, noticing its lack of control. The leatherfeather twisted down, its mate winging powerfully after it. Just

194

for a moment she thought it was going to straighten: then it struck the mountainside with an audible thwack!

Yattmur stood up. She could see the leatherfeather, a motionless heap above which the bereft mate fluttered.

She was not the only one who had observed the fatal dive. Farther over on the big slope, one of the tummy-belly men began running towards the fallen bird, crying to his two companions as he went. She heard the words, "Come and look see with eyes the fallen bird of wings!" clear in the clear air, she heard the sound of his feet thudding on the ground as he trotted down the slope. Mother-like, she stood watching, clasping Laren and regretting any incident that disturbed her peace.

Something else was after the fallen bird. Yattmur glimpsed a group of figures farther down the hill, coming rapidly from behind a spur of stone. Eight of them she counted, white-clad figures with pointed noses and large ears, outlined sharply against the deep blue gloom of a valley. They dragged a sleigh behind them.

She and Gren called these beings Mountainears, and kept a sharp watch out for them, for the creatures were fast and well-armed, though they had never offered the humans any harm.

For a moment the tableau held: three tummy-belly men trotting downhill, eight mountainears moving up, and the one surviving bird wheeling overhead, uncertain whether to mourn or escape. The mountainears were armed with bows and arrows; tiny but clear in the distance, they lifted their weapons, and suddenly Yattmur was full of anxiety for the three plump halfwits with whom she had travelled so far. Clutching Laren to her breast, she stood up and called to them.

"Hey, you tummies! Come back!"

Even as she called, the first fierce mountainear had unleashed his arrow. Swift and sure it went—and the surviving leatherfeather spiralled down. Beneath it, the leading tummy-belly ducked and squealed. The falling bird, its wings still faintly beating, hit him between the shoulder blades as it dropped.

195

Staggering, he fell, while the bird flopped feebly about him.

The group of tummy-bellies and mountainears met.

Yattmur turned and ran. She burst into the smoky cave where she, Gren, and the baby lived.

"Gren! Please come! The tummy-bellies will be killed. They are out there with the terrible big-eared white ones attacking them. What can we do?"

Gren lay propped against a column of rock, his hands clasped together on his stomach. When Yattmur entered, he fixed her with a dead gaze, then dropped his eyes again. Pallor marked his features, contrasting with the rich livery brown that glistened about his head and throat, framing his face with its sticky folds.

"Are you going to *do* anything?" she demanded. "What is the matter with you these days?"

"The tummy-bellies are useless to us," Gren said. Nevertheless, he stood up. She put out her hand, which he clutched listlessly, and dragged him to the cave mouth.

"I've grown fond of the poor creatures," she said, almost to herself.

They peered down the steep slope to where figures moved against a backdrop of hazy shadow.

The three tummy-belly men were walking back up the hill, dragging one of the leatherfeathers with them. Beside them walked the mountainears, pulling their sleigh, on the top of which lay the other leatherfeather. The two groups went amicably together, chattering with plentiful gesticulation from the tummy-bellies.

"Well, what do you make of that?" Yattmur exclaimed.

It was an odd procession. The mountainears in profile were sharp-snouted; they moved in an irregular fashion, sometimes dropping forward to pace on all fours up the incline. Their language came to Yattmur in short barks of sound, though they were too far away for her to distinguish what was being said— even provided that what they said was intelligible.

"What do you make of it, Gren?" she asked.

He said nothing, staring out at the little crowd that was now clearly heading for the cave in which he had directed the tummy-bellies to live. As they passed beyond the stalker grove, he saw them point in his direction and laugh. He made no sign.

Yattmur looked up at him, suddenly struck with pity at the change that had recently possessed him.

"You say so little and you look so ill, my love. We have come so far together, you and I with only each other to love, yet now it is as if you were gone from me. From my heart flows only love for you, from my lips only kindness. But love and kindness are lost things on you now, O Gren, O my Gren!"

She put her free arm round him, only to feel him move away. Yet he said, as if the words came wrapped one by one in ice, "Help me, Yattmur. Be patient. I am ill."

Now she was half-preoccupied with the other matter.

"You'll be better. But what are those savage mountainears doing? Can they be friendly?"

"You'd better go and see," Gren said, still in his bleak voice. He disengaged her hand, went back inside the cave and lay down, resuming his former position with his hands clasped over his stomach. Yattmur sat down at the cave mouth, undecided. The tummy-bellies and mountainears had disappeared into the other cave. The girl stayed helplessly where she was, while clouds piled up overhead. Presently it began to rain, the rain turning to snow. Laren cried and was given a breast to suck.

Slowly the girl's thoughts grew outwards, eclipsing the rain. Vague pictures hung in the air about her, pictures that despite their lack of logic were her way of reasoning. Her safe days in the tribe of herders was represented by a tiny red flower that could also, with just the tiniest shift of emphasis, be her, as her safe days had been her: she had not seen herself as a phenomenon distinct from the phenomena about her. And when she tried to do so now, she could only picture herself distantly, in a crowd of bodies, or as part of a dance, or as a girl whose turn it was to take the buckets to Long Water.

Now the red flower days were over, except that a new bud put forth petals at her breast. The crowd of bodies had gone, and vanished with it was the yellow shawl symbol. The lovely shawl! Perpetual sun overhead like a hot bath, innocent limbs, a happiness that did not know itself—these were the strands of the yellow shawl she pictured. Distinctly she saw herself throw it away to follow the wanderer whose merit was that he was the unknown.

The unknown was a big withered leaf in which something crouched. She had followed the leaf—the tiny figure of herself grew nearer and somehow more spiky—while shawl and red petals blew merrily off in the one way wind of time. Now the leaf turned flesh, rolling with her. She became a big figure, swarming with traffic, a land of milk and honeyed pubic parts. And in the red flower had been no music like the music of the fleshy leaf.

Yet it all faded. The mountain came marching in. Mountain and flower were opposed. Mountain rolled on for ever, in one steep slope that had no bottom or top, though the base rested in black mist and the peak in black cloud. Black mist and cloud were reaching everywhere through her reverie, long-handed shorthand for evil; while by another of those tiny shifts of emphasis, the slope became not just her present life, but all her life. In the mind are no paradoxes, only moments; and in the moment of the slope, all the bright flowers and shawls and flesh were as if they had never been.

Thunder snored over the real mountain, rousing Yattmur from her reverie, scattering her pictures.

She looked back into the cave at Gren. He was unmoving. He did not look at her. Her daydreaming brought her the comprehension she sought, and she told herself, "It is the magic morel that has brought us this trouble. Laren and I are victims of it as much as poor Gren. Because it preys on him, he is ill. It is on his head and in his head. Somehow, *I* must find a way to deal with it."

Comprehension was not the same as comfort. Gathering up the baby, tucking her breast away, she stood up.

"I'm going to the cave of the tummy-bellies," she said, half-expecting to get no reply.

Gren answered her.

"You cannot take Laren through that pouring rain. Give him to me and I will take care of him."

She crossed the floor towards him. Though the light was bad, she thought the fungus in his hair and round his neck looked darker than before. Certainly it was expanding, standing out over his forehead in a way it had never done. Sudden revulsion checked her movement as she began to offer him the baby.

He glanced up at her from under the morel with a look she could not recognize as his; it held the fatal mixture of stupidity and cunning that lurks at the bottom of all evil. Instinctively, she jerked her child back.

"Give him to me. He won't be hurt," Gren said. "A young human could be taught so much."

Though his movements were generally lethargic, he jumped up with all swiftness. She leapt away angrily, hissing at him, drawing her knife, afraid in all her fibres. She showed him her teeth like an animal.

"Keep away."

Laren sent out an irritable wail.

"Give me the baby," Gren said again.

"You are not yourself. I'm frightened of you, Gren. Sit down again! Stay away! Stay away!"

Still he came forward in a curiously slack way as if his nervous system was having to respond to two rival centres of control. She raised her knife, but he took absolutely no notice of it. In his eyes hung a blind look like a curtain.

At the last moment, Yattmur broke. Dropping her knife, she turned and sprinted from the cave, clutching her baby tightly.

Thunder came tumbling down the hill at her. Lightning sizzled, striking one strand of a great traverser web that stretched from nearby up into the clouds. The strand spluttered and flared until rain quenched it. Yattmur ran, making for the cave of the tummy-bellies, not daring to glance back.

Only when she reached it did she realize how unsure she was of her reception. By then it was too late to hesitate. As she burst in out of the rain, tummy-bellies and mountainears jumped up to meet her.

24

Gren sank to his hands and knees among the painful stones at the mouth of the cave.

Complete chaos had overtaken his impressions of the external world. Pictures rose like steam, twisting in his inner mind. He saw a wall of tiny cells, sticky like a honeycomb, growing all about him. Though he had a thousand hands, they did not push down the wall; they came away thick with syrup that bogged his movements. Now the wall of cells loomed above his head, closing in. Only one gap in it remained. Staring through it, he saw tiny figures miles distant. One was Yattmur, down on her knees, gesticulating, crying because he could not get to her. Other figures he made out to be the tummy-bellies. Another he recognized as Lily-yo, the leader of the old group. And another—that writhing creature!—he recognized as himself, shut out from his own citadel.

The mirage fogged over and vanished.

Miserably, he fell back against the wall, and the cells of the wall began popping open like wombs, oozing poisonous things.

The poisonous things became mouths, lustrous brown mouths that excreted syllables. They impinged on him with the voice of the morel. They came so thickly on him from all sides that for a while it was only their shock and not their meaning that struck him. He screamed creakingly, until he realized the morel was speaking not with cruelty but regret; whereupon he tried to control his shivering and listen to what was being said.

"There were no creatures like you in the thickets of Nomans-

200

land where my kind live," the morel pronounced. "Our role was to live off the simple vegetable creatures there. They existed without brain; we were their brains. With you it has been different. In the extraordinary ancestral compost heap of your unconscious mind, I have burrowed too long.

"I have seen so much to amaze me in you that I forgot what I should have been about. You have captured me, Gren, as surely as I have captured you.

"Yet the time has come when I must remember my true nature. I have fed on your life to feed my own; that is my function, my only way. Now I reach a point of crisis, for I am *ripe*."

"I don't understand," Gren said dully.

"A decision lies before me. I am soon to divide and sporulate; that is the system by which I reproduce, and I have little control over it. This I could do here, hoping that my progeny would survive somehow on this bleak mountain against rain and ice and snow. Or . . . I could transfer to a fresh host."

"Not to my baby."

"Why not to your baby? Laren is the only choice for me. He is young and fresh; he will be far easier to control than you are. True, he is weak as yet, but Yattmur and you will look after him until he becomes able to look after himself."

"Not if it means looking after you as well."

Before Gren finished speaking he received a blow, scattering directly over his brain, that sent him huddling against the cave wall in pain.

"You and Yattmur will not desert the baby under any circumstances. You know that, and I see it in your thought. You know also that if any opportunity came you would get away from these barren miserable slopes to the fertile lands of light. That also fits in with my plan. Time presses, man; I must move according to my needs.

"Knowing every fibre of you as I do, I pity your pain—but it can mean nothing at all to me when set against my own nature. I must have an able and preferably witless host that will carry me rapidly back into the sunlit world, so that I can seed there. So I have chosen Laren. That would be the best course for my progeny, don't you think?"

"I'm dying," Gren moaned.

"Not yet," twanged the morel.

At the back of the tummy-belly cave sat Yattmur, half-asleep. The foetid air of the place, the yammer of voices, the noise of the rain outside, all combined to dull her senses. She dozed, and Laren slept on a pile of dead foliage beside her. They had all eaten scorched leatherfeather, half-cooked, half-burnt over a blazing fire. Even the baby had accepted titbits.

When she appeared distraught at the cave entrance, the tummy-bellies welcomed her in, crying "Come, lovely sandwich lady, out of the raining wetness where the clouds fall. Come in with us to cuddle and make warmth without water."

"Who are these others with you?" She looked anxiously at the eight mountainears, who were grinning and jumping up and down at the sight of her.

Seen close to, they were very formidable: a head taller than the humans, with thick shoulders on which long fur stood out like a mantle. They had grouped together behind the tummy-bellies, but now began circling Yattmur, showing their teeth and calling to each other in a weird perversion of speech.

Their faces were the most fearsome Yattmur had ever seen. Long-jawed, low-browed, they had snouts and brief yellow beards, while their ears curled out of fuzzy short fur like segments of raw flesh. Quick and irritable in movement, they seemed never to leave their faces in repose: bars of long, sharp ivories appeared and disappeared behind grey lips as they snapped out questions at her.

"You yap you live here? On the Big Slope you yakker-yakker live? With the tummy-bellies, with the tummy-bellies live? You and them together, yipper-yap slap-sleeping running living loving on the Big Big Slope?"

202

One of the largest mountainears asked Yattmur this rapid fire of questions, jumping before her and grimacing as he did so. His voice was so coarse and guttural, his phrases so chopped into barks, that she had difficulty in understanding him at all. "Yipper yapper yes live you on Big Black Slope?"

"Yes, I live on this mountain," she said, standing her ground.

"Where do you live? What people are you?"

For answer he opened his goat eyes at her until a red brink of gristle showed all round them. Then he closed them tight, opened his cavernous jaws and emitted a high clucking soprano chord of laughter.

"These sharp-fur people are gods, lovely sharp gods, sandwich lady," the tummy-bellies explained, the three of them hopping before her, jostling each other in an agony to be first to unburden their souls to her. "These sharp-fur people are called sharp-furs. They are our gods, missis, for they run all over the Big Slope mountain, to be gods for dear old tummy-belly men. They are gods, gods, they are big fierce gods, sandwich lady. They have *tails!*"

This last sentence was delivered in a cry of triumph. The whole mob of them went streaming round the cave, shrieking and whooping. Indeed the sharp-furs had tails, sticking out of their rumps at impudent angles. These the tummy-bellies chased, trying to pull and kiss them. As Yattmur shrank back, Laren, who had watched this rout for a moment wide-eyed, began to bawl at the top of his voice. The dancing figures imitated him, interposing shouts and chants of their own.

"Devil dance on the Big Slope, Big Slope. Teeth many teeth bite-tear-chew night or light on Big Slope. Tummy-belly men are singing for tails of sharp-fur gods. Many big bad things to sing about on the Bad Slope. Eat and bite and drink when rain comes raining. Ai, ai, ai-yah!"

Suddenly as they galloped by, one of the fiercest sharp-furs snatched Laren out of Yattmur's arms. She cried out—he was gone, whirled away with startlement on his small red face. The long-jawed creatures tossed him from one to another, first high then low, almost striking the floor or nearly scraping the ceiling, barking with laughter at their game.

Outraged, Yattmur flung herself on the nearest sharp-fur. As she tore at his long white fur, she felt the muscles beneath it, rippling as the creature turned. A leathery grey hand flashed up, rammed two fingers up her nostrils, and pushed. Scissoring pain cut between her eyes. She fell back, her hands going up to her face, lost her footing, and sprawled on the ground. Instantly the sharp-fur was on to her. Almost as quickly, the others piled on as well.

This was Yattmur's saving. The sharp-furs began to fight among themselves and forgot her. She crawled away from them to rescue Laren, who lay now drugged with surprise, perfectly unharmed on the ground. Sobbing with relief, she hugged him to her. He began at once to cry—but when she looked fearfully round, the sharp-furs had forgotten about her and the fight, and were preparing to cook the dead leatherfeathers again.

"Oh don't have wet rain in the eyes, lovely sandwich lady," said the tummy-bellies, clustering round her, patting her clumsily, trying to stroke her hair. She was alarmed at their familiarity with her when Gren was not about, but she said in a low voice, "You were so afraid of Gren and me: why have you no fear of these terrible creatures? Do you not see how dangerous they are?"

"Do you not see see see how these gods of sharp-fur have tails? Only tails that grow on people have people with tails to be gods to us poor tummy-belly men."

"They will kill you."

"They are our gods, so we make happiness to be killed only by gods with tails. Yes, they have sharp teeth and tails! Yes, and the teeth and tails are of a sharpness."

"You are like children, and they are dangerous."

"Ai-ee, the sharp-fur gods wear danger in their mouth for teeth. Yet the teeth do not call us hard names like you and the brain man Gren. Better to have a jolly death, miss!"

As the tummy-bellies huddled round Yattmur, she peered over their hairy shoulders at the group of sharp-furs. Momentarily they were almost still, tearing up one of the leather-feathers and cramming it into their mouths. At the same time, a large leathern flask passed between them; from this, with much squabbling, they gulped in turn. Yattmur observed that even among themselves they spoke a broken version of the tongue the tummy-bellies spoke.

"How long are they staying here for?" she asked.

"In the cave they stay often because they love us in the cave," one tummy-belly said, stroking her shoulder.

"They have visited you before?"

Those fat faces grinned at her.

"They come to see us before and again and again because they love lovely tummy-belly men. You and the hunter man Gren do not love lovely tummy-belly men, so we weep on the Big Slope. And the sharp-furs soon take us away to find a green mummy-tummy. Yep, yep, sharp-furs take us?"

"You are leaving us?"

"We go away from you to leave you on the cold and nasty dark Big Slope, where it is so big and dark, because the sharp gods take us to tiny green place with warm mummy-tummies where slopes cannot live."

In the heat and stink, and with Laren grizzling, she grew confused. She made them say it all again, which they did volubly, until their meaning was all too clear.

For a long while now, Gren had been unable to conceal his hatred for the tummy-bellies. This dangerous new sharp-snouted race had offered to take them off the mountain and back to one of the fleshy trees which succoured and enslaved tummy-belly men. Yattmur knew instinctively that the long-toothed mountainears were not to be trusted, but it was impossible to make the tummy-bellies feel this. She saw that she and her child were soon to be left alone on the mountain with Gren.

205

Overcome by several varieties of wretchedness, she began to weep.

They clustered nearer, trying inadequately to comfort her, breathing in her face, patting her breasts, tickling her body, making faces at the baby. She was too miserable to protest.

"You come with us to the green world, lovely sandwich lady, to be again far from the huge Big Slope with us lovely chaps," they murmured. "We let you have lovely sleeps in with us."

Encouraged by her apathy, they began to explore the more intimate parts of her body. Yattmur offered no resistance, and when their simple prurience was satisfied, they left her alone in her corner. One of them returned later, bringing her a portion of scorched leatherfeather, which she ate.

While she chewed, she thought, "Gren will kill my baby with that fungus. So I must take a chance for Laren's sake, and leave when the tummy-bellies leave." Once the decision had been made, she felt happier, and sank into a doze.

She was wakened by Laren's crying. As she attended to him, she peered outside. It was as dark as she had ever known it. The rain had stopped temporarily; now thunder filled the air, as if it rolled between earth and packed cloud seeking escape. The tummy-bellies and sharp-furs slept together in an uncomfortable heap, disturbed by the noise. Yattmur's head throbbed, and she thought, I'll never sleep in this rumpus. But a moment later, with Laren cuddled against her, her eyes were closed again.

The next time she was roused, it was by the sharp-furs. They were barking with excitement and scampering out of the cave.

Laren was sleeping. Leaving the child on a pile of dead foliage, Yattmur went to see what was happening. She drew back momentarily on coming face to face with the sharp-furs. To protect their heads from the rain—which was coming down again with full force—they were wearing helmets carved from the same sort of dried gourd that Yattmur used for cooking and washing in.

Holes had been cut in the gourds for their ears, eyes and

snouts. But the gourds were too large for the furry heads they covered; they rolled from side to side with every movement, making the sharp-furs look like broken dolls. This, and the fact that the gourds had been clumsily smeared with various colours, gave the sharp-furs a grotesque air, from which the element of fear was not missing.

As Yattmur ran into the pouring rain, one of the creatures jumped forward with its nodding wooden head and barred her way.

"Yagrapper yow you stay sleeping in the sleeping cave, mother lady. Coming through the rap-yap-rain is coming bad things that we fellows have no like. So we bite and tear and bite. Brrr buff best you stay away yap yay from sight of our teeth."

She flinched from its clutch, hearing the drum of rain on its crude helmet mingle with its baffling mixture of growls, yaps, and words.

"Why should I not stay out here?" she asked. "Are you afraid of me? What is happening?"

"Catch-carry-kind come yum yap and catch you! Grrr, let him catch you!"

It pushed Yattmur and leaped away to join its mates. The helmeted creatures were leaping about over their sledge, quarrelling as they sorted out their bows and arrows. The tummy-belly trio stood close by, cuddling each other and pointing along the slope.

The cause of all the excitement was a group of figures moving slowly towards Yattmur's party. At first, squinting through the downpour, she thought only two things were approaching; then they separated to reveal themselves as three—and for the life of her she could not make out what, in their oddity, they might be. But the sharp-furs knew.

"Catchy carry kind, catchy carry kind! Killy catchy carry kind!" they seemed to be calling, growing frenzied about it. But the trio advancing through the rain, for all their peculiarity, did not look menacing even to Yattmur. The sharp-furs, however, were leaping in the air in lust; one or two were already taking aim with their bows through the wavering curtains of rain.

"Stop! Don't hurt them, let them come!" Yattmur shouted. "They can't harm us."

"Catchy carry kind! You you yap you keep quiet, lady, and be not any harm or take harm!" they called, unintelligible with excitement. One of them charged at her, head first, banging his gourd helmet against her shoulder. In fear of him she turned and ran, blindly at first and then with purpose.

She could not deal with the sharp-furs: but probably Gren and the morel could.

Squelching and splashing, she ran back to her own cave. Unthinkingly, she plunged right in.

Gren stood against the wall by the entrance, half-concealed. She was past him before she realized it, only turning as he began to bear down on her.

Helpless with shock, she screamed and screamed, her mouth sagging toothily wide at the sight of him.

The surface of the morel was black and pustular now—and it had slipped down so that it covered all his face. Only his eyes gleamed sickly in the midst of it as he jumped forward at her.

She sank to her knees. It was all she could manage at the moment in the way of evasive action, so completely had the sight of that huge cancerous growth on Gren's shoulders unnerved her.

"Oh Gren!" she gasped weakly.

He bent and took her roughly by her hair. The physical pain of this cleared her mind; though she trembled like a hill under a landslide of emotion, her wits returned to her.

"Gren, the morel thing is killing you," she whispered.

"Where's the baby?" he demanded. Though his voice was muffled, it had too an additional remoteness, a twanging quality, that gave her one more item for alarm. "What have you done with the baby, Yattmur?"

Cringing, she said, "You don't speak like yourself any more, Gren. What's happening? You know I don't hate you—tell me what's happening, so that I can understand."

"Why have you not brought the baby?"

"You're not like Gren any more. You're—you're somehow the morel now, aren't you? You talk with his voice."

"Yattmur—*I need the baby.*"

Struggling to her feet though he still clasped her hair, she said, as steadily as possible, "Tell me what you want Laren for."

"The baby is mine and I need him. Where have you put him?"

She pointed to the gloomy recesses of the cave.

"Don't be silly, Gren. He's lying back there behind you, at the back of the cave, fast asleep."

Even as he looked, as his attention was diverted, she wrenched herself out of his grip, ducked under his arm, and ran. Squeaking with terror, she burst into the open.

Again the rain soused down on to her face, bringing her back to a world she had left—though that horrifying glimpse of Gren had seemed to last for ever—little more than a moment before. From where she stood, the hillside cut off that strange trio the sharp-furs had called the catchy-carry-kind, but the group about the sledge was clearly visible. It stood in a tableau, tummy-bellies and sharp-furs motionless, looking over towards her, diverted from their other business by her screams.

She ran over to them, glad for all their irrationality to be with them again. Only then did she look back.

Gren had followed her from the cave mouth and there had stopped. After pausing indecisively, he went back and disappeared. The sharp-furs muttered and chattered to themselves, evidently awed by what they had seen. Taking advantage of the situation, Yattmur pointed back at Gren's cave and said, "Unless you obey me, that terrible mate of mine with the deadly sponge face will come and devour you all. Now, let these other people approach, and don't harm them until they offer us harm."

"Catchy-carry-kind no yap yap good!" they burst out.

"Do as I say or the sponge-face will devour you, ears and fur and all!"

The three slowly moving figures were nearer now. Two of them were human in outline, if very thin, though the weird biscuit light pervading everywhere made detail impossible to discern. The figure that most intrigued Yattmur was the one bringing up the rear. Though it walked on two legs, it differed considerably from its companions in being taller and seeming to have an enormous head. At times it appeared to have a second head below the first, to possess a tail, and to be walking with its hands clutched round its upper skull. But the deluge, as well as part-concealing it, gave it a shimmering halo of rebounding rain drops which defied vision.

To add to Yattmur's impatience, the odd trio now stopped. Although she called to them to come on, they ignored her. They stood perfectly still on the flooded hillside—and gradually one of the human figures blurred round the edges, became translucent, disappeared!

Both tummy-bellies and sharp-furs, obviously impressed by Yattmur's threat, had fallen silent. At the disappearance, they set up a murmur, although the sharp-furs showed little surprise.

"What's going on over there?" Yattmur asked one of the tummy-bellies.

"Very much a strange thing to take in the ears, sandwich lady. Several strange things! Through the nasty wet rain come two spiriters and a nasty catchy-carry-kind creature having a nasty carry on a number three spiriter in the wet rain. So the sharp-fur gods are crying with many a bad thought!"

What they said made little sense to Yattmur. Suddenly angered with them, she said, "Tell the sharp-furs to keep quiet and get back into the cave. I'm going to meet these new people."

"These fine sharp gods do not do what you say with no tail," the tummy-belly replied, but Yattmur ignored him.

She began to walk forward with her arms outspread and her

hands open to show she intended no harm. As she went, though the thunder still bumped over the nearby hills, the rain petered to a drizzle and stopped. The two creatures ahead became more clearly visible—and suddenly there were three of them again. A blurred outline took on substance, becoming a thin human being who stared ahead at Yattmur with the same watchful gaze as his two companions.

Disturbed by this apparition, Yattmur came to a halt. At this the bulky figure moved forward, calling out as he came, pushing past his companions.

"Creatures of the evergreen universe, the Sodal Ye of the catchy-carry-kind comes to you with the truth. See you are fit to receive it!"

His voice had a richness and fruitiness, as though it travelled through mighty throats and palates to become sound. Moving under the shelter of its mellowness, the two human figures also advanced. Yattmur could see that they were indeed human— two females in fact of a very primitive order, utterly naked except for elaborate tattoos over their bodies, and expressions of invincible stupidity upon their faces.

Feeling that something was called for by way of reply, Yatt-mur bowed and said, "If you come peacefully, welcome to our mountain."

The bulky figure gave out a roar of inhuman triumph and disgust.

"You do not own this mountain! This mountain, this Big Slope, this growth of dirt and stone and boulder, owns you! The Earth is not yours: you are a creature of the Earth."

"You take my meaning a long way," Yattmur said, irritated. "Who are you?"

"Everything has a long way to be taken!" was the reply, but Yattmur was no longer listening; the bulky figure's roar had precipitated activity behind her. She turned to see the sharp-furs preparing to leave, squealing and jostling, pushing each other as they swung their sledge about until it pointed downhill.

"Carry us with you or come running gently beside your lovely riding machine!" cried the tummy-bellies, darting distractedly about and even rolling in the mud before their fierce-featured gods. "Oh please kill us with lovely death only take us with you running and riding away from this Big Slope. Take us away from this Big Slope with the sandwich people and now this big roaring scratchy-carry-kind. Take us, take us, cruel lovely gods of sharp gods!"

"No, no, no. Gup gup go away, sprawly men! Sharpish we go, and come back in a quiet time for you soon!" cried the sharp-furs, bounding about.

All was activity. In no time, despite apparent chaos and indirection, the sharp-furs were moving, running beside and behind their sledge, pushing or braking as was needed, leaping over and on top of it, screaming, chattering, throwing up their gourd helmets and catching them, travelling over the uneven ground at speed, heading towards the glooms of the valley.

Bewailing their fate with gusto, the deserted tummy-bellies slunk back towards their cave, averting their eyes from the newcomers. As the yipping progress of the sharp-furs dwindled, Yattmur heard her baby's cry from the cave. Forgetting everything else, she ran and picked him up, dandled him until he gurgled with joy at her, and then took him outside to speak once more with the bulky figure.

It began to orate directly Yattmur reappeared.

"Those sharp-teeth sharp-fur kind have fled from me. Leaf-brained idiots they are—nothing more, animals with toads in their heads. Though they will not listen to me now, the time will come when they will have to listen. Their kind will be driven like hail on the winds."

As the creature talked on, Yattmur observed him thoroughly, with growing amazement. She could not understand him properly, for his head, an enormous fish-like affair with a broad lower lip which turned down so far that it nearly concealed his lack of chin, was out of all proportion with the rest of his body.

His legs, though bowed, were human in appearance, his arms were wrapped unmoving behind his ears, while from his chest a hairy, head-like growth seemed to emerge. Now and again she caught a glimpse of a large tail hanging behind him.

The pair of tattooed women stood by him, staring blankly ahead without appearing to see or think—or indeed to perform any activity more elaborate than breathing.

Now this strange bulky figure broke off his oration to gaze up at the thick clouds that masked the sun.

"I will sit," he said. "Place me on a suitable boulder, women. Soon the sky will clear, and then we shall see what we see."

The order was not addressed to Yattmur, or the tummy-bellies, who clustered forlornly at their cave mouth, but to the tattooed women. They watched as he moved forward with his dull retinue.

A tumble of boulders lay nearby. One was large and flat-topped. By this the odd trio halted—and the bulky figure split into two as the woman lifted the top part off the bottom! Half of him lay flat and fishy on the boulder, the other half stood bowed nearby.

Comprehension made Yattmur gasp, even as the tummy-bellies behind her wailed in dismay and raced each other into the cave. The bulky creature, the catchy-carry-kind as the sharp-furs called him, was two separate creatures! A giant fish shape, much like one of the dolphins she had seen during their voyage over the wastes of the ocean, had been carried by a stooped old human.

"You are two people!" she exclaimed.

"Indeed I am not!" said the dolphin-thing from its slab. "I am known as the Sodal Ye, greatest of all Sodals of the catch-carry-kind, Prophet of the Nightside Mountains, who brings you the true word. Have you intelligence, woman?"

About the man who had carried him clustered the two tattooed women. They did nothing effectual. They waved their hands at him without speaking. One of them grunted. As for the man, he had obviously been at his carrying for many seasons of fruit. Though the weight had gone from his shoulders, he remained bent as if he bore it yet, standing like a statue of dejection with his withered arms still circling the air above him, his back bowed, his eyes fixed only on the ground. Occasionally he shifted his stance; otherwise he was immobile.

"I asked you if you had intelligence, woman," said the being who called himself Sodal Ye, his voice as thick as liver. "Speak, since you can speak."

Yattmur pulled her eyes away from this horrifying porter and said, "What do you want here? Have you come to be helpful?"

"Spoken like a human woman!"

"Your women here don't seem to speak much!"

"They're not human! They cannot speak, as you should know. Have you never met any of the Arablers, the tattoo tribe before? Anyhow, why do you ask Sodal Ye for help? I am a prophet, not a servant. Are you in trouble?"

"Grave trouble. I have a mate who——"

Sodal Ye flipped one of his fins.

"Cease. Don't bother me with your tales now. Sodal Ye has more important things to do—such as watching the mighty sky, the sea in which this tiny seed Earth floats. Also, this Sodal is hungry. Feed me and I'll help you if I can. My brain is the mightiest of all things on the planet."

Ignoring this boast, Yattmur said, indicating his motley retinue, "What of these companions of yours—aren't they hungry too?"

"They'll be no trouble to you, woman; they eat the bits that Sodal Ye leaves."

"I'll feed you all if you will truly try to help me."

She bustled off, ignoring the new speech on which he had launched himself. Already Yattmur felt that this was a creature —unlike the sharp-furs—with which she could deal: a conceited and intelligent being that was nevertheless vulnerable; for she saw clearly that she had only to kill his porter to render the sodal helpless—should that be necessary. Meeting someone with whom she could negotiate from a position of strength was like a tonic; she felt nothing but goodwill towards the sodal.

The tummy-belly men had always been as gentle as mothers with Laren. She handed him to them, seeing that they settled contentedly to amuse him before gathering food for her strange guests. Her hair dripped as she went, her clothes began to dry on her, but she took no notice.

Into a big gourd she crammed the remains of the leather-feather feast and other edibles the tummy-bellies had collected: sprouts from the stalker grove, nuts, smoked mushrooms, berries and the fleshy fruits of the gourd. Another gourd stood full of water that had dripped through the fissured roof of the cave. She carried that out too.

Sodal Ye still lay on his boulder. He was bathed in an eerie cream light and did not move his eyes from the direction of the sun. Setting the food down, Yattmur looked where he did.

The clouds had parted. Over the dark and rugged sea of landscape, low hung the sun. It had changed its shape. Distorted by atmosphere, it was oblate: but no distortion of atmosphere could account for the great red-white wing which it had sprouted, a wing grown almost as large as its parent body.

"Oh! The blessed light takes wing to fly away and leave us!" Yattmur cried.

"You are safe yet, woman," Sodal Ye declared. "This I fore-saw. Do not worry. To bring me my food would be more useful. When I tell you about the flames that are about to consume our world, you will understand, but I must feed before I preach."

But she fixed her eyes on the strange sight in the heavens. The storm centre had passed from the twilight zone into the regions of the mighty banyan. Above the forest, the clouds piled cream on purple; lightning flashed almost without cease. And in the centre of it hung that deformed sun.

Uneasily, when the Sodal called again, Yattmur brought the food forward.

At this moment, one of the two wretched women began to vanish from where she stood. Yattmur almost dropped the gourds, staring in fascination. In very little time, the woman existed only as a smudge. Her tattoo lines alone remained, a meaningless scribble in the air. Then they too faded and were gone.

The tableau held. Slowly the tattoos returned. The woman followed, dull-eyed and meagre as before. She made a movement with her hands to the other woman. The other woman turned to the sodal and mouthed two or three slurred syllables.

"Good!" exclaimed the sodal, slapping his fish tail on the boulder. "You wisely did not poison the food, mother, so I will eat it."

The woman who had made the mockery of speech now came forward and took the gourd of food over to the sodal. Dipping her hand in, she commenced to feed him, thrusting handfuls into his fleshy mouth. He ate noisily and with relish, pausing only once to drink some water.

"Who are you all? What are you? Where do you come from? How do you vanish?" Yattmur asked.

Thickly through his mastication, Sodal Ye replied, "Something of all that I may tell you or I may not. You may as well know that only this one mute female can 'vanish', as you call it. Let me eat. Keep quiet."

At last he had finished.

In the bottom of the gourd he had left some scraps, and on these the three woebegone humans made their meal, drawing to one side in pitiful modesty to do so. The women fed their stooped fellow, whose arms were still fixed as if paralysed over his head.

"Now, I am prepared to hear your story," announced the sodal, "and to do something to help you if possible. Know that I come of the wisest race of this planet. My kind have covered all the vast seas and most of the less interesting land. I am a prophet, a Sodal of the Highest Knowledge, and I will stoop to help you if I consider your need interesting enough."

"Your pride is remarkable," she said.

"Pah, what is pride when the Earth is about to die? Proceed with your silly tale, mother, if you are going to proceed at all."

25

Yattmur wished to present the sodal with her problem concerning Gren and the morel. But because she possessed no skill in unfolding a story and selecting the telling details for it, she gave him virtually the history of her life, and of her childhood with the herders who lived on the edge of the forest by Black Mouth. She then related the arrival of Gren with his mate Poyly, and spoke of Poyly's death, and of their subsequent wanderings, until fate like a heavy sea had cast them upon the shores of Big Slope. Then finally she told of the birth of her baby, and of how she knew it to be threatened by the morel.

During all this, the sodal of the catchy-carry-kind lay with seeming indifference on his boulder, his lower lip hanging low enough to reveal the orange rims round his teeth. Beside him—with total indifference—the pair of tattooed women lay on the grass flanking the bowed porter, who still stood like a monument to care with his arms above his skull. The sodal surveyed none of them; his gaze roved over the heavens.

At last he said, "You make an interesting case. I have heard details of many infinitesimal lives not unlike yours. By fitting them all together—by synthesizing them in my extraordinary intelligence—I can construct a true picture of this world in its last stages of existence."

Angrily Yattmur stood up.

"Why I could knock you off your perch for that, you deboshed fish!" she exclaimed. "Is that all you have to say when previously you offered help?"

"Oh I could say a deal more, little human. But your problem is so simple that for me it scarcely seems to exist. I have met with these morels before in my travels, and though they are clever fellows, they have several points of vulnerability upon which anyone of my intellect will quickly seize."

"Please make a suggestion quickly."

"I have only one suggestion: that you entrust your baby to your mate Gren when he calls for it."

"That I can't do!"

"Ah ha, but you must. Don't back away. Come here while I explain why you must."

She did not like the sodal's plan. But behind his conceit and pomposity lay a stubborn stony force; his presence too was aweing; the very way he chewed out his words made them seem incontrovertible; so Yattmur clutched Laren with ill-ease and agreed to his dictates.

"I dare not go and face him in the cave," she said.

"Get your tummy-creatures to fetch him here then," ordered the sodal. "And hurry up about it. I travel on behalf of Fate, a master who at present has too much on his hands to bother with your concerns."

A rumble of thunder sounded, as if some mighty being signalled agreement with his words. Yattmur looked anxiously towards the sun, still wearing its cocky feather of fire, and then went to speak to the tummy-bellies.

They sprawled together in the cosy dirt, arms round each other, chattering. As she entered the cave mouth, one of them picked up a handful of earth and gravel and flung it at her.

"Before now you don't come in our cave or ever come here or want to come here, and now you are wanting to come here is too late, cruel sandwich lady! And the fishy-carry-man is your bad company—we don't belong. Poor tummy-men not want you come here—or they make the lovely sharp-furs crunch you up in the cave."

She stopped. Anger, regret, apprehension, ran through her, then she said firmly, "Your troubles are only just beginning if you feel like that. You know I wish to be your friend."

"You make all our troubles! Go quickly away!"

She backed away and, as she began to walk towards the other cave where Gren lay, she heard the tummy-bellies crying out to her. Whether their tone was one of abuse or supplication she did not know. Lightning snickered, stirring her shadow about her ankles. The baby wriggled in her arms.

"Lie still!" she said sharply. "He shall not harm you."

Gren sprawled at the back of the cave where she had last seen him. Lightning stabbed the brown mask through which his eyes peered. Though she saw him staring at her, he did not move or speak.

"Gren!"

Still he neither moved nor spoke.

Vibrant with strain, torn between love and hate of him, she leant there indecisively. When the lightning sparked again, she waved a hand before her eyes as though to brush it away.

"Gren, you can have the baby if you want him."

Then he moved.

"Come outside for him; it's too dark in here."

Having spoken, she walked away. Sickness rose in her as she felt the miserable difficulty of life. Over the saturnine slopes below her played inconstant light, adding to her dizziness. The catchy-carry-kind still lay on his boulder; beneath his shadow were the gourds, now empty of food and drink, and his forlorn retinue, hands to the sky, eyes to the ground. Yattmur sat down heavily with her back to the boulder, cradling Laren on her lap.

After a pause, Gren came out of the cave.

Walking slowly, slack-kneed, he approached her.

She could not tell whether she sweated from the heat or the tension. Because she was afraid to gaze on that pulpy mash that covered his face, Yattmur shut her eyes, opening them again only when she felt him near, fixing them on him as he stooped over her and the child. Uttering his pleased noise, Laren stretched up his arms with complete confidence.

"Sensible boy!" said Gren in his alien voice. "You are going

219

to be a child apart, a wonder child, and I shall never leave you."

Now she shivered so violently that she could not hold the baby still. But Gren was bending close now, down on his knees, so near she caught an acrid and clammy odour from him. Through the fluttering fringes of her eyelashes she saw the fungus on his face begin to move.

It hung above Laren's head, gathering ready to drop on him. Her vision was full of it, peppered with spongy spores, and with a slab of the big boulder and one of the empty gourds. She believed herself to be breathing in short screams, so that Laren commenced to cry—and again the tissue slid over Gren's face with the reluctant movement of stiff porridge.

"Now!" cried Sodal Ye in a voice which twitched her into action.

Yattmur whipped the empty gourd forward, over her child. The morel was caught in the bottom as it fell, trapped by the plan the sodal had devised. As Gren sagged sideways, she saw his true face twisted like rope in a knot of pain. The light ebbed and flowed, quick as a pulse, but she only knew something screamed, not recognizing her own high note before she collapsed.

Two mountains clashed together like jaws with a bloated and squalling version of Laren lost between them. Thrown back to her senses, Yattmur sat up with a jerk and the monstrous vision fled.

"So you are not dead," said the catchy-carry-kind gruffly. "Kindly get up and silence your child, since my women are unable to do so."

It was incredible that everything was much as it had been before she fainted, so long had she seemed to be enveloped in night. The morel lay inert in the gourd that had trapped it, with Gren face down beside it. Sodal Ye was atop his boulder. The pair of tattooed women hugged Laren to their withered breasts without being able to hush his cries.

Yattmur stood up and took him from them, putting his mouth to one of her own plump breasts, where he at once began pulling greedily and was silent. To feel him there gradually stilled her trembling.

She stooped over Gren.

He turned his face towards her when she touched his shoulder.

"Yattmur," he said.

Weak tears stood in his eyes. All over his shoulders, in his hair, across his face, ran a red and white stippling where the probes of the morel had gone down into his skin for nourishment.

"Has it gone?" he asked, and his voice was his own again.

"Look at it," she said. With her free hand, she tilted the gourd over so that he could see in.

For a long while he stared down at the still-living morel, helpless and motionless now, lying like excrement in the gourd. His inner vision was looking back—more with amazement now than fear—at the things that had been since the morel first dropped on him in the forests of Nomansland, the things that had passed like a dream: how he had travelled through lands and performed actions and above all held knowledge in his mind in ways that would have been unknown to his former free self.

He saw how all this had come about under the agency of the fungus that now was no more potent than a burnt mess of food in the bottom of a dish; and quite coolly he saw how he had at first welcomed this stimulus, for it had helped him overcome the limitations natural to him. Only when the morel's basic needs conflicted with his own had the process become evil, driving him almost literally out of his own mind, so that in working to the dictates of the morel he had almost preyed on his own kind.

It was over. The parasite was defeated. He would never again hear the inner voice of the morel twanging through his brain.

At that, loneliness more than triumph filled him. But he searched wildly along the corridors of his memory and thought, He has left me something good: I can evaluate, I can order my mind, I can remember what he taught me—and he knew so much.

Now it seemed to him that for all the havoc the morel had caused, he had found Gren's mind like a little stagnant pool and left it like a living sea—and it was with pity he looked down into the bowl that Yattmur held out to him.

"Don't weep, Gren," he heard Yattmur's voice say. "We are safe, we are all safe, and you will be all right."

He laughed shakily.

"I shall be all right," he agreed. He formed his scarred face into a smile and stroked her arms. "We shall all be all right."

Then reaction hit him. He rolled over and was instantly asleep.

Yattmur was busy, when Gren woke, attending to Laren who squealed with delight as she washed him by the mountain stream. The tattooed women were also there, carrying water back and forth to pour over the catchy-carry-kind on his slab, while nearby stood the carrying man, cramped into his habitual gesture of servitude. Of the tummy-bellies, there was no sign.

He sat up gingerly. His face was puffy but his head clear; what then was the jarring he could feel that had woken him? He caught a glimpse of movement from the corner of his eye, and turning saw a trickle of stones roll down a gully some way off. At another point, more stones rolled.

"An earthquake is in progress," said Sodal Ye in a cavernous voice. "I have discussed it with your mate Yattmur and have told her there is no need for alarm. The world is ending on schedule, according to my predictions."

Gren rose to his feet and said, "You have a big voice, fish face; who are you?"

"I delivered you from the devouring fungus, little man, for I am the Sodal and Prophet of the Nightside Mountains, and all the denizens of the mountains hear what I have to say."

Gren was still thinking this over when Yattmur came up and said, "You've slept so long since the morel left you. We too have slept, and now we must prepare to move."

"To move? Where is there to go from here?"

"I will explain to you as I explained to Yattmur," said the sodal, blinking as his women threw another gourd full of water over him. "I devote my life to travelling these mountains, giving out the Word of Earth. Now it is time for me to return to the Bountiful Basin, where my kind live, to gather fresh instructions. The Basin lies on the fringe of the Lands of Perpetual Twilight; if I take you as far as that, you can easily return to the eternal forests where you live. I will be your guide and you shall help attend me on the way."

Seeing Gren hesitate, Yattmur said, "You know we cannot stay here on Big Slope. We were carried here against our wishes. Now we have the chance to go, we must take it."

"If you wish it, it shall be so, though I'm tired of travel."

The earth trembled again. With unconscious humour, Yattmur said, "We must leave the mountain before it leaves us." She added, "And we must persuade the tummy-bellies to come with us. If they stay here, either the sharp-fur mountainears or starvation will kill them."

"Oh no," Gren said. "They've been trouble enough. Let the wretched creatures remain here. I don't want them with us."

"Since they don't want to come with you, that question is settled," said the sodal with a flick of his tail. "Now, let us move, since I must not be kept waiting."

They had next to no possessions, so close were their lives to nature. To make ready was merely to check their weapons, to stow a little food for carrying and to cast a backward glance at the cave that had sheltered the birth of Laren. Catching sight of a nearby gourd and its contents, Gren asked, "What about the morel?"

"Leave it there to fester," Yattmur said.

"We take the morel with us. My women will carry it," said the sodal.

His women were already busy, their tattoo lines merging with their wrinkles as they strained to lift the sodal from his perch and on to the back of his carrying man. Between themselves they exchanged only grunts, although one of them was capable of making monosyllabic replies accompanied by gesture when the sodal addressed her, using a tongue Gren did not recognize. He watched fascinated until Sodal Ye was firmly in place, clutched round the middle by the stooped man.

"How long has that poor wretch been doomed to carry you about?" he asked.

"The destiny of his race—it is a proud one—is to serve the catch-carry-kind. He was trained to it early. He neither knows nor wishes to know any other life."

They began to move, going downhill with the two slave women leading. Yattmur glanced back to see the three tummy-bellies staring mournfully at them from their cave. She raised her hand, beckoning and calling to them. Slowly they stood up and began to jostle forward, almost tripping over one another in their efforts to stay close together.

"Come on!" she called encouragingly. "You fellows come with us and we'll look after you."

"They've been trouble enough to us," Gren said. Stooping, he collected a handful of stones and flung them.

One tummy-belly was hit in the groin, one on the shoulder, before they broke and fled back into the cave, crying aloud that nobody loved them.

"You are too cruel, Gren. We should not leave them at the mercy of the sharp-furs."

"I tell you I've had enough of those creatures. We are better on our own." He patted her shoulder, but she remained unconvinced.

As they moved down Big Slope, the cries of the tummy-bellies died behind them. Nor would their voices ever reach Gren and Yattmur again.

26

They descended the ragged flank of Big Slope and the shadows of the valley rose up to meet them. A moment came when they waded in dark up to their ankles; then it rose rapidly, swallowing them, as the sun was hidden by a range of hills ahead.

The pool of darkness in which they now moved, and in which they were to travel for some while, was not total. Though at present no cloud banks overhead reflected the light of the sun, the frequent lightning traced out their path for them.

Where the rivulets of Big Slope gathered into a fair-sized stream, the way became precipitous, for the water had carved a gully for itself, and they were forced to follow along its higher bank, going in single file along a steep cliff edge. The need for care slowed them. They descended laboriously round boulders, many of them clearly dislodged by the recent earth tremors. Apart from the sound of their footsteps, the only noise to compete with the stream was the regular groaning of the carrying man.

Soon a roaring somewhere ahead told them of a waterfall. Peering into the gloom, they saw a light. It was burning on what, as far as they could discern, was the lip of the cliff. The procession halted, bunching protectively together.

"What is it?" Gren asked. "What sort of creature lives in this miserable pit?"

Nobody answered.

Sodal Ye grunted something to the talking woman, who in turn grunted at her mute companion. The mute companion began to vanish where she stood, rigid in an attitude of attention.

Yattmur clasped Gren's arm. It was the first time he had seen this disappearing act. Shadows all about them made it the more uncanny, as a ragged incline showed through her body. For a while her tattoo lines hung seemingly unsupported in the gloom. He strained his eyes to see. She had gone, was as intangible as the resonance of falling water.

They held their tableau until she returned.

Wordlessly the woman made a few gestures, which the other woman interpreted into grunts for the sodal's benefit. Slapping his tail round his porter's calves to get him moving again, the

225

sodal said, "It's safe. One or two of the sharp-furs are there, possibly guarding a bridge, but they'll go away."

"How do you know?" Gren demanded.

"It will help if we make a noise," said Sodal Ye, ignoring Gren's question. Immediately he let out a deep baying call that startled Yattmur and Gren out of their wits and set the baby wailing.

As they moved forward, the light flickered and went over the lip of the cliff. Arriving at the point where it had been, they could look down a steep slope. Lightning revealed six or eight of the snouted creatures bouncing and leaping into the ravine, one of them carrying a crude torch. Ever and again they looked back over their shoulders, barking invective.

"How did you know they'd go away?" Gren asked.

"Don't talk so much. We must go carefully here."

They had come to a sort of bridge: one cliff of the gully had fallen forward in a solid slab, causing the stream to tunnel beneath it before splashing down into the nearby ravine; the slab rested against the opposite cliff, forming an arch over the flood. Because the way looked so broken and uncertain, its hazards increased in the twilight, the party moved hesitantly. Yet they had hardly stepped on to the crumbling bridge when a host of tiny beings clattered up startlingly from beneath their feet.

The air flaked into black flying fragments.

Savage with startlement, Gren struck out, punching at small bodies as they rocketed past him. Then they had lifted. Looking up, he saw a host of creatures circling and dipping over their heads.

"Only bats," said Sodal Ye casually. "Move on. You human creatures have a poor turn of speed."

They moved. Again the lightning flashed, bleaching the world into a momentary still life. In the ruts at their feet, and just below them, and over the bridge side, reaching down to the tumbling waters, glistened such spiders' webs as Gren and Yattmur had never seen before, like a multitude of beards growing into the river.

She exclaimed about them, and the sodal said loftily, "You don't realize the facts behind the curious sight you see here. How could you, being mere landlivers?—Intelligence has always come from the seas. We sodals are the only keepers of the world's wisdom."

"You certainly didn't concentrate on modesty," Gren said, as he helped Yattmur on to the farther side.

"The bats and the spiders were inhabitants of the old cool world, many eons ago," said the sodal, "but the growth of the vegetable kingdom forced them to adopt new ways of life or perish. So they gradually moved away from the fiercest competition into the dark, to which the bats at least were predisposed. And in so doing the two species formed an alliance."

He went on discoursing with the smoothness of a preacher even while his porter, aided by the tattooed women, heaved and strained and groaned to pull him up a broken bank on to firm ground. The voice poured forth with assurance, as thick and velvety as the night itself.

"The spider needs warmth for her eggs to hatch, or more warmth than she can get here. So she lays them, sews them into a bag, and the bat obligingly carries them up to Big Slope or one of these other peaks that catch the sun. When they hatch, he obligingly brings the progeny back again. Nor does he work for nothing.

"The grown spiders weave two webs, one an ordinary one, the other half in and half out of the water, so that the lower part of it forms a net below the surface. They catch fish or small living things in it and then hoist them out into the air for the bats to eat. Any number of similar strange things go on here of which you land-dwellers would have no knowledge."

They were now travelling along an escarpment that sloped down into a plain. Emerging as they were from under the bulk of a mountain, they slowly gained a better view of the terrain round about. From the tissue of shadows soared an occasional crimson cone of a hill lofty enough to bathe its cap in sunlight.

227

Gathering cloud threw a glow over the land that changed minute by minute. Landmarks were thus by turns revealed and hidden as though by drifting curtains. Gradually the clouds blanketed the sun itself, so that they had to travel with additional caution through a thicker obscurity.

Over to their left appeared a wavering light. If it was the one they had seen by the ravine, then the sharp-furs kept pace with them. The sight reminded Gren of his earlier question.

"How does this woman of yours vanish, Sodal?" he asked.

"We have a long way yet to go before reaching the Bountiful Basin," declared the sodal. "Perhaps it will therefore amuse me to answer your question fully, since you seem a mite more interesting than most of your kind.

"The history of the lands through which we travel can never be pieced together, for the beings that lived here have vanished leaving no records but their unwanted bones. Yet there are legends. My race of the catchy-carry-kind are great travellers; we have travelled widely and through many generations; and we have collected these legends.

"So we learned that the Lands of Perpetual Twilight, for all their apparent emptiness, have offered shelter to many creatures. Always these creatures are going the same way.

"Always they come from the bright green lands over which the sun burns. Always they are heading either for extinction or for the lands of Night Eternal—and often the two mean the same thing.

"Each wave of creatures may stay here for several generations. But always it is forced farther and farther from the sun by its successors.

"Once there flourished here a race we know as the Pack People because they hunted in packs—as the sharp-furs will do in a crisis, but with far more organization. Like the sharp-furs, the Pack People were sharp of teeth and brought forth living young, but they moved always on all-fours.

"The Pack People were mammal but non-human. Such distinctions are vague to me, for Distinguishing is not one of my subjects, but your kind once knew the Pack People as wolves, I believe.

"After the Pack People came a hardy race of some kind of human, who brought with them four-footed creatures which supplied them with food and clothing, and with which they mated."

"Can that be possible?" Gren asked.

"I only repeat to you the old legends. Possibilities are no concern of mine. Anyhow, these people were called Shipperds. They drove out the Packers and were in turn superseded by the Howlers, the species that legend says grew from the matings between the Shipperds and their creatures. Some Howlers still survive, but they were mainly killed in the next invasion, when the Heavers appeared. The Heavers were nomadic—I've run into a few of them, but they're savage brutes. Next came another off-shoot of humanity, the Arablers, a race with some small gift for cultivating crops, and no other abilities.

"The Arablers were quickly overrun by the sharp-furs, or Bamboons, to give them their proper name.

"The sharp-furs have lived in this region in greater or lesser strength for ages. Indeed, the myths say they wrested the gift of cooking from the Arablers, the gift of sledge transport from the Heavers, the gift of fire from the Packers, the gift of speech from the Shipperds, and so on. How true that is, I don't know. The fact remains that the sharp-furs have overrun the land.

"They are capricious and untrustworthy. Sometimes they will obey me, sometimes not. Fortunately they are afraid of the powers of my species.

"I should not be surprised if you tree-dwelling humans—Sandwichers, did I hear the belly men call you?—aren't the forerunners of the next wave of invaders. Not that you'd be aware of it if you were. . . ."

Much of this monologue was lost on Gren and Yattmur, particularly as they had to concentrate on their progress across a stony valley.

"And who are these people you have as slaves here?" Gren asked, indicating the carrying man and the women.

"As I should have thought you might have gathered, these are specimens of Arablers. They would all have died out but for our protection.

"The Arablers, you see, are devolving. I may possibly explain what I mean by that some other time. They have devolved furthest. They will turn into vegetables if sterility does not obliterate the race first. Long ago they lost even the art of speech. Although I say lost, this was in fact an achievement, for they could only survive at all by renouncing everything that stood between them and vegetative level.

"This sort of change is not surprising under present conditions on this world, but with it went a more unusual transformation. The Arablers lost the notion of passing time; after all, there is no longer anything to remind us daily or seasonally of time: so the Arablers in their decline forgot it entirely. For them there was simply the individual life span. It was—it is, the only time span they are capable of recognizing: the period-of-being.

"So they have developed a co-extensive life, living where they need along that span."

Yattmur and Gren looked blankly through the gloom at each other.

"Do you mean these women can move forward or backward in time?" Yattmur asked.

"That wasn't what I said: nor was it how the Arablers would express it. Their minds are not like mine nor even like yours, but when for instance we came to the bridge guarded by the sharp-fur with the torch, I got one of the women to move along her period-of-being to see if we crossed the bridge uneventfully.

"She returned and reported that we did. We advanced and she was proved right, as usual.

"Of course they only operate when danger threatens; this spanning process is primarily a form of defence. For instance, when Yattmur brought us food the first time, I made the spanning woman span ahead to see if it poisoned us. When she returned and reported us still alive, then I knew it was safe to eat.

"And similarly when I first saw you with the sharp-furs and —what do you call them?—the belly-tummy men, I sent the spanning woman to see if you would attack us. So you see even a miserable race like the Arablers have their uses!"

They were forging slowly ahead through foothills, travelling through a deep green gloom nourished by sunshine reflected from cloud banks overhead. Ever and again they caught a glimpse of moving lights over on their left flank; the sharp-furs were still following them, and had added more torches to their original one.

As the sodal talked, Gren stared with new curiosity at the two Arabler women leading their party.

Because they were naked, he could see how little their sexual characteristics were developed. Their hair was scanty on the head, non-existent on the mons veneris. Their hips were narrow, their breasts flat and pendulous, although, as far as one could judge their age, they did not seem old.

They walked with neither enthusiasm nor hesitation, never glancing back. One of the women carried on her head the gourd that held the morel.

Through Gren ran a sort of awe to feel how different must be the understandings of these women from his own; what could their lives be like, how would their thoughts flow, when their period-of-being was not a consecutive but a concurrent vista?

He asked Sodal Ye, "Are these Arablers happy?"

The catchy-carry-kind laughed throatily.

"I've never thought to ask them such a question."

"Ask them now."

With an impatient flip of his tail, the sodal said, "All you human and similar kinds are cursed with inquisitiveness. It's a horrible trait that will get you nowhere. Why should I speak to them just to gratify your curiosity?

"Besides, it needs absolute nullity of intelligence to be able to span; to fail to distinguish between past and present and future needs a great concentration of ignorance. The Arablers have no language at all; once introduce them to the idea of verbalization and their wings are clipped. If they talk, they can't span. If they span, they can't talk.

"That's why it is always necessary for me to have two women with me—women preferably, because they are even more ignorant than the men. One woman has been taught a few words so that I can give her commands; she communicates them by gesture to her friend, who can thus be made to span when danger threatens. It is all rather roughly devised, but it has saved me much trouble on my journeys."

"What about the poor fellow who carries you?" Yattmur asked.

From Sodal Ye came a vibrating growl of contempt.

"A lazy brute, nothing but a lazy brute! I've ridden him since he was a lad and he's very near worn out already. Hup, you idle monster! Get along there, or we'll never be home."

Much more the sodal told them. To some of it Gren and Yattmur responded with concealed anger. To some of it they paid no heed. The sodal orated unceasingly, until his voice became merely another factor in the lightning-cluttered gloom.

They kept moving even when rain fell so heavily that it turned the plain about them to mud. The clouds swam in a green light; in their discomfort they felt that it was growing warmer. Still the rain fell. Because nowhere in the open country afforded shelter, they kept doggedly trudging forward. It was as though they walked in the middle of a bowl of swirling soup.

By the time the rainstorm died, they had begun to climb again. Yattmur insisted on stopping for the baby's sake. The sodal, who had enjoyed the rain, reluctantly agreed. Under a bank they managed with difficulty to start a poor smouldering grass fire. The baby was fed. They all ate sparingly.

"We are nearly at Bountiful Basin," declared Sodal Ye. "From

232

the tops of this next range of mountains you will see it, its sweet salt waters dark, but with one long bar of sunlight falling across it. Ah, it'll be good to be back in the sea. It's lucky for you land-goers that we are a dedicated race, or we'd never leave the water in exchange for your benighted medium. Well, prophecy is our burden and we must shoulder it cheerfully. . . ."

He began shouting at the women to hurry and fetch more grass and roots for the fire. They had placed him on top of the bank. The unfortunate carrying man was down in the hollow, standing with his arms above his head almost on top of the fire, letting smoke swirl round him as he attempted to induce heat into his body.

Seeing that Sodal Ye's attention was distracted, Gren hurried over to the man. He grasped his shoulder.

"Can you understand what I am saying?" he asked. "Do you speak in my tongue, friend?"

The fellow never raised his head. It hung down on to his chest as if his neck was broken, rolling slightly as the man muttered something unintelligible. When next lightning spread its palsy over the world, Gren glimpsed scars about the top of the man's spinal cord. In a flash of understanding as swift as the lightning, Gren knew the man had been mutilated so that his head would not lift.

Dropping on to one knee, Gren peered upward at that bowed countenance. He had a view of a twisted mouth and an eye like a gleaming coal.

"How far can I trust this catchy-carry-kind, friend?" he asked.

The mouth writhed slowly, as if from an agony of which it had long grown bored. It dropped words thick as matter.

It said: "No good . . . I no good . . . break, fall, die filth . . . see, I finish . . . one more climb. . . . Ye of all sins—Ye you carry . . . you strong back . . . you carry Ye . . . he know. . . . I filth finish. . . ."

Something splashed on to Gren's hand as he fell back; whether it was tears or saliva he could not tell.

233

"Thanks, friend, we'll see about all that," he said. Moving over to where Yattmur was cleaning Laren, he told her, "I felt in my bones this talkative fish was not to be trusted. He has a plan to use me as his beast of burden when this carrying man dies—or so the man says, and he should know the ways of the catchy-carry-kind by now."

Before Yattmur could answer, the sodal let out a roar.

"Something's coming!" he said. "Women, get me mounted at once. Yattmur, smother that fire. Gren, come up here and see what you can see."

Scrambling on to the top of the bank, Gren peered about while the women pulled Sodal Ye into position on the carrying man's back. Even above the noise of their panting, Gren heard the other sounds that the sodal must have heard: a distant and insistent yowling and howling that rose or fell in angry rhythm. It sent the blood draining from his face.

He saw with ill ease a group of about ten lights spread out not far away on the plain, but it was from another quarter that the eerie sound came. Then moving figures caught his eye; he strained to observe them more closely, his heart thudding.

"I can see them," he reported. "They—they glow in the dark."

"They are Howlers then, for sure—the man-animal species I told you of. Are they coming this way?"

"It looks like it. What can we do?"

"Get down with Yattmur and stay quiet. Howlers are like sharp-furs; they can be nasty if they are upset. I'll send my woman spanning to see what is happening soon."

The pantomime of grunting and gesture was undergone, both before the woman vanished and after she reappeared. All the while the eerie howling grew in volume.

"The woman spanned and saw us climbing up the slope ahead, so we evidently shall not be harmed. Just wait quietly until the Howlers have gone by; then we will move on. Yattmur, keep that baby child of yours quiet."

Somewhat reassured by what the sodal said, they stood by the bank.

Presently the Howlers sped past, travelling in a single file not more than a stone's throw away. Their yipping cry, designed to intimidate, rose and fell as they went. It was impossible to say whether they ran or leaped or hopped over the ground. So fast and recklessly they travelled, they were like visions from a maniac's dream.

Though they glowed with a dim white light, their shapes were ill-defined. Were their outlines mockeries of human figures? It was clear at least how tall they were, and as thin as wraiths, before they went bounding away across the plain, trailing their awful cry behind them.

Gren found he was clutching Yattmur and Laren and trembling.

"What were those things?" Yattmur asked.

"I told you, woman, they were the Howlers," said the sodal, "the race about which I was telling you, that was driven into the lands of Night Eternal. That party was probably on a hunt-. ing expedition and is now returning home. We too must be on the move. The sooner we get over this next mountain, the better pleased I shall be."

So they moved on again, Gren and Yattmur without the ease of mind they had previously enjoyed.

Because Gren developed the habit of glancing back, he was the one to see that the lights on their left flank which they took to be the torches of sharp-furs were coming nearer. Occasionally a bark floated to him on the stillness like a twig drifting across water.

"Those sharp-furs are closing in on us," he told the sodal. "They've followed us almost the whole journey, and if we aren't careful they'll catch us on this hill."

"It's unlike them to follow so consistently. They generally forget a course of action almost as soon as they have thought of it. Something ahead must be attracting them—a feast, possibly.

All the same, they're bold in the dark; we don't want to risk attack. Move faster. Hup, you ambling Arabler, hup ho!"

But the torches gained on them. As they ascended up the long, long pull of the mountain, the filtered light overhead gradually increased, until they could see a blur of bodies about the torch-bearers. A considerable mob of creatures was pursuing them, although as yet at some distance.

Their worries were piling up. Yattmur observed more creatures on their right flank, heading tangentially towards them. Faint barks and yippings echoed through the wastes. Un-doubtedly they were being overtaken by large numbers of sharp-furs.

Now the small party was leaning forward against the drag of the hill and almost running in its anxiety.

"We'll be safe when we get to the top. Hup ho!" cried the sodal encouragingly. "Not much farther before we see Bountiful Basin. Hup hey there, you lazy, ugly brute!"

Without word or warning his carrying man collapsed under him, pitching him forward into a gully. For a moment the sodal lay half-stunned on his back; then a flick of his powerful tail put him right way up again. He began to curse inventively at his steed.

As for the tattooed women, they stopped, and the one carrying the gourd with the morel in set it down on the ground, but neither went over to the aid of the fallen man. Gren did that, running to the bundle of bones and turning it over as gently as possible. The carrying man made no sound. The eye like an ember had closed.

Breaking into Sodal Ye's swearing, he said angrily, "What have you to complain of? Didn't this poor wretch carry you un-til the last lungful of air left his body? You flogged all you could out of him, so be content! He's dead now, and he's free of you, and he'll never carry you again."

"Then you must carry me," answered the sodal without hesitation. "Unless we get out of here quickly, we shall all be

236

torn to bits by those packs of sharp-furs. Listen to them—
they're getting nearer! So look smart, man, if you know what's
good for you, and make these women lift me on to your back."

"Oh no! You're staying there in the gully, sodal. We can get
on more quickly without you. You've had your last ride."

"No!" The sodal's voice rose like a foghorn. "You don't
know what the crest of this mountain's like. There's a secret
way down the other side into Bountiful Basin that I can find and
these women can't. You'll be trapped on the top without me,
that I promise you. The sharp-furs will have you."

"Oh Gren, I'm so afraid for Laren. Let's take the sodal rather
than stand here arguing, please."

He stared at Yattmur through the dull dawnlight. She was a
blur, a chalk drawing on a rock face, yet he clenched his fist as if
she were a real antagonist.

"Do you want to see me as a beast of burden?"

"Yes, yes, anything rather than have us all torn apart! It's
only over one mountain, isn't it? You carried the morel far
enough without complaint."

Bitterly he motioned to the tattooed women.

"That's better," said the sodal, wriggling between Gren's en-
circling arms. "Just try and keep your head a little lower, so that
no discomfort is caused to my throat. Ah, better still. Fine, yes,
you'll learn. Forward, hup ho!"

Head well down, back bent, Gren struggled up the slope with
the catchy-carry-kind on top of him, Yattmur carrying the babe
beside him and the two women going on ahead. A desolate
chorus of sharp-fur cries floated to them. They scrambled along
a stream bed with water washing cold about their knees, helped
each other up a precipitous gravel bank, and came on to less
taxing ground.

Yattmur could see that over the next rise lay sunshine. When
she thought to take in the landscape about them, she observed a
new and more cheerful world of slopes and hill tops showing all

round. The sharp-fur parties had fallen from view behind boulders.

Now the sky was streaked with light. An occasional traverser sailed overhead, making for the night side or heading up into space. It was like a sign of hope.

Still they had some way to go. But at last the sun lay hot on their backs and after a long steady pull they stood panting on the crest of the mountain. The other side of it fell away in a great ravaged cliff down which it would be impossible for anything to climb.

Nestling in a hundred intersecting curtains of shadow lay an arm of the sea, wide and serene. Fanning straight across it, casting a glow over the whole basin of cliffs in which the sea rested, was a swathe of light, just as Sodal Ye had predicted. Creatures moved in the water, leaving their marks momentarily upon it. On a strip of beach, other figures moved, winding between primitive white huts as tiny as pearls in the distance.

The sodal alone was not staring down.

His eyes went to the sun and to the narrow section of fully illumined world that could be seen from this vantage point, the lands where the sun shone perpetually. There the brilliance was almost intolerable. He needed no instruments to tell him that the heat and light had increased in intensity even since they left Big Slope.

"As I predicted," he cried, "all things are melting into light. The day is coming when the Great Day comes and all creatures become a part of the evergreen universe. I must talk to you about it some time."

The lightning which had almost played itself out over the lands of Perpetual Twilight still flittered over the bright side. One particularly vivid shaft struck down into the mighty forest —and stayed visible. Writhing like a snake caught between earth and heaven it remained; and from the base it began to turn green. Green rose up it into the sky, and the shaft steadied and thickened as it went, until something like a pointing finger

238

stretched into the canopy of space and the tip of it was lost to view in the hazy atmosphere.

"Aaaah, now I have seen the sign of signs!" said the sodal. "Now I see and now I know the end of the Earth draws near."

"What in the name of terror is it?" Gren said, squinting up from under his burden at the green column.

"The spores, the dust, the hopes, the growth, the essence of the centuries of Earth's green fuse, no less. Up it goes, ascending, for new fields. The ground beneath that column must be baked to brick! You heat a whole world for half an eternity, stew it heavy with its own fecundity, and then apply extra current: and on the reflected energy rises the extract of life, buoyed up and borne into space on a galactic flux."

The island of the tall cliff returned to Gren's mind. Though he did not know what the sodal meant by talking of extracts of life being buoyed up on galactic fluxes, it sounded like his experience in the strange cave with eyes. He wished he could ask the morel about it.

"The sharp-furs are coming!" Yattmur cried. "Listen! I can hear them shouting."

Looking back down the way they had come, she saw tiny figures in the gloaming, some still bearing smoky torches, climbing slowly but climbing steadily, swarming uphill mainly on all fours.

"Where do we go?" Yattmur asked. "They'll be upon us if you don't stop talking, Sodal."

Shaken out of his contemplation, Sodal Ye said, "We have to move higher up the crest of the mountain. Only a little way. Behind this big spur sticking up ahead is a secret way leading down among the rocks. There we strike a passage leading right through the cliff down to Bountiful Basin. Don't worry—those wretches have some distance to climb yet."

Gren had started moving towards the spur before Sodal Ye stopped speaking.

239

Anxiously propping Laren over one shoulder, Yattmur ran forward. Then she paused.

"Sodal," she said. "Look! One of the traversers has crashed behind the spur. Your escape way will be completely blocked!"

The spur stood up crazily on the sheer edge of the cliff, like a chimney built on top of a steeply-pitched roof. Behind it, massive and firm, lay the bulk of a traverser. Only the fact that they viewed its shadowed side, which rose up like part of the ground, had prevented their noticing it earlier.

Sodal Ye let out a great cry.

"How are we to get under that great vegetable?" he demanded, and he slapped Gren's legs with his tail in a fury of frustration.

Gren staggered and fell against the woman carrying the gourd. They sprawled together on the grass while the sodal flopped beside them, bellowing.

The woman gave a cry of something between pain and rage, covering her face while her nose trickled blood. She took no notice when the sodal croaked at her. As Yattmur helped Gren up, the sodal said, "Curse her dung-devouring descendants, I'm telling her to make the spanning woman get spanning and see how we can escape from here. Kick her and make her pay attention—and then get me on to your back again and see you're less careless in future."

He started shouting at the woman again.

Without warning, she jumped up. Her face was as distorted as a squeezed fruit. Seizing the gourd by her side, she brought it swinging down hard on to the sodal's skull. The blow knocked him unconscious. The gourd split under the impact, and the morel slid out like treacle, covering the sqdal's head with a sort of lethargic contentment.

Gren's and Yattmur's eyes met, worried, questioning. The spanning woman's mouth split open. She cackled soundlessly. Her companion sat down to weep; her period-of-being's one moment of revolt had come and gone.

"Now what do we do?" asked Gren.

"Let's see if we can find the sodal's bolthole; that's the first worry," Yattmur said.

He touched her arm for comfort.

"If the traverser's alive, perhaps we can light a fire under it and drive it away," he said.

Leaving the Arabler women to wait vacantly beside Sodal Ye, they moved up towards the traverser.

27

As the sun's output of radiation increased towards that day, no longer so far distant, when it would turn nova, so the growth of vegetation had increased to undisputed supremacy, over-whelming all other kinds of life, driving them either to extinction or to refuge in the twilight zone. The traversers, great spider-like monsters of vegetable origin that sometimes grew up to a mile in length, were the culmination of the might of the kingdom of plants.

Hard radiation had become a necessity for them. The first vegetable astronauts of the hothouse world, they travelled between Earth and Moon long after man had rolled up his noisy affairs and retired to the trees from whence he came.

Gren and Yattmur moved along under the green and black fibrous bulk of the creature, Yattmur hugging Laren, who gazed at everything with alert eyes. Sensing danger, Gren paused.

He looked up. A dark face stared down at him from high up that monstrous flank. After a startled moment, he made out more than one face. Concealed in the fuzz covering the traverser was a row of human beings.

Instinctively he drew his knife.

Seeing they were observed, the watchers emerged from hiding and began to swarm down the flank of the traverser. Ten of them appeared.

"Get back!" Gren said urgently, turning to Yattmur.

"But the sharp-furs——"

The attackers took them by surprise. Spreading wings or cloaks, they jumped down from a height well above Gren's head. They started to surround Gren and Yattmur. Each one brandished a stick or a sword.

"Stand steady or I'll run you through!" Gren shouted savagely, leaping in front of Yattmur and the baby.

"Gren! You are Gren of the group of Lily-yo!"

The figures had stopped. One of them, the one who exclaimed, came forward with open arms, dropping her sword.

He knew her dark face!

"Living shades! Lily-yo! Lily-yo! Is it you?"

"It is I, Gren, and no other!"

And now two others were coming up to him, crying in pleasure. He recognized them, faces forgotten but ever familiar, the faces of two adult members of his tribal group, Haris the man, and Flor, clasping his hand. Although they were so changed, he hardly noticed that in his surprise at meeting them again. He looked at their eyes rather than their wings.

Seeing his questioning gaze run over their faces, Haris said, "You are a man now, Gren. We too have altered much. These others with us are our friends. We have returned from the True World, flying through space itself in the belly of this traverser. The creature became ill on the way and crashed here, in this miserable land of shadows. With no way to get back to the warm forests, we have been caught here for far too long, suffering attacks from all sorts of unimaginable creatures."

"And you're about to suffer the worst one yet," Gren said. He was not pleased to see people that he admired like Haris and Lily-yo consorting with flymen. "Our enemies gather against us. Time for stories later, friends—and I'll guess mine is more strange than yours—because a great pack, two great packs, of sharp-furs are nearly on us."

"Sharp-furs you call them?" Lily-yo said. "We could see a little of their approach from on top of the traverser. What makes

242

you think they are after us? In this miserable land of starvation they must surely be after the traverser for food?"

To Gren this idea was unexpected; yet he recognized its likelihood. Only the considerable bulk of food the traverser represented would have drawn so many sharp-furs so far so consistently. He turned to see what Yattmur thought. She was not there.

Immediately, he pulled out the knife he had just sheathed and jumped round, searching for her, calling her name. The members of Lily-yo's band who did not know him fingered their swords anxiously, but he ignored them.

Yattmur stood a short way off, clutching their child and scowling in his direction. She had gone back to where the sodal lay; the Arabler women stood fruitlessly by, gazing ahead. Muttering angrily, Gren pushed by Haris to go to her.

"What are you doing?" he called. "Bring Laren here."

"Come and get him if you want him," she replied. "I will have nothing to do with these strange savages. You belong to me—why do you turn from me to them? Why do you talk to them? Who are they?"

"O shades protect me from foolish women! You don't understand——"

He stopped.

They had left their escape from the ridge too late.

Moving in an impressive silence, perhaps because they needed their breath, the first lines of sharp-furs appeared over the crest of the hill.

They halted on confronting the humans, but the back ranks jostled them forward. With their mantles standing out stiff about their shoulders and their teeth bared, they did not have the look of friends. One or two of them wore the ridiculous helmets shaped out of gourds on their heads.

Through cold lips, Yattmur said, "Some of these were the ones who promised they would help the tummy-bellies to get home."

"How can you tell? They are so much alike."

"That old one with the yellow whiskers and a finger missing—I'm sure I recognize him at least."

Lily-yo, coming up with her group, asked, "What are we going to do? Will these beasts trouble us if we let them have the traverser?"

Gren made no reply. He walked forward until he stood directly in front of the yellow-whiskered creature Yattmur had pointed out.

"We bear you no ill-will, sharp-fur bamboon people. You know we never fought you when we were on Big Slope. Do you have the three tummy-belly men who were our companions with you?"

Without answering, Yellow Whisker shambled round to consult with his friends. The nearest sharp-furs reared upon their hind legs and talked yappingly to each other. Finally Yellow Whisker turned back to Gren, showing his fangs as he spoke. He cuddled something in his arms.

"Yip yip yap yes, skinny one, the bouncing-bellies are wiff wiff with us. See! Look! Catch!"

With a quick motion, he threw something at Gren—who was so close he could do nothing but catch it.

It was the severed head of one of the tummy-bellies.

Gren acted without thought. Dropping the head, he flung himself forward in scarlet fury, thrusting out with his knife as he did so. His blade caught the yellow-whiskered sharp-fur in the stomach before he could dodge. As the creature staggered sideways screaming, Gren grabbed his grey paw with both hands. He spun completely round on one heel, and cast Yellow Whiskers right over the edge of the tall cliff.

Absolute silence fell, a silence of surprise, as Yellow Whiskers' cries died.

In the next moment, our fate is decided, Gren thought. His blood ran too high for him to care. He sensed Yattmur, Lily-yo, and the other humans behind him, but did not deign to look back at them.

Yattmur leant forward to the broken and bloodied object lying at their feet. The head by its severance had been reduced to a mere thing, a thing of horror. Looking into the watery jelly that had been eyes, Yattmur read there the fate of all three tummy-belly men.

Unheard she cried, "And they were always so gentle with Laren!"

Then the noise broke out behind her.

A terrible roar burst forth, a roar of alien cadence and power, a roar—breaking over their heads so unexpectedly—that turned their blood to snow. The sharp-furs cried in awe: then they turned about, jostling and fighting to get back into the safety of the shadows below the crest of the mountain.

Deafened, Gren looked round. Lily-yo and her companions were heading back towards the dying traverser. Yattmur was trying to pacify the baby. Hands over their heads, the Arabler women lay prone on the ground.

Again the noise came, swelling with an anguished despair. Sodal Ye had recovered consciousness and cried aloud his wrath. And then, opening his fleshy mouth with its huge lower lip, he spoke, in words that only gradually merged into sense.

"Where are your empty-headed heads, you creatures of the darkling plains? You have toads in the head, not to understand my prophecies where the green pillars grow. Growing is symmetry, up and down, and what was called decay is not decay but the second part of growth. One process, you toad-heads—the process of devolution, that carries you down into the green well from which you came. . . . I'm lost in the mazes—Gren! Gren, like a mole I tunnel through an earth of understanding. . . . Gren, the nightmares—Gren, from the fish's belly I call to you. Can you hear me? It's I—your old ally the morel!"

"Morel?"

In his astonishment, Gren dropped to his knees before the catchy-carry-kind. Blank-faced, he stared at the leprous brown crown that now adorned its head. As he stared, the eyes opened, filmily at first, and then they focused on him.

"Gren! I was near death. . . . Ah, the pain of consciousness. . . . Listen, man, it is I, your morel, who speaks. I hold the sodal in check, and am using his faculties, as once I had to use yours; there's so much richness in his mind—coupling it with my own knowledge . . . ah, I see clearly not just this little world but all the green galaxy, the evergreen universe. . . ."

Frantically, Gren jumped up.

"Morel, are you crazed? Do you not see what a position we are in here, all about to be killed by these sharp-furs when they gather courage to charge? What are we to do? If you are truly here, if you are sane, help us!"

"I'm not crazed—unless to be the only wise creature in a toad-minded world is to be crazed. . . . All right, Gren, I tell you help comes! Look into the sky!"

The landscape had long been suffused with an uncanny light. Away in the distant and unbroken ranks of jungle stood the green pillar, joined now by another which had formed some way off. They seemed to taint the lower atmosphere with their glow, so that it did not surprise Gren to see cloud bars of viridescent hue striping the sky. From one of these clouds dropped a traverser. Falling at leisurely speed, it seemed to aim at the promontory on which Gren and the others stood.

"Is it coming here, morel?" Gren asked. Though he resented the resurrection of the tyrant that had recently sapped his life blood, he saw that the fungus, dependent on the legless sodal, could offer him only help, not harm.

"It's descending here," the morel answered. "You and Yattmur and the baby come and lie down here so that it does not crush you when it lands. It is probably coming to mate—to cross-fertilize—with the dying traverser. Directly it gets down, we must climb on to it. You must carry me, Gren, do you understand? Then I'll tell you what else to do."

As he spoke through the sodal's blubber mouth, wind ruffled the grass. The hairy body overhead expanded until it filled almost their whole view: and gently the traverser landed on the brink of the cliff, perching on top of its dying mate. Its great legs came down, steadying it like buttresses on which rank mosses grew. It scratched for a hold and then was still.

Gren, with Yattmur and the tattooed women trailing behind, came up to it and stared up its height. He released the tail of the sodal, which he had dragged over the ground.

"We can't climb up there!" he said. "You're mad to consider such a thing, morel. It's far too big!"

"Climb, man creature, climb!" bellowed the morel.

Still hesitating, Gren stood while Lily-yo and the others of her land came round. They had hidden behind the tall crag, and were anxious to get away.

"As your fish-creature says, this is our only way to safety," Lily-yo said. "Climb, Gren! You can come with us and we'll look after you."

"You don't have to fear a traverser, Gren," Haris said.

He still stood there, not encouraged by their prompting. The thought of clinging to something that flew through air made him sick; he remembered his ride on the back of the vegbird that crashed in Nomansland, remembered too the journeys by boat and stalker, each landing him in a worse situation than the last. Only on the journey just concluded, which he had undertaken under his own control with the sodal, had the destination seemed preferable to the starting point.

As he wavered, the morel was again bellowing with the sodal's voice, goading the others to climb the fibrous leg, even goading the tattooed women to carry him up, which they did with the aid of Lily-yo's party. They were soon all perched high up on the immense back, looking down and calling at him. Only Yattmur stood by him.

"Just when we are free of the tummy-bellies and the morel, why should we have to depend on this monstrous creature?" he muttered.

"We must go, Gren. It will take us away to the warm forests,

247

far from the sharp-furs, where we can live with Laren in peace. You know we can't stay here."

He looked at her, and at the big-eyed child in her arms. She had endured so much trouble for him, ever since the time the Black Mouth sang its irresistible song.

"We will go if *you* wish it, Yattmur. Let me carry the boy." And then with a flash of anger he peered up, calling to the morel. "And stop your stupid shouting—I'm coming!"

He called too late: the morel had already stopped. When Gren and Yattmur finally pulled themselves panting on to the top of the living hill, it was to discover the morel busily directing Lily-yo and her company in a new enterprise.

The sodal turned one of its piggy stares at Gren and said, "As you know as well as anyone, it is time for me to divide, to propagate. So I'm going to take over this traverser as well as the sodal."

"Mind it doesn't take you over," Gren said feebly. He sat down with a thud as the traverser moved. But the huge creature, in the throes of fertilization, had so little sensitivity that it remained engrossed in its own blind affairs as Lily-yo and the others, working savagely with their knives, cut into its epidermis.

When they had a crater exposed, they lifted the Sodal Ye so that he hung head down into it; though he wriggled weakly, the morel had him too much under control for him to do more. The ugly pitted brown shape of the morel began to slide; half of it dropped into the hole, after which—under direction—the others covered it with a sort of bung of flesh. Gren marvelled at the way they hurried to do the morel's bidding; he seemed to have developed an immunity to orders.

Yattmur sat and suckled her child. As Gren settled beside her, she pointed a finger across the dark side of the mountain. From their vantage point, they could see sad and shadowy clusters of sharp-furs moving away to safety to await events; here and there their torches gleamed, punctuating the gloom like blossoms in a melancholy wood.

"They're not attacking," Yattmur said. "Perhaps we could

248

climb down and find the secret way to Bountiful Basin?'

The landscape tilted.

"It's too late," Gren said. "Hold tightly! We're flying. Have you got Laren safely?"

The traverser had risen. Below them flashed the high cliff and they were falling down it, sweeping rapidly over rock. Bountiful Basin spun toward them, growing as it turned and came nearer.

Into long shade they slipped, then into light—their shadow pasted across the stippled water—into shade again, and then once more into light as they rose, gained certainty, and headed towards the plumed sun.

Laren gave a yelp of alarm and then returned to the breast, shutting his eyes as if it was all too much for him.

"Gather round, everyone," cried the morel, "while I speak to you through this fish's mouth. You must all listen to what I have to say."

Clinging to fibrous hairs, they settled about him, only Gren and Yattmur showing any reluctance to do so.

"Now I am two bodies," pronounced the morel, "I have taken control of this traverser; I am directing its nervous system. It will go only where I wish. Have no fear, for no harm will come to any of you immediately.

"What is more fearful than flight is the knowledge I have drained from this fishy catchy-carry-kind, Sodal Ye. You must hear about it, for it alters my plans.

"These sodals are people of the seas. While all other beings with intelligence have been isolated by vegetable life, the sodals in the freedom of the oceans have been able to keep in contact with all their communities. They can still rove the planet un-interruptedly. So they have gained rather than lost knowledge.

"They have discovered that the world is about to end. Not immediately—not for many generations—but certainly it will end, and those green columns of disaster rising from the jungle to the sky are signs that the end has already begun.

"In the really hot regions—regions unknown to any of us,

249

where the burning bushes and other fire-using plants live—the green columns have already been for some time. In the sodal's mind I find knowledge of them. I see some blazing on shores glimpsed from a steaming sea."

The morel was silent. Gren knew how he would be dredging down for more intelligence. He shuddered, admiring somehow the morel's excitement for facts, yet disgusted by his nature.

Underneath them, floating slowly by, bobbed the coast of the Lands of Perpetual Twilight. They showed appreciably brighter before the heavy lips moved and once more the voice of the sodal carried the thoughts of the morel.

"These sodals don't always understand all the knowledge they have gained. Ah, the beauty of the plan when you see it. . . . Humans, there is this burning fuse of a force called devolution. . . . How can I put it so that your tiny brains will understand?

"Very long ago, men—your remote ancestors—discovered that life grew and evolved from, as it were, a speck of fertility: an amoeba, which served as the gateway to life like an eye of a needle, beyond which lay the amino acids and the inorganic world of nature. And this inorganic world too, they found, evolved in its complexity from one speck, a primal atom.

"These vast processes of growth men came to understand. What the sodals have discovered is that growth incorporates also what men would have called decay: that not only does nature have to be wound up to wind down, it has to wind down to be wound up.

"This creature I now inhabit knows the world is in a winding down phase. This he has vaguely been trying to preach to you lesser breeds.

"At the beginning of this sun system's time, all forms of life were blurred together and by perishing supplied other forms. They arrived on Earth from space like motes, like sparks, in Cambrian times. Then the forms evolved into animal, vegetable, reptile, insect—all varieties and species that flooded the world, many of them now gone.

"Why are they gone? Because the galactic fluxes which determine the life of a sun are now destroying this sun. These same fluxes control animate life; they close it down as they will close Earth's existence. So nature is devolving. Again the forms are blurring! They never ceased to be anything but inter-dependent —the one always living off the other—and now they merge together once more. Were the tummy-bellies vegetable or human? Are the sharp-furs human or animal? And the creatures of the hothouse world, these traversers, the killerwillows in Nomansland, the stalkers that seed like plants and migrate like birds— how do they stand under the old classifications?

"I ask myself what am I?"

For a moment the morel was silent. His listeners looked at each other covertly, full of unease, until a flick of the sodal's tail recalled them to the discourse.

"All of us here have by accident been swept aside from the main stream of devolution. We live in a world where each generation becomes less, and less defined. All life is tending towards the mindless, the infinitesimal: the embryonic speck. So will be fulfilled the processes of the universe. Galactic fluxes will carry the spores of life to another and new system, just as they once brought it here. Already you see the process at work, in these green pillars of light that draw life from the jungles. Under steadily increasing heat, devolutionary processes accelerate."

While the morel was speaking, its other half controlling the traverser had brought them steadily lower. Now they floated over dense jungle, over the banyan that covered all of this sunlit continent. Warmth wrapped itself round them like a cloak.

Other traversers were here, moving their great bulks lightly up and down their threads. With hardly a jolt, morel's traverser alighted in the tips of the jungle.

Gren stood up at once, helping Yattmur to her feet.

"You are the wisest of creatures, morel," he said. "I feel no sorrow in leaving you, because you seem now so well able to look

251

after yourself. After all, you are the first fungus to solve the riddle of the universe. Yattmur and I will speak of you when we are safe in the middle levels of the jungle. Are you coming also, Lily-yo, or is your life given over to riding vegetables?"

Lily-yo, Haris, and the others were also on their feet, facing Gren with a mixture of hostility and defensiveness he recognized from long ago.

"You're not leaving this splendid brain, this protector, this morel who is your friend?" Lily-yo asked.

Gren nodded.

"You are welcome to him—or he is welcome to you. You in your turn must decide as I have had to whether he is a power for good or evil. I have decided. I am taking Yattmur, Laren, and the two Arabler women back to the forest where I belong." When he snapped his fingers, the tattooed women rose obediently.

"Gren, you are as hard-headed as ever you were," Haris said, with a touch of ill-temper. "Come back to the True World with us—it's a better place than the jungle. You just heard the fish-morel say the jungle is doomed."

To his delight, Gren found he could use argument in a way that once would have been impossible to him.

"If what the morel says is correct, Haris, then your other world is doomed as surely as this one."

The morel's voice came back, booming and irritable.

"So it is, man, but you have yet to hear about my plan. In the dim thought centre of this traverser I find awareness of worlds far beyond this, far beyond and basking round other suns. The traverser can be driven to make that journey. I and Lily-yo and the others will live inside it, safe, eating its flesh, until we get to those new worlds. We simply follow the green columns and ride on the galactic fluxes of space and they will lead us to a good fresh place. Of course you must come with us, Gren."

"I'm tired of carrying or being carried. Go and good luck! Fill a whole empty world with people and fungus!"

"You know this Earth will suffer a fire death, you fool man!"

252

"So you said, O wise morel. You also said that that would not come for many generations. Laren and his son and his son's son will live in the green, rather than be cooked into the gut of a vegetable making an unknown journey. Come along, Yattmur. Hup hey, you two women—along you come with me."

They moved to go. Ushering the tattooed women before her, Yattmur handed Laren to Gren, who rested him over his shoulder. Haris took a step forward with his knife out.

"You were always as difficult to deal with. You don't know what you're doing," he said.

"That may be true; but at least I know what you are doing."

Ignoring the man's blade, he climbed slowly down that vast shaggy flank. They lowered themselves until they could reach a slender bough, helping the submissive Arablers to gain a foothold. With a wonderful gladness in his heart, Gren looked down into the leafy depths of the forest.

"Come on," he said encouragingly. "This shall be home, where danger was my cradle, and all we have learnt will guard us! Give me your hand, Yattmur."

Together they climbed down into a bower of leaves. They did not look back as the traverser with its passengers rose slowly, slowly floated from the jungle up into the green-flecked sky, and headed for the solemn blues of space.